Joshua Whittaker was born in the West Midlands, England. From a young age, he was a fan of sci-fi, fantasy books and movies. Later, he also developed an interest in horror. The author identifies himself as bisexual.

Dedicated to my loving and caring mother, Collette Whittaker

Joshua Whittaker

THE MENAGERIE

AUSTIN MACAULEY PUBLISHERS™
LONDON * CAMBRIDGE * NEW YORK * SHARJAH

Copyright © Joshua Whittaker 2023

The right of Joshua Whittaker to be identified as author of this work has been asserted by the author in accordance with sections 77 and 78 of the Copyright, Designs and Patents Act 1988.

All rights reserved. No part of this publication may be reproduced, stored in a retrieval system, or transmitted in any form or by any means, electronic, mechanical, photocopying, recording, or otherwise, without the prior permission of the publishers.

Any person who commits any unauthorised act in relation to this publication may be liable to criminal prosecution and civil claims for damages.

This is a work of fiction. Names, characters, businesses, places, events, locales, and incidents are either the products of the author's imagination or used in a fictitious manner. Any resemblance to actual persons, living or dead, or actual events is purely coincidental.

A CIP catalogue record for this title is available from the British Library.

ISBN 9781398499102 (Paperback)
ISBN 9781398499119 (Hardback)
ISBN 9781398499133 (ePub e-book)

www.austinmacauley.com

First Published 2023
Austin Macauley Publishers Ltd®
1 Canada Square
Canary Wharf
London
E14 5AA

I want to thank Austin Macauley and everybody who contributed to making this book what it is now. By doing this they have helped turn my dream into reality. I also want to thank you, the reader, for purchasing this book.

Introduction

What you're about to read are the recovered writings from a Mr Robert Smith.

August 1921

Once I considered myself a man of science. I said to myself there is nothing that can't be explained or disproven by the use of science, but that was before that day, before my eyes were truly opened up to the world around me, and if these are the last words, I am going to write then I would like to go back to the very beginning.

R. Smith

30 August 1921

I was in London in my study, perusing my notes on the solar eclipse, for you see that is my field of science the study of the eclipse. I have always found it fascinating how something as luminous as the Sun can, just for a few minutes, be totally blocked out of view by this dark ominous empty looking void of nothingness. Yes, the popular opinion is that it's just the moon's shadow crossing the earth's surface, but what if it's something more than that? Something that is unexplainable.

So I did some digging around in books that were unpronounceable, or not in any known language of this world that I could understand, but as I flicked through the pages of these decrepit, dusty, cobweb filled books, I found some pages that were in English and learned that people worshipped the eclipse by leaving offerings outside their homes. When the eclipse was due, these offerings would vary, it says in the books, from raw meat to dead family members.

Were these things true or were they just stories and myths passed down through time, I asked myself, either way, I had to go and find out for myself but the only location in these books that kept popping up was a place called Lemming, and beside it was a latitude and longitude that read 8.7832*S and 124.5085*W.

I went to check my map that I had in my desk draw, and as I walked, the dilapidated floor beneath my feet was creaking and groaning at me with every step, until eventually I reached my desk. When I opened the draw, the map was indeed inside, so I unrolled the map and blew off dust that had gathered on it, and started my search for this place called Lemming.

It took me a while because of my limited knowledge of map reading but I eventually found it. It looked like a miniscule island somewhere out in the Pacific Ocean, separated from all other parts of the world, so getting there would be hard but I'm determined, and I'm sure I will make a great discovery.

31 August 1921

Today, I started to pack my essentials and get ready for my trip to Lemming. Since it's an island in the Pacific, I decided I would travel by ship. I knew this would be a long method of travel but I preferred it. As I finished packing, I had a nagging feeling in the back of my mind and heard an incoherent whisper but as I looked around my study, no one was to be seen.

Then as I was about to leave, there it was again, the nagging in the back of my mind, the incoherent whisper but this time when I looked around something stood out to me, it was those books; it was as if they were calling to me. I walked over to my bookcase to get them, but as I walked over, with every step I took, the whispers grew louder and louder and the nagging in the back of my mind turned into a headache, until suddenly I was unconscious.

When I awoke, I was on the ship with the books in my cabin and all my essentials unpacked. The only logical explanation I could think of was that one of the crew members must have brought me here after my episode or whatever strange thing it was that occurred in my study. After I gathered myself, I went on to explore the ship before we set sail.

As I looked around, I saw the decaying, rotting, moss engulfed, maggot filled wood of the ship that was taking over my senses. It made me want to throw up but I managed to hold it back as I carried on exploring. Then out the corner of my eye, I saw a crew member. I saw that his face was covered in deep, and what seemed like unending scars, and one of his eyes were missing, but he didn't wear anything to conceal it.

I couldn't help but look, and as I looked at this hole where his eye used to be, it felt like staring down into the vast emptiness of space itself. Then suddenly, he smiled at me and I felt this great sense of dread come over me, so I retreated to go and talk to the captain about setting our course.

I started to make my way to the captain's cabin. When I got there, I made sure to knock so as not to disturb him but before my hand even touched the door, he opened it as if he knew I was there. Then the captain went on to introduce himself, "My name's Samuels and I'm happy that you have chosen my ship and crew to serve your needs."

He was a very well-spoken man, even though his voice was husky. He appeared well groomed. His clothes were of high quality and were very clean for a man who spends most of his time at sea. He was also a very stout person with a rugged almost shiny grey bushy beard.

The wolf grey, bushy crop of hair he had, seemed to blend into his weather-beaten face. His acorn eyes danced around anxiously. He offered me a wrinkled hand with bloody bitten finger nails as a gesture.

After introducing himself, he then offered me a seat inside his cabin but when I walked in, I was shocked at what I saw. It was very different from the impression I got from the captain himself, the cabin was in disrepair. I saw papers and documents strewn about and many empty bottles of whiskey on the floor, and even some smashed and broken glass as far as my eyes could see.

I then sat down and was about to ask about the course to Lemming, when unexpectedly, he took a bottle of whiskey out from some unknown crevice that could not be seen and went to open it, but struggled profusely. As he started to get frustrated, he suddenly yelled and smashed the top of the bottle on the table in his cabin.

Shards of glass went flying everywhere but the captain was not fazed by this, he just drank from the broken bottle with the serrated edges cutting and scrapping his mouth, and with every sip he took, blood flooded out of his mouth like a heavy down pour of rain.

Then he stopped sipping for a moment and spoke, "I know why you're here, we get folks like you every so often, thinking they can go to that island of horrors and come back alive. If you're so determined to go there, I will take you, but don't think this will be an easy and quick journey. The seas are perilous and no mortal truly knows what lies beneath the murky depths."

I didn't know what to say, I was taken aback by what he said. How did he know where Lemming was, had he come upon it when travelling, had he set foot on the island and who were these other people? So many questions were running through my mind all at once.

As I looked at Samuels, he knew I was confused, but he was waiting for an answer, so I replied, "Yes, I am determined. Whatever is on that island is important to my research and…"

Before I could continue my reply, he just laughed in a loud and undermining way, and replied, "Ok, I will take you," and as I got up to leave, he said one last thing, "Oh and keep away from the crew, trust me it's for your own safety."

Then the ship started to set sail, so I went back to my cabin to rest and ponder on what the captain had said. Was he really telling me the truth or was it just the drink, that overflowed my sinuses every time he spoke? I would have to trust him if I were to get to Lemming in time for the eclipse.

1 September 1921

I was awoken by the sound of men shouting orders at each other above me. Then I realised, this was the first day of my sea voyage to the mysterious island of Lemming. I pulled myself from my bed and started to get dressed. I then decided that today I would go around the ship and ask the crew if they knew anything about Lemming, even though Captain Samuels said to keep away from them.

The crew, I thought, what could be the harm in asking a few questions? So I exited my cabin and proceeded to the main deck, and as I opened the weathered and beaten door, I was hit in the face with a burst of air from the sea and the door behind me slammed itself shut. As this happened, I could now see that all the crew members were staring at me and I started to feel the intense sense of dread come over me once again.

Like before when the crew member with the one eye had smiled at me, but I had to find out more about Lemming. So I started to cautiously walk towards the crew, and as I did this, all the crew turned away as if they were trying to hide themselves and didn't want to be bothered. One crew member didn't turn away, so I approached him.

This man was of average build with what looked to be red stained overalls on. He was also wearing leather gloves and a leather cap with a white strip across the front to hide his baldness. He had an untidy, scraggly, dense moustache with sideburns coming up from it going all the way up his face, to underneath his cap.

His skin appeared to be rough, like sandpaper and was coated with what I could describe as filth. His keen cerulean eyes peered slyly from beneath the brim of his cap. I introduced myself, "Hello, my name is Robert Smith. Is it OK if I ask you some questions about our destination?"

He looked me up and down, and then answered in a low gruff voice, "You mean Lemming, Huh? Sure, why not."

I then proceeded with my questions. "Have you ever seen Lemming?" I asked.

"Yea, I seen it a couple of times. The captain sometimes docks there and goes on the island. He tells me to stay on the boat but all the other guys go with him. I guess it's because I'm the new guy."

"So how long have you been working on this ship?"

"Not long just started a couple of weeks ago," He replied puffing on his pipe.

"So do you know why the captain docks at Lemming and why he goes onto the island?"

"He doesn't tell me that much, except that he is making good money on Lemming."

As I took all this information in, I was startled because the people of Lemming worship the eclipse. So has Captain Samuels got something to do with it? What is he hiding from me?

Is it chance or fate that I was on this ship with a captain who has set foot on Lemming, and knew where it was without needing a map? Whatever is happening I must find out and I'm sure I will find the answer in those mysterious obscure and other worldly books I have in my cabin.

2 September 1921

I didn't get any sleep last night. I stayed up trying to understand the language in these books, trying to find something that could explain the Lore behind the island of Lemming. Tell me if there is any connection with sea captains but the words in these books are not of this Earth.

I compared the writings in the books with writings from all over the globe that I have some knowledge in. Chinese, Hindi, Arabic, Bengali, Japanese and Punjabi, but the more and more I compared the writings in the books, the less and less they made sense. My body and mind grew weaker every time I read the books' unknown language and when the thought of giving up seemed so appealing, I suddenly saw something that I hadn't seen before.

It was the title of the books. How stupid must I have been not to see it before? Out of the many times I have handled these suspicious unnerving things, and to my luck the title was in a language I could understand. In clear Chinese, it said chi which means to eat, to suffer, to annihilate and as I soaked this in I thought to myself how did I get these books?

I could not remember ever purchasing them. One day I just had them, where did they come from and I never questioned having them before I just accepted it. It's just now that I realise these books just appeared into my life out of nowhere. All these events started to make my brain spin, and then I focused myself and went back to looking at the title of the books, Chi and the meaning behind the word.

Was the meaning of the title representing what the words inside couldn't convey? Danger maybe or were they instructions for the inhabitants of Lemming who worship the eclipse? Either way, I needed to find out more, but who was I to ask for help?

The captain who goes to Lemming frequently for some unknown reason? No I thought, not the Captain. I must find out more about him before conversing with him again. Maybe some member of his crew, no I thought, they are loyal to him and not so welcoming of strangers. Also they help the Captain in his unknown dealings on the island of Lemming.

Then I suddenly remembered, there was one crew member who was welcoming of me and helped me before. If I could just find him then I am certain he would be willing to help me again.

I swiftly made my way to the main deck of the ship, and when I got there, I saw him in his red stained overalls and ran rapidly to him. When I reached him, I tapped him hurriedly on his shoulder, and as he turned, it was if he didn't recognise me, he just stared blankly at my face. Just as I was about to ask him what was wrong, Captain Samuels bellowed out an order for him to come to his cabin.

I tried to stop him from going but as I was doing this, I could see all the crew staring at me and the captain just gave me a bone chilling look. I gave up and started to slink away back to my cabin, but as I was about to open the door, I heard someone inside. I didn't know whether to burst in and catch them in the act or wait outside to see who it was.

While I was thinking this, I heard someone climbing the steps up to the door that I was hiding behind. As I heard this, I panicked and tried to hide. Then instantaneously, my cabin door swung open and it was him, the crew member with the deep unending cuts on his face, with the one eye and dread-inducing smile. I waited till there was a good amount of distance between us and sped into my cabin, and immediately started to look around to see if anything had been taken, but to my surprise nothing had been. There was just a note on my table like desk that read:

Whatever you do, trust no one!

3 September 1921

After getting some much needed rest, I started to think about the note that the sinister crew member left in my cabin. Does he know something I don't? He must, so if I speak with him then maybe I will find something out about Lemming and Captain Samuels. Maybe he could bridge the connection between the two, but the struggle was finding him and in what way to find him.

I dare not ask any crew member or the Captain. Then as I went to put the note back on my table, I got this overpowering feeling to look on the back of the note, and as I did this my problem was solved. The sinister crew member had written on the back of the note a place to meet and what time to meet.

It read, *meet in storage at midnight.* Midnight was very far away. What would I do on this ship till then? Then I remembered the crew member who helped me, the one who was called to the captain's cabin. I must check if he is OK and see if he knows anything about the books I have in my cabin.

So I set out towards the main deck and when I got there, my eyes started to dart around searching for him, like an animal hunting its next meal but as I looked around the deck of the ship I saw him nowhere. I sensed my only option was to go to Captain Samuels and ask him if he had seen him, (even though I had a deep suspicion that he may have done something to him.), so I marched my way up to the captain's cabin and flung open the door.

There I saw something that took me by surprise. It was him the crew member with the red stained overalls, but there was something off about him. I approached him calmly and when he turned to look me in the eyes, he had this dead expression on his face. He then started to whisper something, but I couldn't make out what he was saying. I moved closer to him, till eventually I lent my ear towards his mouth, and what I heard gave me a shiver down my spine.

"Burn those books; burn them till they are nothing but ash!"

He kept repeating this sentence over and over again. I thought to myself, *How did he know about the books?* I haven't shown them to him, I hadn't mentioned them to him, so how does he know about them? Then it hit me, was he the crew member who brought me to the ship when I fell unconscious in my study? Did he bring all my essentials that I packed and the books to my cabin?

Was he curious about them and decided to read them? But what did he see that I could not? Before I could ask him anything, he was rushing towards the main deck and then hurled himself off the ship into the shimmering crystal blue ocean below. My eyes and brain could not fathom what they had just witnessed.

I stood there petrified as all the crew raced around the deck trying to gather something to pull him back onto the ship. It was, however, too late. The sea had swallowed him up. The man I thought was my last hope of knowing something, anything about what was happening on this ship.

I then remembered the note from the member of the crew member with the one eye who wanted to meet at midnight! I collected myself together and thought to myself that there still is a glimmer of hope as to finding out what the captain has to do with Lemming. Also what was in those books? So I retired to my cabin to wait for midnight.

After hours of waiting in my dull depressing prison cell, midnight finally came. I slowly opened my door and looked through the sliver of a crack that I had made. I looked but I saw no one on the deck except for the crew member steering the ship.

I proceeded to open my door and walk to the storage room on the other end of the ship, beneath the ship, and as I walked, I heard the wind snapping, whipping and cracking against the sails. The ocean was crashing up the side of the ship and every time this happened, the vessel would sway and I would lose my footing.

I reached the storage room door that lead underneath the ship. As I was about to open the door, I heard multiple voices, so I squinted through the metallic and rusty keyhole and saw almost the whole crew down there whispering to each other. I listened for a while before I managed to grasp what one of them was saying, "How should we do him in, like we did the others?"

As I heard this, my mind jumped to a thousand assumptions. What did that person mean do him in? Were they going to kill me? Were these others they talked about the same others the captain mentioned and did they kill them? I didn't understand, what was this captain and crew doing that was so centred on Lemming?

I wanted to find out but at the same time all the events leading up to this moment filled me with apprehension. I so want to find out but as I was thinking all this, I suddenly noticed that the whispers had stopped. What if they heard me? But I had made no noise.

I hastily made my way back to my cabin, trying not to be observed. I entered and locked the door. I was now very unnerved but being a man of science I tried to think of some logic explanation. I thought this could easily be some kind of practical joke, yes that's it, it's just a practical joke that they are playing on me, that they pull on everyone. As I thought of this, it calmed me for this could be the only reason and no other reason could possibly exist could there?

That night I slept with my loaded pistol beneath my pillow.

4 September 1921

Today I was awoken by the thunderous thrashing of ocean waves all around me. I sprang up from my bed and went to the main deck to see what was happening. As I opened my cabin door, I saw that the sea was in a fit of rage, throwing huge waves left and right which were slamming into the ship.

This was causing huge splinters of wood to separate themselves from the boat, which were then flung into the air, whizzing in every direction like a swarm of bees, ready to attack.

The crew were obviously running around like mad dogs, making sure that the ship stayed on course, and as for me, I just tried to stay standing and not throw up everywhere. Then I observed the captain through a window in his cabin, not really looking effected by what was happing. I tried to walk towards his cabin holding on to the side of the boat as to not fall over, but with every step I took, it grew harder and harder to reach his door.

As the wind furiously gained in strength and speed, I felt like I was about to be carried off my feet and swept away into the sea. I fought the fury of the wind and carried on towards Captain Samuels's cabin. Then suddenly, I felt a splash of cold sea water on my face, and as I looked to where it came from, I saw that a mountain of a wave was about to hit the ship.

I turned around and tried to go back to my cabin but it was too late. The momentous wave had struck the main deck of the ship and I was about to be carried out to sea, but as the wave hit the main deck and my body was pushed back by this force of nature, I suddenly felt someone grab my arm and save me from death. I couldn't see who it was but then as the waves around the boat subsided I saw that it was Captain Samuels who had saved me.

But how? I thought, how did he get to me in time, did the furious winds not affect him, and how wasn't he almost pulled over into the sea as well, and then I thought, *Why did he save me if he knows I suspect him of shady dealings with the eclipse worshipers of Lemming. Why didn't he let me die, or maybe he doesn't know I suspect him, in which case I must now make sure that whatever I do I draw as little or no attention to myself as possible.*

Then the captain and I engaged in a conversation.

"Are you OK?" the captain asked.

"Yes, I, I'm fine. Thank you for your help. I feared I was a goner," I replied.

"It's no problem, just be careful. I told you that the sea is a perilous place, and if I were you I would be prepared, because the closer we get to Lemming, the more and more dangers the sea will throw at us."

"Yes quite, err, well thank you again and don't worry. From now on, I will be very careful," I muttered.

Then I started to make my way back to my cabin and as I did, I began to think about what happened the night before and what was down beneath the ship in storage. Was it something they were trying to hide? Could there be something down there that would unlock the secret of what connects Lemming and Captain Samuels together, and was there a secret hatch or door down there that the crew had disappeared into.

I had to find out, but I could not just walk down there during the day. The crew would almost certainly stop me or even follow me and do me in, whatever they meant by that. So I would have to wait till night (even though I favoured this even less), and then hopefully, I would discover whatever secret they all were hiding on this sick inducing ship.

For now I would wait and get some rest, for I felt that I needed some after what the sea had just threw at me. So when I reached my cabin and was inside, I made sure to lock the door and get out of the disgustingly sea drenched clothes and into bed. I started to think how I would get into the storage area beneath the ship.

Would I need a key? Would I need to break down the door and what if someone does see me? What would they do to me? I dare not think of it. Whatever happens, I just hope that I find out what Captains Samuels' connection is with that unfathomable island that goes by the name of Lemming.

5 September 1921

When I woke up, a plan had formed itself in my mind, stirring me in my dreams. I thought the captain must have the key to the storage area that was beneath the ship. He must have the keys to all the doors on the ship. Why shouldn't he, the only problem that occurred now was getting the key from him.

Then it came to me, I would wait till tonight when the captain and the crew were sleeping, and go to his cabin to find and retrieve the key. That, I thought, is the only way to get into the storage area without drawing any attention to myself, and I did not want to draw any attention to myself, mainly because I don't know what these crew members and especially Captain Samuels are capable of.

Plus after what I heard one of the crew members say, down in that mysterious storage area, *Do him in, do me in*, well I would not like to find out what that unknown devilish crew member meant by that, but then all of a sudden, I thought how will I know which key is the key to the storage area door? I guess I would just have to deal with that when it came to it.

Having arisen, I got dressed and started to exit my cabin. I decided I would take in the view today, but tonight I would finally find out what is behind that door, and hopefully I will find something that connects Captain Samuels with the island of Lemming so that I can make some sense of what that helpful crew member told me; the one who wore the red stained overalls and sadly threw himself over the side of the ship.

As I remembered him, some other thoughts came rushing into my mind. It's what he said to me before he threw himself overboard, "Burn those books, burn them till they are nothing but ash!" As I thought of this, I regretted not being able to ask him something about the books sooner.

Perhaps, he could have helped me understand the words that are scribbled in the pages, and maybe by understanding the words in the books pages, I could have understand what he saw in the books that I seem unable to see. Did I miss something when I was studying them? I must go back and study them closer. Then I refocused myself and finally exited my cabin.

I walked over to the side of the ship and what I saw was beyond any beauty I had ever seen.

I saw the never ending ocean shinning like a gem underneath the golden radiant sun above in the blue ethereal sky. I was amazed at what I saw and how gorgeous the sea can be when it's not trying to kill you. I then glanced back down to the ocean and saw little waves. It looked as if they were dancing as the rays of the sun shone down upon them.

I lost myself for a moment, letting all my fears evaporate into the sea mist, almost forgetting my reason for this journey and the dangers I had encountered. Then I made my way back to my cabin to have a nap and get myself ready for the night.

When I awoke from my nap, I went onto the main deck, but to my shock it was almost night. *I must have over slept a bit*, I thought to myself, but at least now, I won't have to wait that long to put my plan into action. So I went back to my cabin and started to read one of my favourite books as I waited for midnight.

When I had finished my book, I saw that an enormous amount of time had elapsed, so I went to check and I saw that it was indeed midnight. All the crew were indeed gone from the main deck except the one steering the ship again. So I slowly and cautiously, started to make my way across the main deck to the captain's cabin.

As I did this, the wood beneath me made an ear-splitting sound, but thankfully the crew member steering the ship couldn't hear this because of the wind and waves that were like a mini tsunami in his ears. So I eventually made it to the captain's cabin. I opened his door and as I did this it made a slight creak due to the salt rusted hinges. Finally, I entered cautiously and saw him asleep, slouched in a chair with multiple empty bottles of whiskey at his feet.

I slowly closed the door and started my search for the storage key. I looked everywhere I thought it might be, when suddenly I realised, I hadn't checked the captain. So I steadily made my way over to him and began to search him. Then

I saw a key with a large letter S carved into it in the top breast pocket of his jacket, so I reached and reached and finally I had it in my hands.

Then suddenly the captain started to stir. I didn't know what to do. Was he about to wake up? I held my breath anxiously, but no he was just getting more comfortable. I left his cabin hastily and made my way to the storage door, which was just below his cabin on the right.

All I had to do was walk down his cabin stairs to the main deck, and I would finally find out what was in there. I walked down the stairs and every time I touched a step, it made an uncomfortably loud sound, but again to my amazement, the crew member steering the ship did not look in my direction. I carried on down the stairs and eventually made it to the storage door.

I unlocked it and then entered, and as I walked down the stairs, I got a feeling that I was unwelcome, and after what seemed like an infinite amount of time, I reached the bottom of the stairs.

I could see nothing but blackness, it was as if I had gone blind, so I felt around in my pockets to see if I had some kind of light source, then I found on my person a lighter. I began to strike it several times until it lit up the room but then I saw something in front of me I wish I hadn't seen. There was blood everywhere, splattered against the walls and floor of the room.

Everywhere I turned to look, all I could see was blood, blood as red as the planet Mars. As I looked closer I saw tools, such as a saws and hammers. I saw that these objects were also covered in a large quantity of blood, but then I saw that the blood was dry, so whatever, or whomever was killed in this room, it must have taken place a while ago.

In my disbelief of what I saw, I still searched the room for some form of a secret hatch or room to explain the crew members unexplainable vanishing that night without using the main and only door that leads in and out of the storage room.

I couldn't find anything or maybe I wasn't looking hard enough, but I decided in the end, to go back to my cabin because I couldn't stomach anymore of what I was seeing. So I steadily made my way back to my cabin. When I got there, I went inside and made sure to lock the door. I was drained both physically and mentally.

Then I retired to bed and started to think of what it was I had just discovered. What was all that blood back there? Are the crew and captain actually killing people, or was it just blood from a very large fish that they had caught? What if it was a person's blood, what do they get out of it? Do they worship the eclipse as well, is that why they dock at Lemming so often?

My brain was now racing with more unanswered questions than ever, but all I knew was from now on, I would have to keep an eye on everyone on this ship. Until I figure out the truth that connects this crew and their captain with the mystifying island known as Lemming, my pistol will be my constant companion.

6 September 1921

A loud yell penetrated its way into my ears and awoke me. I sprang up from my bed in shock and scurried towards my cabin door. I pressed my ear against it to listen to what was happening out on the main deck. It was Captain Samuels, he was yelling and screaming at the top of his lungs saying, "Who has it, who has the storage key?"

Then I suddenly remembered, I had forgotten to return the storage key back to his cabin the previous night. I had borrowed it to discover what was in the storage area beneath the ship. I then started to panic, I locked my cabin door and started to pace up and down in what little space I had, thinking of what I was going to do.

Would I just give it to him saying I had found it somewhere on the ship, or would I confront him about what I had seen in the storage area and see what he had to say for himself? I then decided I would do neither of these things and chose to return the key to his cabin later on today when he wasn't in there. Then hopefully that would be the end of the matter and he would forget it had even gone missing.

Then it occurred to me, how was I going to get him out of his cabin, because he never leaves his cabin, he just stays in there all day and night drinking whiskey. The only time he comes out is to get more whiskey. Then it struck me like a lightning bolt. I would hide the crate containing the bottles of whiskey.

I would hide them in my cabin, then when Captain Samuels comes out to get another bottle he would have to search around for a while and that would give me some time to replace the key back in his cabin. I then swiftly dressed and exited my cabin.

I saw that the large crate of whiskey was directly beside the stairs that led up into the captain's cabin, so I made my way over towards it, and then as gently and as quietly as I could, I picked up the create and started to move it towards my cabin. When eventually I reached my cabin, I went inside and placed the crate of whiskey underneath my bed to hide it from view, just in case Captain Samuels checked my cabin.

Then I went back onto the main deck and waited for Captain Samuels to leave his cabin. I heard the rusty hinges of his door and saw him march down the stairs looking like he was on the prowl, and when he noticed the crate of whiskey was missing, I could tell he was perplexed. He went to the makeshift kitchen that was on the ship and started to search for whiskey in there.

It was at that moment that I took my chance. I made my way into the captain's cabin. When I entered, I placed the key on his table then as I was about to leave, I couldn't help myself but look at the documents that where on the table, just lying there for me to see. As I looked, I saw one document that recorded the trips that he had took to Lemming, so I stuffed it in my pocket.

Then suddenly I heard the cabin door slam shut behind me, and as I slowly turned, Captain Samuels was standing there in front of me with this menacing look on his face. He motioned me to sit down and started to speak. "Did you take this key?" He said in a deep and sinister voice.

I replied with a stuttering answer, "N…no I found it and thought I should to return it to you immediately, in case it was of some importance."

He then motioned for me to leave his cabin. I left and made my way to my cabin. I couldn't believe I had gotten away with it but then I remembered, I needed to put the crate of whiskey back. When I got back to my cabin, I removed the crate from under my bed and placed it back on the main deck of the ship.

I then returned to my cabin to get some sleep, and as I was lying in bed, I couldn't help but think, did I miss my opportunity back there to confront him and find out the truth that connects this crew and Captain Samuels with the island of Lemming? Could I have also found out what happened down in that storage area and find out where that tidal wave of blood came from that was down there.

No, I thought, I will have more opportunities to confront him. Now I have this document that I took from Captain Samuels's cabin. I will study it to try and find out more information that may let me in on the secret that connects this crew and Captain Samuels with that mystifying island called Lemming.

7 September 1921

When I awoke from my sleep, I rose from my bed and went over to the table that was in the middle of my cabin. I then sat down in the most inhumanly uncomfortable chair that I had ever sat in, and pulled the document out of my pocket, where I had hidden it and forgotten to take it out of last night. I placed it on the table and as I was about to inspect it, I heard someone knock at my door.

It was a crew member. *What does he want?* I thought. I made a response to the knocking, "Yes, who is it?"

Then the crew member replied, in a raspy voice, "My name is John, sir. I was wondering if you were planning on coming onto the main deck today."

"No, I shall be staying in my cabin all day. I have work to do," I replied in a stern voice.

Then I focused my attention back to the table and started to inspect the document that I had taken from Captain Samuel's cabin the day before. As I looked at it, I could see no particular thing that stood out, but then as I started to look closer, I could see something next to where it said Lemming dock. It also said cargo drop off. So does this mean that every time that Captain Samuel's and his crew dock at Lemming they drop something off?

What is it? Could it be fish? No, it can't be. Lemming is an island in the Pacific Ocean and there are plenty of fish there. So if not fish, then I need to know what Captain Samuels is dropping off at Lemming.

Then I thought to myself could this be the link that connects everything together and at the same time another thought made its way into my mind. I thought is this the right moment to confront Captain Samuels, and as I thought this, it was as if my body had taken over and my brain was just a passenger inside my body. Suddenly, I was leaving my cabin and making my way to the captain's cabin.

I swung open my cabin door and stomped my way to the captain's cabin, and when I got there I kicked open his cabin doors. There, I saw him jolt up from his seat in shock and then I entered, and when I was about to speak it was as if my vocal cords had been cut. I would think of what I wanted to say but the words refused to come out of my mouth.

Then Captain Samuels started to speak to me, "What do you think you're doing, boy. Throwing your weight around if you've got something to say. Say it!"

Then suddenly it was if a blast of courage came over me and I confronted him saying, "I know about the blood in the storage area and I know you have been to Lemming multiple times. I also know that every time you dock there, that you drop off some unknown object."

He then sat back down and slunk in his chair and replied, "We were just trying to help the people of Lemming. We didn't mean to hurt anyone."

I then engaged in further conversation with him, "What do you mean hurt anyone?"

He looked away, avoiding eye contact. "You see all the myths are true. There's an evil on that island that can only be quenched by human flesh. OK, so we did what we had to do to help keep the people of Lemming alive."

Curiosity pushed me on. "Ok, let's say I believe you and this myth is true, and there is an evil on the island, what did you do to quench it and help the people of Lemming?"

"Me and my crew we…we killed people, many people. First, we would lure them back to the ship, then get them down into the storage room out of sight and then knock them on the back of the head with a hammer multiple times until we knew for certain they were dead. Then we would take a saw and start cutting their body into pieces. When we had finished, we would put the body parts in a crate, nail it shut and drop it off at Lemming when we docked there."

I didn't know how to react; I didn't know how to reply. I just ran frantically back to my cabin and made sure I locked the door. Then I started to ask myself if he was telling the truth. But with all the blood splattered everywhere down in the storage area as well as the hammers and the saws that I had found that were also covered in blood down there, it all now made sense.

But is he telling me the whole truth, or is there something more to this? Could Samuels and all his crew be worshipping the eclipse like the people of Lemming? Could they be slaughtering innocent people and taking them to Lemming as some sort of sacrifice. If he is telling me the truth why would the people of Lemming need body parts?

There is no mention of this in the books, unless I just haven't researched hard enough. I guess I need to study and find out what I can from those disconcerting books, but it will be hard since nearly all the writing in the books is in some unknown, other earthly language. Thus I will have to work harder than ever before, to see what I can uncover and to see if anything in those books can help me understand the lore behind Lemming better before I reach its ominous waters.

8 September 1921

The questions from the night before were still going through my mind when I woke. Was what Captain Samuels had said to me yesterday when I confronted him true? I couldn't get it out of my head. Were he and all his crew really murders? Then I remembered my thoughts from the day before.

I would need to study those books more try and uncover whatever I could, something that I could not see before. So I walked over to the bookshelf that was in my cabin and pulled the books from it. I then dropped them on the table and as I did this a cloud of dust exploded and drifted away piercing the beams of light breaking in through the cracks.

I sat down and opened the books. I started to turn the rotting pages of the books, studying each page very closely, but I saw nothing! I could still not understand the writings in the books. I was adamant that I was not giving up, so I kept on turning the pages until suddenly, I came upon a page that had no writing on it.

There was just an image on the page. The image seemed to depict a solar eclipse but there were people underneath running away in what looked like fear into houses and makeshift huts. I didn't understand what I was seeing and what this meant, so I decided to go with my gut and ask Captain Samuels for his help. I slowly walked over to his cabin and asked him if he wouldn't mind returning to my cabin with me to look at this image I had discovered.

He was willing and so we went back to my cabin. When we entered my cabin, I went straight to the table but the captain was very silent and walked slowly towards the books. Then when he eventually reached the table and saw the image, he gaped as if he was shocked and threw the books out of my cabin window. I was outraged and demanded an answer. "Why on earth did you do that?"

He then replied, "Those books, they're dangerous."

I engaged in conversation with him. "Books, dangerous, don't be so ridiculous."

"Where did you get those books," the captain asked.

I paused, trying to recall events. "I, well…well I don't know. I just had them. I can never remember buying them or where I purchased them. Why is that important anyway?"

Captain gave me a sideways glance, looking me up and down. "You're doomed."

I looked at him. "Oh do shut up! Now do you know anything about that image or not, Captain Samuels?"

"Yes, I know something. The image depicts the people of Lemming running from an eclipse in fear because you see; they do not worship the eclipse like you think. Many others before you have thought they fear the eclipse and fear what it brings with its darkness.

"For the people of Lemming have an evil among them, and every time an eclipse hits their island, the evil comes and they are forced to leave out raw meat and dead family members. But that was before we started to help them. Yes, we supplied them with dead body parts from the people we killed; you see that is what they use the body parts for and why we drop them off at Lemming.

"We killed people, bad people, people of no use to society. Not because we wanted to, we didn't enjoy it. We did it so the people of Lemming, good, God fearing innocents, didn't have to use their dead family members of their food anymore!"

Before I could think of a reply, Captain Samuels left my cabin and I didn't know what to think. Was there something darker going on the island of Lemming that I just discovered? Of course I don't believe in monsters and bogeymen, there's no such thing, so if there is an evil on the island it has to be a physical human causing this trouble, making people run in terror.

That is the only logical explanation that doesn't involve these immature fascinations of monsters. What did the captain mean by bad people, people of no use? I was left with more confusion, more questions that had to be answered and answered before we reached the island.

9 September 1921

I was awoken by a loud thudding on my cabin door and as I heard this, my eyes shot open and I readied myself for what the day had in store for me. I got off bed but someone was still banging on my cabin door, so I yelled out in response to the banging, "Yes, who is it?"

"It's me, John, sir."

"What do you want?"

"I just came to tell you that all the crew have decided to stay up tonight to put extra effort in making sure that the ship stays on course and gets to Lemming as fast as possible, so we are estimated to arrive at Lemming tomorrow morning."

"Thank you," I replied tiredly.

I heard the floor beneath his feet creak as he walked away, and then thought to myself that if this is true, then where are the raging tides and winds that Captain Samuels warned me about? Could he have just been joking to try and get a reaction out of me, or were we lucky and had we avoided the raging waves and winds.

As I was thinking this, another thought popped into my head, I thought I must check to see if an eclipse does indeed happen tomorrow. So I took all my notes that I had on solar eclipses that occurred in the Pacific Ocean out from my draw and placed them upon the table that is in my cabin, and started to go over them. It was then I noticed, one does indeed occur tomorrow at 1 pm and lasts for 7 minutes.

Then I sighed in relief that we had made it in time for the eclipse, so I could study it and see the Lemmings people reaction. I then started to think to myself that when I reach Lemming, I will finally find out the truth and put these foolish monster stories that Captain Samuels has been telling me. Out of my mind will I find out if Captain Samuels has been lying to me all this whole time about the reason for killing.

I will soon find out, for tomorrow I will question the people of Lemming to see if their stories and his are linked, but what if Captain Samuels worships the eclipse like I have often thought so many times? Then the people of Lemming would obviously lie for him to protect their own, but what if the people of Lemming don't worship the eclipse?

There was so much doubt now clouding my thoughts and judgements after all the things I had found and all the things Captain Samuels had told me that could have fitted neatly together I didn't know what to think anymore. I would just have to wait till tomorrow and see what I could find out from the people of Lemming, if they were willing to talk.

10 September 1921

Again I was awoken by aloud thudding on my cabin door. I didn't bother to reply but then the thudding noise grew louder, so I shouted out towards the direction of the door, "Yes! What is it?"

"It's me again John. I've just come to tell you that we are coming up on Lemming now, and I didn't know if you wanted to come out and see the island as we approached it?"

"Yes, I do, thank you for informing me." I then again heard the creak of the floor beneath his feet as he walked away, but when he was gone I bolted out of bed, dressed myself and went straight to the main deck of the ship to see the island of Lemming.

As we approached it, I prepared myself and then from what my eyes could see, it was literally an island in the Pacific Ocean, not connected to any other main source of land. I mean I had an idea that it would be something like this, that's why I chose to travel by ship, but at the very least I thought there would be some other islands around it, but for miles and miles there was nothing.

The island of Lemming was the only island in sight. It was as if someone had just picked it up from its original place and just placed it here in the Pacific Ocean and left it bobbing around on top of the briny blue depths of the ocean. Then finally we arrived and docked at Lemming. The island's dock was made from wood and had a stair case that would join directly to the ship when it docked.

When I finally walked down the stairs and got off that vomit enduing moss ridden ship and was on the dock, I scanned the area. The dock was about average size and had many wooden barrels and crates on it. I started to make my way to the main part of the island where the houses and the inhabitants of Lemming reside.

When I eventually got there, I was startled. This looked like no normal island. The grass looked like it had been burned. It was so black, it almost looked like charcoal. The houses were all different sizes, some were of a monumental size, as if for a giant. Then others were tiny as if they were made for a rat.

I also saw that there were not many people living on this island, but then again the island is not very big. I stepped onto the grass and breathed a sigh of relief as I thought to myself that I had finally made it. I looked at my watch and saw that it was 6 am and thought why are there so many people walking around?

Shouldn't they be getting rest, but at the same time I thought to myself this was a great chance to go around and ask the locals a few questions before the solar eclipse happens at 1 pm. I hastily made my way over to a local and started to ask some questions. *I would mainly ask them questions about the eclipse and Captain Samuels*, I thought to myself. When I finally reached one of the locals I had a friendly smile and spoke calmly.

The islander turned around and it was a woman. The woman was elderly with bags under her eyes that looked like they were weighing her down. She had very messy hair that was almost winter white and looked like ocean waves. Her skin was leathered, tanned and ravaged by time.

Her eyes were jade in colour and full of life despite the crows' feet. The clothes she wore were dusty and moth eaten, her fingers appeared brittle and twisted. When she walked towards me, it was spiritless and wilting.

"Hello, my name is Robert; can I ask you some questions regarding Captain Samuels?"

She then replied to me, her voice weak and fragile.

At first her words were undistinguishable in a language unknown, but the more she spoke, the clearer it became as if by some magic.

"Oh Captain Samuels, sure ask me anything about him," she said.

I then engaged in a conversation with this woman.

"So what is your name," I enquired.

"My name is Mary."

"So how long have you lived on this island, Mary."

"Oh I couldn't say. I was born here and I will die here," she glanced at the sky.

"So about Captain Samuels, do you and everyone on the island know him on a personal basis because from what I have learned he seems to come here very often."

She looked at me cautiously, "Oh no, he just helps us."

"In what way does he help you," I asked.

"Hasn't Captain Samuels told you?"

"Yes, he has, but I would like to hear it from your perspective."

"Ok, well, Samuels saved us and whether you believe me or not, there is a demon on this island that only comes when the solar eclipse comes, and for some reason it doesn't attack us if we leave out meat for it. So when we learned this, we started to leave out our uncooked raw meat, but then when we ran out of that we had to go to drastic measures.

"We began to leave out family members who had died or dig up past family members from their graves to leave on our doorsteps. Then Captain Samuels came and offered us a solution, he would get us an alternative source. We no longer had to use our own food and deceased family members as long as we paid him a small amount. So we did.

"At first, we were suspicious to see if he was going to follow through and not just take off with the money, but he did as promised. Then we saw what he had brought back for us, human body parts. Of course none of us questioned it because we would rather use them than our own food source and dead relatives, so you see he saved us."

I started to think back and connect everything Captain Samuels had told me. The same story of how the people of Lemming use dead body parts and that he supplied them. That way they didn't have to use raw meat and their dead family members anymore. He also referred to the people of Lemming as not worshiping the eclipse because of some evil.

Both Mary and Captain Samuel's stories seemed to match almost exactly, except for the part of him getting paid. Samuels never told me anything about that. Then I suddenly remembered the crew member with the red stained overalls on had said that Captain Samuels makes a profit on Lemming.

Could this be the profit he was referring to? Everything seemed to make sense. The reason why Captain Samuels came to Lemming so often was to supply the people of Lemming with body parts from the people he had killed, so they didn't have to use raw meat and dead family members anymore, and every time he docked and dropped these crates off here, he got paid.

All of these statements from people seemed to make sense and connect with each other, but there was one thing I still did not believe in. This beast, this monster, this demon that Samuels and Mary talked about. I asked Mary about it.

"What is this beast or demon you are talking about?"

She replied, "Well no one on the island knows for sure what it looks like, but we can hear its rumbling, growling and snarling as we lay in our beds."

"I guess if this monster is real and does appear when the eclipse comes, I will be the first to see it then."

"No, you should not go out when the eclipse comes and whatever you do, not look at the eclipse for if you look at the sun on the day of an eclipse, the gates of hell will open and drag you down into its volcanic pits!"

Of course I didn't believe a word she had just uttered, then I realised that she and all the people of Lemming were rushing into their homes. I looked at my watch and saw that it was almost 1 pm, the eclipse was almost coming. That must be the reason for this. Of course I was still a bit suspicious about them and if they worship the eclipse or not, but I had to study the eclipse, so I ran to the ship but when I got to the dock, there he was, that dread-inducing crew member with the one eye. He said nothing.

I saw in his hand my bag that had my essentials for studying the eclipse. What was he going to do with them? Then as I thought this, he threw the bag to my feet and walked back onto the ship. I thought it was odd behaviour but had no time to dwell on it, so made my way to a position where I could study the eclipse.

As I started to do this, I could see that the people of Lemming were now placing the human body parts that Captain Samuels had provided them with on their doorsteps, and as I walked past the houses the smell was overwhelming. I could see that some of the body parts were decaying and bones were showing through the skin and flesh.

I also saw that there were many maggots and flies chewing on the various body parts that they had left on their door steps. The sight of this made me want to throw up, but I eventually saw a spot that looked good enough for me to stop and study the eclipse. As I reached the spot I saw that the grass here was green and not charcoal black like the rest of the island, which threw me off but the eclipse was still just a few minutes away.

I unlocked my case and took out my telescope that I had modified to see solar eclipses, and as I was setting up my telescope I heard the people of Lemming locking their doors and bolting their windows. Eventually, I finally finished setting up my telescope and sat looking through the barrel, ready with my notebook to see the eclipse and take notes. I saw it slowly taking over the sun then within a blink of an eye, the sun almost completely disappeared and I could see the sun shining through a valley on the moons edge to form a diamond ring.

I looked down from my telescope and started to take notes in my notebook. It was then I noticed something that was very peculiar. I saw a shadow on the grass where I was sitting. I noticed that the shadow got larger and grew until it covered the whole area around me.

As I looked behind me I saw that the shadow had covered the whole island. I thought to myself, *what is this, how is this possible*. A solar eclipse doesn't do this. I looked through my telescope again but this time there was nothing. Nothing but darkness. No bits of Sun peeking through.

Then I did what the old woman told me not to do. I looked at the solar eclipse and saw that the Sun was not there but instead there was just blackness. How could this be usually? You cannot actually see an eclipse without equipment but here I am looking at it, and this is what is causing the island to be shrouded in darkness.

Then I tried to look away but couldn't. Then suddenly, the shadow over the island grew darker and darker and then I heard something. A snarling, but as I looked around, I could not see anything because the island was shrouded in too much darkness. Then I remembered about my lighter that I had in my pocket, so I searched around in my many pockets until I found it.

When I had it, I struck it with my thumb and a flame came dancing from it. But even with the light I could still barely see, but I walked around to see what the noise was. As I walked around, the air around me was getting colder and colder, and as I was breathing I could see my breath appear in front of me as a cloud of smoke.

Then I heard it again, the snarling and as I turned around, I saw it and thought to myself, they had not been lying. Captain Samuels was telling the truth and so was Mary. The people of Lemming do not worship the eclipse and the proof was right in front of me. The beast, the monster, the demon, the evil that comes with every eclipse, I can see everything now.

They all were telling the truth and as my mind came back to focus on what was in front of me, I couldn't fathom what I was seeing.

My hands trembled as I looked this unknown creature up and down, and as I did this, I saw that its body was black almost tar like and this tar like substance was dripping from its body. I also saw that bubbles would form on the creatures' body going up and down as it breathed. Its feet were also very odd. It had five claw like toes that were all webbed, and it didn't have a head but instead there were 15 blue tentacles that took its place.

As I looked at the torso, I saw that it didn't have arms and I also saw that scattered around its chest were 10 deeply imbedded eyes, but I saw no mouth. I did not want to think about anything right now except getting away from this creature. So I slowly backed away and as I did, this the creatures stomach opened and what I saw was frightful.

Inside the stomach there were 50 sword like teeth and then a tongue came out. The tongue was a tentacle as well but it was black and dripping a black tar substance like the creature. As I saw this, I panicked and ran. I didn't care that I couldn't see where I was going.

I just knew if I ran in the opposite direction of that thing then I would be safe. So I kept running and running, and every time I heard the snarling noise of that creature I ran faster, panting and breathing heavily but I could still here it behind. I didn't know what to do and as my legs grew weak and tired, I suddenly saw a light.

It was the dock. I kept up my speed and ran towards the docks but when I got there the ship was gone. Captain Samuels and his crew had abandoned me. What was I to do? But even as I thought this, I felt something slimy grab my ankle and as I looked down, I knew it was a blue tentacle.

I tried to free myself but nothing worked and I got dragged backwards. The creature dangled me above its grotesque stomach that opened up. Then it slowly lowered me in, but as this was happening the eclipse was starting to finish. I then remembered 7 minutes, that's how long the eclipse lasts.

I glanced at my watch and saw the eclipse was almost over, and thought surely if this creature is bought here by the eclipse, then when the eclipse is finished, it should hopefully go away to where it came from. I then took my lighter and burned the tentacle that was holding my ankle. The creature then screamed in agony dropping me and I then ran while I had the chance.

I ran back towards where I had set up my telescope. I could hear the creature following me, I just hoped I got there in time and I did. When I got there, there was a tiny little ray of sunlight shining on the grass that was now charcoal black like the rest of the island but I dived into the little ray of sunlight and the creature just stood there watching me.

As the sun slowly spread its light over the island again, I watched it slowly step backwards. Every time the Sun moved closer towards it, it retreated but when there was only a small amount of darkness left the creature slunk into the ocean and the island of Lemming was now fully submerged by the Sun.

I then heard the people of Lemming unlock their doors and come outside, but I didn't bother with them for my eyes have seen something no human should ever see. Now my eyes were truly open to the true reality of our universe and the mystery that lie within it. But, if there is anything to take away from this then it is this: NEVER LOOK AT THE SUN ON THE DAY OF AN ECLIPSE OR THE GATES OF HELL WILL OPEN, AND DRAG YOU DOWN INTO ITS VOLCANIC PITS.

Escape Room

The oldest and strongest emotion of mankind is fear, and the oldest and strongest kind of fear is fear of the unknown.

H.P. Lovecraft

Chapter 1

The day was as normal as any other day. I arose slowly from my bed and made my way down the stairs to the kitchen. The kitchen is a pearl white colour and it looks especially beautiful as the sunrays shine in through the large, arched windows and bounce around the room from wall to wall almost making it seem as if you were in heaven. I started to make breakfast. I had wholemeal toast with butter and a cup of coffee.

I looked up at the clock and noticed I was going to be late for my new job as bank manager at the cities 'In us you trust' local bank. I rushed up stairs to my bedroom leaving my half eaten toast behind. I chose the only nice suit I owned, a dark blue blazer and trousers with a white shirt and black tie.

I got changed at rapid speed and went back down stairs. I grabbed what was left of my toast to finish it walking up to the bank. I walked to the door and put on my high shine, polished leather shoes, my brown fuzzy trench coat, and just before I walked out the door, I picked up my light brown, battered and beaten leather briefcase and left for my first day at work.

Chapter 2

As I started walking down the cobbled street, a wave of nervousness came over me. As this happened, I could feel every stone beneath my feet. I could tell if they were even uneven, and as I looked to the road the cars seemed to be moving in slow motion. It was like something from a film or a book, but the feeling left me as fast as it had begun.

I just thought to myself that its first day nerves and brushed it off. I resumed eating my toast and carried on walking down the street. When I had finished my toast, I brushed the minuscule crumbs off my suit and from around my mouth but realised I desperately needed a drink, as my mouth felt dry like a desert. I walked into the nearest shop and went straight to the drinks section.

As I looked, my eyes were bombarded with hundreds of drinks, in hundreds of flavours and colours with unusual names such as 'Blue Bang' which was a very light blue colour and on the label it had a blueberry with a piece of dynamite stuck to it. There were others like 'Red Death' which was a dark red colour and on the label it had a rat eating a cherry. A staff member came up to me from behind and said, "Would you like some help sir?"

I quickly spun round my head and saw a young woman with long golden hair and green eyes. I replied, "Yes, uh, do you sell water?"

She looked confused then replied, "Are you sure, sir? Red Death is quite popular." I was taken aback but didn't have time for an early morning sales pitch, so just walked out the shop and carried on down the street towards the bank. I thought to myself, I will have a drink when I get to work, not long to go now.

Chapter 3

I carried on towards the bank and I could see it in the distance. From the outside, it looked like a greenhouse, nearly all of it was made from glass. It glistened like a jewel as the sun shone down on it. I could tell it was the bank because of the sign that towered in the sky like a skyscraper.

I came to a crosswalk and as I waited, thought about what my first day would be like? Will I make friends? Will everyone hate me? Then suddenly as I was thinking, I heard what sounded like tyres squealing like a pig.

I stopped daydreaming and looked around to see a black van speeding up the road towards the crosswalk. I couldn't see who was driving because the windows were tinted but as it reached the crosswalk, the van came to a stop and almost flipped forward because of the speed it was going. I made my way to the other side of the crosswalk but as I did this I had an unpleasant feeling.

I felt as though the driver of the van was watching me, but when I reached the other side, the van quickly sped off so it was probably nothing. I carried on towards the bank and as I did this, I started to become more confident that this job and this day would be one of the best of my life.

Chapter 4

I finally made it to the bank. It was just across the street, all I had to do was cross the road. I could see people moving around inside like busy worker ants, everybody doing their bit to keep the wheels in motion. I crossed the road noticing it was there again. The same black van from earlier.

It sped up the road towards me, almost running me over. I was lucky not to get hit, but I just brushed it off and finally reached the doors of the bank. I grabbed the cold metallic door handle and swung it open. I stepped inside, the banks floor was light wood, and its walls were painted white.

In the centre of the bank was a cream coloured rug, with three leather cream chairs and opposite a brown bench. Above this, there were two lamp lights hanging from the ceiling with cyan coloured lamp covers. All the other lights were imbedded into the walls except for the natural sources of light coming from the windows and the skylight.

There were also dotted about, four small light brown wooden tables that had leaflets on top of all of them. Then there were the desks. There were eight desks for the customers to go to. They were made from a light brown wood, beech coloured, with a computer at each one and they all were in a line like sardines in a can.

There were also private rooms so customers could speak to staff alone about their account or any other problems, but as I was taking all this in someone tapped me on my shoulder. I turned in response and saw it was a man with thick rugged black hair and dark hazel eyes.

He said, "Yes, hello, my names Jason. I'm your assistant/secretary so anything you need just shout for me, ok…ok so, if you just want to follow me to your office, Mister Bank Manager." I had no reply, I stayed silent and followed him.

When we reached my office, I looked proudly at the door. I saw my name written on it in bright gold. It read, 'Zac S' Branch Manager. I was overcome with happiness. I had a door with my name on. Jason then opened my office door and it wasn't much but I loved it.

There was a large walnut brown desk in the centre, with a large black leather chair behind it. Then against the wall were three white and brown cabinets with three draws each. A large gold and black clock hung on the wall and there were two other chairs in which the client/customer/visitor would sit during a meeting.

I thanked Jason and I slowly entered trying to absorb every detail. Then I sat in the most comfortable chair I have ever sat in. I put my briefcase under the desk, then Jason asked, "Would you like anything before I leave you?"

I instantly replied, "Yes, can I have a water please."

Jason didn't hesitate in replying, "Yes, no problem." He closed the door and I just sat in silence spinning in my large chair.

It was peaceful; it was perfect; it was mine, but I knew I had work to do. Then thud! thud! thud! on the door. I cautiously uttered "Come in?"

It was Jason. "Here's your water, call me if there's anything else." I grabbed the plastic water bottle unscrewing the lid as fast as I possibly could.

"Thanks," and took a giant gulp of water. I breathed a sigh of relief and thought back to that staff member at the shop, didn't she know what water was or was she just trying to be as annoying as possible. Either way, I finally have gotten a drink. I screwed the lid back on the water bottle, put it to one side and started my work.

Chapter 5

As I was about to start my work, I realised I have no idea what I'm supposed to be doing so quickly called Jason. "Jason!"

He came running in. "Yes, what's wrong?"

I replied, "Well what do I do in this job exactly?"

To which he replied quite calmly, "Well you are responsible for coordinating and directing the operational functions of financial institutions such as banks, building societies or credit unions. You oversee front office operations, provide high levels of customer service and direct regular team meetings and training sessions."

I replied, "WHAT?"

Jason replied, "It's OK just stay here until one of the staff needs something approved, for example a loan."

I replied, "Oh that seems simple when you put it like that. I thought it was going to be harder. That's all then I guess, thanks, Jason." He left and closed the door behind him. So I've worked all my life to get this position and all I have to do is sit here and do nothing…sounds perfect for me. Hope I'm still getting paid for it.

So I sat waiting and waiting and waiting for someone to knock on my office door but no one did. I got here at 8 am, and 4 hours have passed and not a single staff member has come to my office, so I decided to take a break from doing nothing and go outside for some fresh air. As I walk towards the doors, I nodded and smiled at the staff and also the customers, some of them smiled back at me, but some of them just looked miserable like they wish this day was over.

I get to the doors and push them open then make my way outside, and just take a big healthy lung full of fresh air, but then I noticed it again for the third time, the same black van parked across the street. I got the same unpleasant feeling that the driver of the van was looking at me, staring straight into my soul. I quickly ran back inside the bank and headed straight for my office.

When I got there, I locked the door and sat down in my chair not understanding what was happening. Were the people in the black van following me, if so why? There's nothing special about me, I'm a normal middle aged guy with blue eyes and short brown hair. I've never done anything Illegal. I calmed myself down.

I just thought of it as a coincidence. I mean there's probably lots of makes of that particular van that have been sold all around the world.

Chapter 6

The work day was finally coming to an end and all the staff were leaving. Jason came in to say bye. They were turning most of the lights off and the janitors were coming in to clean, so I decided to go home as well, I mean there's nothing to do here so I made my way outside. When I got outside, I noticed that it was dark and that the street lamps had come on, but another thing I noticed was that the black van that had been parked across the street was gone.

I knew I thought to myself, I was just getting worked up about nothing, so I started to make my way home and as I walked down the street, it was so quiet. I could hear my own heartbeat. I was the only person walking down this street for some reason, but as a I continued down the street the street lamps started to flicker.

I heard what sounded like a car. I turned around and saw the black van speeding up the road. I started to walk at a faster pace. Then I heard it speed up, that's when I started running, but the black van caught up to me and when it did it halted and its doors swung open.

I tried to see if there was anyone inside but all I could see was blackness. It felt as if something was pulling me closer, and as I looked down something was pulling me closer. My body was being dragged through the air as if by magic. Then suddenly, I was violently pulled into the van and as this happened, I hit my head on something and passed out.

Chapter 7

When I awoke, I looked around to see where I was and I found myself in a small and confined room. The room was almost circular in shape with no doors in sight. The only source of light, though bright, came from a solitary light bulb hanging over the middle of the room.

There was a round dark wooden table in the middle of the room with three maroon coloured chairs around it. Beneath the table, there was a maroon coloured rug with some white diamonded shapes on it. Apart from these things, the room was almost empty. A glass book shelf stood in the corner and two paintings on one of the walls.

The glass book shelf was not very full. As I looked inside it, I could see that the books had accumulated a thick layer of dust from not being used, as well as the glass its self was very dirty. I looked at the paintings. They were the same size with the same wooden frames but were different styles. One of the paintings looked like a giant mushroom growing in a forest and the other one looked like a house or a cottage that was on fire.

I gathered myself and started to think about the situation that I was in. I had been kidnapped and as this realisation came over me, I felt like the room was closing in around me. I felt claustrophobic. I started to panic, my breathing became fast and heavy, my vision started to blur and my body went limp. I fell to the floor and fainted.

Chapter 8

I woke up groggy and disorientated. My head was spinning. I slowly got my bearings and realised where I was. I vomited, knowing that this was real, this was not a dream. I got to my feet and sat at the table wiping the left over vomit from around my mouth with my sleeve.

I then noticed something that had not there before, a jigsaw puzzle box. Now I was more confused because that had not been there earlier. I thought perhaps, maybe I hadn't noticed it with everything happing so fast and brushed it off. I examined the jigsaw puzzle box.

It was brand new, still sealed in its plastic wrap. The box was plain white with no picture or any indication of what the jigsaw could be. The only words on the box were in the left corner in big bold letters. It said 'PUZZLE BOX'. I looked around the room.

I thought to myself that I may as well do the puzzle. I mean there is nothing else to do here. It could help pass the time while I was waiting to hear from my kidnappers to see what their demands were going to be.

Chapter 9

I tore off the plastic wrap and eagerly opened the box. When I opened it I saw that there was no leaflet to help you with the puzzle, not even a picture to help you know what pieces go where. I realised I would have to try and put the jigsaw together just using my imagination, determination, perseverance and some smarts, so I dumped all the pieces onto the table.

The first thing I did was spread the pieces out and then turn all the pieces picture side up. I started sorting the jigsaw pieces into separate groups, for example I sorted all edge pieces into one pile, then if pieces had the same colour or bits of picture on I would sort them into the same pile. For example, some pieces had grass on others had trees on so I sorted them into different piles.

By the end, I had four large piles of jigsaw pieces. I then started to assemble the puzzle. I started with the border of the jigsaw so I took the edge pieces and started to join them together. This took a while and when I had finished, it gave me no clue to what it could be. I couldn't tell what it was; it was just green I was thinking maybe a jungle.

I sat back and looked at the frame on the table. I felt tired, hungry and thirsty. What time was it? Was it day or night? I had no way of knowing. I took another pile of puzzle pieces and started to assemble the main part of the jigsaw. I started to assess where the pieces were going to go but as I looked through the pile, I saw that the pictures on the pieces looked like grass.

I thought that would obviously be at the bottom of the jigsaw, now it's just trying to fit the pieces in the right place. For this I would need to pay close attention to the shape of each jigsaw piece because jigsaw puzzle pieces come in six basic shapes, ranging from zero knobs and four holes, to four knobs and zero holes and all permutations in between.

So I guess, if I was more experienced with jigsaws, the easier I would be able to tell if an individual piece had a chance to fit in a certain spot, but I guess I would just have to test my luck. I started to pick certain puzzle pieces to see if they would fit. It was trial and error, some fit perfect and some I had to rearrange a few times, but eventually I got it done, well some of it done anyway. I looked down at the jigsaw and as I suspected it was grass, so maybe it is a jungle of some kind.

Chapter 10

I stood up slowly. I needed to stretch my legs. I walked slowly around the room, touching the cold, clammy walls. I tried to feel for a door but nothing. I found myself back at the table, looking down at the puzzle. I sat down and grabbed the next pile of jigsaw pieces and started to examine them. These were also green but with some brown thrown in what looked to be twigs or branches perhaps.

I started to try and place the puzzle pieces, looking at what I had completed so far to see where certain pieces could fit. It was trial and error for the most part because there was still a lot of the puzzle that needed to be filled in, but as I slowly placed the pieces in I saw that it was coming together. It looked like a forest. Then I noticed something.

The puzzle bared a resemblance to the one of the paintings I saw when I first got here. It was the painting of the forest with a large mushroom growing in it. I looked back and forth many times to reassure myself that it was indeed the same image. I got up and walked over to the painting on the wall and tried to take it down and bring it back to the table with me for reference, but no matter how hard I pulled it was if it was glued to the wall.

I grew weary, my arms tired and I gave up and went back to the table. I sank down into my chair in defeat but I realised the painting is still on the wall, I can still see it so I can still use it as reference. With a renewed energy, I grabbed the last pile of jigsaw pieces and went to work, glancing every so often at the painting.

My hands couldn't move quickly enough, my head was swivelling back and forth so fast that I felt a little lightheaded. I was looking at the painting then looking at the puzzle, and repeating this over and over until finally I was finished. I breathed a little sigh of relief and felt some small warmth of pride.

Then I looked down and saw to my horror that there were three pieces missing. I felt a rage bubbling up inside me and could feel my body heating up. I screamed in anger and frustration.

I calmed down and started to search. How could there be three missing pieces? The box was sealed and unopened and I didn't drop any. I got up throwing the chair away. I don't understand. All the time I'd wasted on this idiotic puzzle and there are pieces missing!

I was pacing angrily back and forth, round and round, my head spinning, my mind racing. I grabbed the glass book shelf and flung it to the floor in a fit of rage. All I saw was crystal like glass flying everywhere around the room, books spread out across the floor, and a dust cloud flew up into the air clouding my vision and choking me.

When the dust cloud had settled and I stopped choking, I tried to pull myself together. I listened for voices, angry bewildered voices running towards the room, wondering what was happening. Nothing, no voices just silence. I looked around trying to calm myself.

I had made a mess, broken glass everywhere, books scattered and torn. What an idiot I was, I was going to have to clean this mess up or there may be repercussions. I moved towards the bookcase, bending to pick it up, and then I saw it. Taped to the back of the bookcase was one of the missing pieces of the jigsaw puzzle.

I was utterly confused. What kind of people had I been kidnapped by? Why had I been taken? I had no money, neither did my family. I had not seen anyone or heard anyone since being locked in this room. Did they want me to do this puzzle so they could play a joke on me? Why? I don't understand.

I looked down at the puzzle piece in my hand. I pulled the bookcase up and placed it back against the wall. I took the puzzle piece and added it to the rest of the jigsaw. I stood looking at it, two more pieces to find. Perhaps they were hidden in the room; perhaps my captors were playing some sadistic, psychological game.

I felt the energy draining from me. When were they going to feed me or give me water? When would they tell me what they wanted? I looked around the room. Where could the other pieces be? I began searching. The two remaining pieces must be in here.

I began picking the books up from the floor and flicking though them, shaking them searching to see if one of them might have a piece inside, but to my disappointment, none of them did. I replaced the final book on the shelf but no piece had I found. I moved on to the chairs ripping them up, breaking their legs and looking inside them but again nothing. I decided to look underneath the table and to my luck a puzzle piece was indeed taped underneath.

I grabbed it and added it to the rest of the jigsaw. I now just needed to find one more piece to complete the jigsaw. I had no idea where to look, I had looked everywhere. I hung my head in defeat, but as I hung my head I saw the rug underneath the table. I moved the table, careful not to disturb the puzzle. I bent down and flipped the rug over.

Nothing! I looked around hopelessly. Where could it be? I sat back and could feel the tears, desperation and frustration building up inside. Why did I felt like this, it was only a stupid puzzle. The truth was that I somehow felt this puzzle was important, that I had to complete it. That it was almost as if my life depended on it. I looked up and found myself staring at the paintings on the wall.

I stayed that way for a while, how long I don't know, staring up at those paintings. Then I noticed that the painting of the cottage was slightly askew, just at an angle instead of straight like the other. I felt light, as if I was floating. I looked down to see I was walking.

I made my way slowly over to the paintings. Maybe I was imagining it. I could be wrong. I gently brushed the picture frame of the cottage painting. It moved. Just a little but it moved. I felt a grin forming as I grabbed the painting from the wall.

I closed my eyes and prayed that it was there. I slowly turned over the painting and there, taped to the back was the final piece of the puzzle. I grabbed the jigsaw piece and laughed joyfully before adding it to the rest of the puzzle. I laughed and felt the tension leave my body.

Suddenly, I heard a loud, almost mechanical sound coming from inside the walls. I made my way over to where, the wall where the paintings were. I put my ear to the wall. The noise stopped and I heard a loud click.

Suddenly, the painting of the forest with the giant mushroom growing in it lifted up and underneath it was a red button. I was hesitant at first. What would this do? Was it a trick? Slowly, cautiously I raised my hand and pressed it. The whole wall moved and opened up like a door to reveal another room behind it.

Chapter 11

After seeing this happen, I was in shock. I didn't know what was happening. I thought I had been kidnapped for money but obviously there was something else going on here. I nervously walked into the dark room that had just been revealed to me. When I got into the room, I couldn't see anything it was pitch black.

It was if I had gone blind, then suddenly behind me the door slammed shut with a loud thud. As this happened, the lights in the room flickered on and I saw that the room I had entered was a very baron room. It was square in shape and larger than the other room that I had been in. It had what looked like rotting wooden walls as well as mould growing in some of the corners.

I almost vomited again but I managed to keep it down. The floor was wooden and looked very decrepit. With every step I made, the floor creaked and groaned beneath my feet. Then I saw the only things that were in the room were a square table with a Rubik's cube on top, as well as one chair.

On the table was also a glass of water and a cold chicken sandwich. Finally food! Then I saw on the opposite side if the room a bright orange door which instantly stood out in this bleak and depressing room. I ran over to the door and started tugging at the handle, pulling as hard as humanly possible, but to my disappointment, the door was locked.

I walked over to the table and sat down in the chair. As I did this, it felt as if the chair was going to break underneath me. It looked like very old and withered but to my surprise it did not break. I started to think about my situation.

What was happening? Why haven't the kidnappers made demands yet? Why are these puzzles here? Were they playing some sadistic game with me? I didn't understand, but I just kept on telling myself that as long as I carry on with what they want me to do, perhaps I won't get hurt.

I picked up the glass of water and at first gulped it down, then I realised that I may not get another for some time so started to sip slowly. I grabbed at the sandwich, taking a huge mouthful. It felt so good. Soft white bread with creamy, silky mayonnaise and moist, flavoursome chicken. It was the most delicious sandwich I had ever eaten; I savoured it slowly but left half for later.

I felt refreshed. I looked down at the Rubik's cube. It was all jumbled up and I as assessed it I assumed that they wanted me to solve it. I grabbed it off the table and as I did so a number appeared on the wall in front of me. The number was twenty. I looked around the room to see where this could be coming from, but I could see no source of light anywhere, so I pushed it from my mind and started to solve the Rubik's cube.

First I started with the white face of the Rubik's cube and made a cross while paying attention to the colour side of the centre pieces. I was about to sort the next move when suddenly the twenty went down to nineteen. I now understood what this number that appeared on the wall was for. It was telling me that I had to solve the Rubik's cube by using twenty moves or less.

Now I understood this, I carried on to the next move. In this move, I arranged all white corner pieces to finish the first face by twisting the bottom layer, so that one of the white corners is directly under the spot where it's supposed to go on the top layer. Then the number on the wall went down again from nineteen to sixteen.

After that, I then made my next move, which was to first turn the cube upside down so the white face was facing down and the uncompleted face was facing me. I made eight moves in order to get the cube close to completion, and then the number on the wall went down again from sixteen to eight. I sighed and made my next move. I was now on the last face of the cube.

I started again by making a cross this time, it was with the yellow cubes; this took four moves. I was now running out of moves. I was getting anxious but I had to carry on, so next, after making the yellow cross I put the yellow edge pieces in their places to match the colours of the side centre pieces. This took me eight moves, so I watched as the number on the wall slowly went down four…three…two…one and then it disappeared.

The numbers disappeared and were no longer there. I didn't know what to do or what had happened, so I tried continuing on with the Rubik's cube but when I tried to move it, it wouldn't budge. It was if it was locked in place, so in sheer confusion, I hurled the Rubik's cube at the floor with all my might. As it hit, I saw an explosion of plastic fly through the air like shrapnel.

I looked over and just saw a plastic pile of rubble and debris on the floor mixed with a few colours from the stickers like green or red.

I panicked. What had I done? What was I thinking? How was I supposed to finish it now? What if I was going to be stuck in this room forever? I fell to my knees, tears welling up, stinging my eyes.

I looked at the pile of plastic on the floor, something caught my eye something shiny was glistening in the rubble. I got up and walked over there to see what it was. I slowly sorted through the mess and I saw to my disbelief that it was a key. I thought to myself that if I had solved that Rubik's cube with twenty moves or less, perhaps the Rubik's cube have opened up revealing the key inside.

I returned to the table and downed the last of the water as my mouth felt like I had eaten sand. I grabbed the key and headed to the bright orange door. I put the key in the lock and turned it. There was a loud click then there it was again, the mechanical noise in the walls.

Then more clicking noises and the door creaked open slowly only to reveal…a third room.

Chapter 12

I stood there in utter shock thinking to myself, *when will this end?* I stepped into the room, as I did this, the door behind me slammed itself shut just like before. This time it locked itself. When it did this, I heard a loud clicking noise that echoed around the room.

I looked around and saw that this room was filled with a numerous objects. There were two dark brown wooden cabinets, one on the left side of the room up against the wall and one on the right side of the room up against the wall. The cabinet on the left side of the room had 5 pale white milk jugs on it, there was also a grey stone like mortar and pestle on top of it.

Above it on the wall was a small mirror in a golden frame. The cabinet on the right side of the room had a golden candle stick holder with four luminescent white candles in it. There was also a piece of paper folded up on top of the cabinet next to a pen, and in front of the cabinet there was a golden chair, with a red velvet cushion. Above the cabinet was a very large mirror with a brown and beaten frame.

The walls were a bright green colour and on the walls were at least 7 picture frames, but in the frames there were no pictures, just writing that read, *nearly there*. I took comfort in knowing this was almost over but what would happen at the end? Would my kidnappers kill me? I didn't want to think about it so I sat down in the chair that was fit for a king.

Then I saw the folded up piece of paper again and wondered what it was, so I gently and slowly unfolded it. On the paper was a Sudoku puzzle, it was then I thought to myself, *every time I complete a puzzle a door opens to another room.* I looked around but I saw no door in this room.

Then I thought maybe there could be a secret door like in the first room. I was in here, where else could I go, what else could I do? So I decided to try and complete the puzzle, to carry on forward perhaps to the next room, and maybe eventually get out of this puzzle prison.

I picked up the pen that was next to the paper and started to work out the puzzle. The Sudoku puzzle was a large nine by nine square inside that was nine small squares, and inside those were even smaller squares to write the numbers in. Some squares had numbers already been filled such as the first square on the first row had an **8** in the top corner.

The first square on the second row had a **3** right next to the middle square. The first square last row had a **7** in the middle square. So I started with this first square. I knew if I use a number I can't use it again in that same column going across or down, so I started easy with **1, 2, 9, 4, 6** and **5,** and if I add the numbers that were already there **8, 1, 2, 9, 4, 3, 6, 7** and **5.**

I finished the first square only eight more left. I saw that the second square also had numbers filled in but this time it was only two. The second square, in the second row left of the middle was a **6,** then the second square final row middle square had a **9** in the middle.

I then started to work out the second square. I knew now what numbers I couldn't use in certain rows and started to work it out. A **7** first, then a **5, 3, 8, 2, 4** and **1;** and now if I add the numbers that were already filled in **7, 5, 3, 6, 8, 2, 4, 9** and **1.** Seven more left to work out.

I moved on to work out the third square. The third square had only one number already filled in. It was the final row in the left corner and it was a **2** but this didn't bother me. I dropped the pen, sat back and stretched my arms out, they were tight and sore.

I wriggled my fingers as they were starting to tense up due to the tightness of my grip on the pen. I felt tired, no not tired, drained, as if the energy was slowly being sucked out of me. I sat up, screwed my head on and got ready to work it out.

But as I was about to, I felt a flash of blue light appear in my brain. Then suddenly these numbers started to imbed themselves into my skull. They were all I could think of **6, 4, 9, 1, 7, 5, 8,** and **3**. I didn't know what they meant but as I looked down at the piece of paper, I thought to myself that these numbers might be the answer to the third square.

So I rapidly wrote them down before they escaped my mind, and as I looked down I saw that they were indeed the answer to the third square. I checked it to make sure and included the numbers that were already filled in **6, 4, 9, 1, 7, 5, 2, 8** and **3.**

I saw it was indeed correct. I then thought about what had made this happen, what made me think of these numbers so abruptly and what was that flash of blue light. The only explanation for it I thought is that I was tired. I hadn't gotten any sleep in a while, so I decided to try and sleep.

With no bed or even a sofa in the room, I curled up on the chair like a cat and went to sleep, trying just for a moment to forget about the situation I was in.

Chapter 13

When I awoke, I immediately vomited. I put it down to lack of food and hydration, and wiped the vomit from around my mouth. I arose slowly as my head felt light and dizzy, and I felt as if I was going to fall over. I stretched even more slowly, feeling my muscles and bones waking up and moaning at me about the position I had slept in.

Then I sat in the chair and as I did this, I started to wonder when this would end. When would I get out of here, and if I would ever see the sun again and feel its warming, healing, rays shine down on my skin. Would I ever feel a cold breeze against my cheeks, or look up and see the ocean blue sky ever again, or walk on the uneven rickety cobblestone street.

Would I see the candyfloss like clouds float on by above my head or hear the rush of traffic swarm by like a bees nest? I would have to focus on what was happening here and now, so I carried on with the Sudoku puzzle.

As I recalled, I have completed three out of nine squares so I only have six left, and I will have then completed the puzzle. So I now started on the fourth square, like the third square, this square only had one space filled in it was on the top row in the middle square the number was **5**. I started to work out the rest of the numbers.

This took me a while as I was a little bit groggy and hadn't woken up properly, but eventually after a few minutes, I worked it out. The answer was **1, 4, 3, 6, 9, 2, 8** and **7**; and if I included the numbers that were already filled in **1, 5, 4, 3, 6, 9, 2, 8** and **7**.

I moved on to the fifth square. This had four numbers already filled in. On the top row in the left corner was a **7**. In the second row, middle square was a **4** and second row; left of the middle square was a **5**. Then bottom row, in the right corner was a **1**. I started to try and work this square out.

This square took me longer than the previous other ones because of how I had filled up almost half of the puzzle, but eventually I completed the square.

The answer was **2, 3, 8, 6** and **9**; and if I add the numbers that were already filled in **2, 3, 7, 8, 4, 5, 1, 6** and **9**.

Now there are only four more squares to solve and I will have finished the puzzle. I moved onto the sixth square. This square had two numbers already filled in. On the second row on the left side of the middle square was a **7**. Then on the final row in the middle square was a **3**.

I then carried on trying to work out the other numbers. This one also took me a while to complete, I noticed the closer I get to the end of the puzzle the harder it gets, so I guess the very end square will be extremely difficult.

After a while I did eventually complete the sixth square. I got up out the chair and walked around the room. I needed to take a break and to stretch my legs. As I got up, I heard almost every bone in my body crack like a twig. I thought maybe it was because of how I slept last night curled up in ball on the chair.

That could be good for my body or anything in general. Then I looked in the mirror at my appearance and just sighed. My brown hair was a mess, my eyes looked like tar pits from lack of sleep and my best suit was covered in vomit. As I looked closer I could see stubble.

I couldn't have been here for that long, but then again who knows, I don't. I've lost track of time and the days of the week, but I then refocused and sat down to continue with the puzzle.

I now only had three squares left to complete and I would be out of this room. I moved on to square number seven. In this square like the others, there were numbers already completed. To my surprise, it did not take me a long time to complete this square. Maybe I finally figured out a system or just got lucky.

I quickly moved on to square number eight, thinking I had finally figured out how to do it because of how fast I had finished the last square. Number eight, unlike the others, only had the one number already in it. In the second row, left of the middle square. It was a **5**. I quickly tried to work it out and again for some unknown reason figured it out as fast as before.

I was now thinking I had definitely figured out how to do these puzzles. I hastily moved on to the last square, number nine. This last square took me a very long time and I got it wrong quite a few times.

So I guess I was just lucky with the other two squares and I was not at all getting the hang of the puzzle. After a couple of hours, I finally figured out the numbers. As I completed the last square, I sighed in relief.

The puzzle was finished. I threw the pen down onto the cabinet. Behind me I could hear a low rumble. As it got louder, I realised it was the same sound I had heard before. It was the mechanical noise that slowly echoed through the hollow walls.

Then suddenly it ended abruptly and the large mirror with the brown beaten frame started to slowly move down like a car window. When it reached the bottom, I heard that familiar noise again, then the click. As I peered in through this large square shaped hole in the wall where the mirror had been, to my amazement, disbelief and dismay, I saw another room.

Chapter 14

I jumped up onto the cabinet and climbed through the large square hole in the wall. When I had eventually crawled through, the mirror quickly zipped up and locked with a clicking noise.

I looked around at the room that I had entered. It was an octagon shaped room, the walls were an almost blinding bright yellow colour. The floor had dark and light brown octagon shaped tiles everywhere, and in the centre of the room, there was a square shaped table with a cream coloured cloth covering it. On top of the table were three sheets of paper and a pen as well as a glass oil lamp.

Behind the table was a black chair and on the three walls behind the chair were three bright white windows. WINDOWS! I could see lush green grass outside, the sunlight making it shine, so I ran over to one of the windows to try on open it and escape.

I rapidly undid the catch on the window and as I did this something fell out of the window. I looked down to see what it was. It was a photograph of some grass. I looked back up at the window and saw a brick wall. I then knew in that moment that there was no way out of here. I would be stuck in this puzzle prison forever.

I stepped slowly and fell into the chair in defeat. Tears began to stream down my face but no sound came forth from my mouth. No sobs, no cries, what would be the point, but the tears still came. Another room and no doubt another puzzle, how much more of this could I take?

I could taste the saltiness of my tears as they stung my lips; I suddenly felt an intense thirst and hunger. I fought a swell of anger inside.

"I'm not going to do this anymore!" I shouted. "I have had enough!"

"I want food and water and a coffee or this game of yours is over."

"Do you hear me? Do you?" I paused hoping to hear something, anything; a reply, a refusal, but nothing. I sat back down in the chair and wiped my face. I leaned forward, resting my arms on the table and then resting my head on my arms. I was tired, so tired. I didn't want to play this stupid game anymore. My eyes felt sore and heavy, and I slowly found myself falling asleep.

I awoke with a start. I thought I had heard something. I looked around the room, nothing. Then there on the table before me was something that at first I thought must be a mirage. There on a silver platter sat a double cheeseburger, large fries, a bottle of water and a large coffee.

The smell hit my nostrils and seemed to fill my whole body. My stomach rumbled, already anticipating the meal that was coming. I picked up the coffee and took a deep breath of its aroma.

It was as if I were smelling it for the first time. I felt dizzy with excitement. I slowly put the cup to my lips and took a sip. It was warm and sweet and I could have carried on drinking it forever.

I carefully placed the cup back onto the table, taking care not to spill any. My hands were shaking; in fact my whole body was shaking. I pulled the double cheeseburger and fries towards me; again I took a deep breath. The tears welled up again but this time they were tears of joy.

I picked up a fry and slowly began to chew. The crunchy, soft, salty texture was like heaven. I grabbed a few more and gobbled them down. Then I turned my attention to the burger. I held it in my hands and looked lovingly at it. The sesame seed bun was warm and soft in my hands and the smell of the cheese and fried onions was intoxicating.

I licked my lips and put the burger to my mouth. I slowly bit into the burger, moving my teeth slowly down through the layers. First the soft bun and then the greasy onions which were sweet and warm. Then cheese and finally the inch thick, moist beef burger. I chewed slowly. I savoured every second of it.

In between bites of burger, I crammed my mouth with French fries. I thought to myself that if this was my final meal I couldn't be happier. When the food was finally gone, I opened the cold bottle and took half of it down in one gulp.

Then I sat back slowly, feeling warm satisfaction, not only of the meal that I had just consumed, but of the fact I had won a battle. I had given them my demands and they had complied. It gave me a new vigour, perhaps I would be able to get out of here. I drank the coffee and wondered what type of puzzle was awaiting me.

Chapter 15

I started to examine the pieces of paper that were on the table and as I read it, I thought to myself hurray another puzzle. I instantly knew this puzzle would be more difficult than the others because it was a riddle and I'm not that good at riddles. The riddle was:

Five houses painted five different colours stand in a row.
One person of a different nationality lives in each house.
The five home owners all drink some type of beverage, smoke a certain cigar brand and have a certain kind of pet but no two are the same.

Underneath that there was a question.
Who owns the fish?

That was on the first sheet of paper. On the second sheet were clues to help me. I knew they were clues because at the top of the paper it read in bold black writing **Clues**. There were fifteen clues in order they read:

The Brit lives in the red house.

1. The Swede keeps dogs as pets.
2. The Dane drinks tea.
3. The green house is on the left of the white house.
4. The green houses owner drinks coffee.
5. The owner who smokes Pall Mall rears birds.
6. The owner of the yellow house smokes Dunhill.
7. The owner living in the centre house drinks milk.
8. The Norwegian lives in the first house.
9. The owner who smokes Blends lives next to the one who keeps cats.
10. The owner who keeps the horse lives next to the one who smokes Dunhill.
11. The owner who smokes Bluemaster drinks beer.
12. The German smokes Prince.

13. The Norwegian lives next to the blue house.
14. The owner who smokes Blends lives next to the one who drinks water.
15. The Brit lives in the red house.

I examined the last piece of paper and saw it was blank and so came to the conclusion that this piece of paper was for me to use work out the riddle.

I first started by making a grid that was six by six down the left side. I put the different categories such as colour, nationality, smoke, drink and then pet, and at the top I put the ordering of the houses from one to five as this I thought would help me visual the answer better. I then started to work it out.

So the Norwegian lives in the first house. That would go in the first column next to nationality. Also the Norwegian lives next to the blue house. I put the blue house in the second column next to colour.

	1	2	3	4	5
Colour		Blue			
Nationality	Norwegian				
Smoke					
Drink					
Pets					

The man living in the centre house drinks milk, so I put that in the third column in the drinks row. The next one is the owner of the green house. It is on the left side of the white house; the owner of the green house also drinks coffee. Which means column four is the only place it can go. The reason for this is if it were to go in column five the one to the right of it would have to be white and there's nothing to the right of five.

It can't be three because the owner of house three drinks milk, whereas green has to drink coffee. I sat back and caught my breath. This was hard going. Colours, drinks and pets etc were all swirling in my head. I took a swig of the remaining water and carried on.

It can't be two because that's already blue and it can't be one because if it were to be one then two would have to be white, but it's not its blue, so four is the only spot it can go which means five has to be the white house.

The next clue is 'Brit lives in a red house' which means three is the only spot that can go because I'm looking for a house which has no nationality yet and no colour because they have to go together which is three. I put them in to the grid, two in that column and now in the colour column there is only one spot left which means it has to be yellow. Now following on from that, I can see that the owner of the yellow house smokes Dunhill, so I went and put Dunhill in the smoke column.

The man who keeps horses lives next to the man who smokes Dunhill. Horses go in column two, and now for drink and house number one. There's only one option, water, so I entered it into the column then read the next clue.

The man who smokes blends lives next to a neighbour who drinks water. Blends have to be number two for smoke. The next clue is the man who smokes Bluemaster drinks beer, which means I'm looking for one of the houses which currently does not have anything in drink or smoke and that's house number five. Bluemaster and beer have to go together which means they can only go there; it's the only possible option.

The next clue the Dane drinks tea, same situation as the last one. I'm looking for a house which has nothing in drink and nothing in nationality so that's number two. Same thing again the German smokes Prince, so I'm looking for something without anything in smoke or nationality so that's house number four. The Swede keeps dogs as pets, same thing nothing in pets nothing in nationality so that would be house number five.

Now the final one, the person who smokes Pall Mall rears birds. That would be house number three and as I finished, I look down at the completed grid and examine it to figure out who the owner of the fish is. I then reach two possible conclusions. It is either house number one or house number four. Then I realised I had missed a clue.

The owner who smokes Blends lives next to the one who keeps cats. This means that house number one has to be cats, which means that house number four is the one that keeps the fish! So the overall answer is house number four, the green house where the German lives, who drinks coffee and smokes Prince cigarettes, that is the owner of the fish!

I thought to myself maybe I'm not as bad at riddles as I had previously thought. Then as I thought this, I suddenly got an intense pain in my skull. I saw it again, the flash of blue light. This time it looked different. I saw a black shadow of something that looked like a person. Then the pain went as fast as it came.

That mechanical noise came creeping through the walls again and stopped. I couldn't see anything happening. I sat back in the chair clasping my hands to my head and wiping the sweat from my brow. I looked up at the ceiling, it was moving slowly sideways to reveal another room above me.

How the hell would I get up there? There were no ladders. Then it struck me like an iron. I could stack the chair on top of the table and climb up. So I did exactly that, I grabbed the black withered chair and balanced it on top of the table.

I carefully climbed onto the chair and it started to wobble precariously. I eventually was standing on top of the chair, trying my hardest to keep my balance but I still couldn't reach the room above. I lunged upward, pushing off from the chair. I grabbed the ledge, hearing the chair crash onto the floor below me, I climbed up into the room.

As I did this, the ceiling, which was now the floor, sealed back up and made a loud clicking noise. I was now locked in this room until I completed the next puzzle.

Chapter 16

I examined the square shaped room which I was now in. The room seemed to have a heavy pirate theme to it. In the corner was a brown, almost golden world globe. On the right side of the room up against the wall was a large dark brown, battered chest with bits of wood splintered from it.

Then in the upper right corner of the room was a miniature cannon. The walls were a dark oak colour with lots of skull and cross bone flags covering them. The floor was a lighter brown colour and then in the middle of the room was a circular table with a stool next to it.

On the table were two pieces of paper as well as a pen, and directly above the table was a chandelier with six pale white skulls attached to it and shining out of their mouths were lights. I sat down on the stool and examined the papers. I noticed on one of the pieces of paper was a riddle the riddle was:

Three gods A, B and C are called in some order True, False and Random.
True always speaks truly,
False always speaks falsely,
But whether Random speaks truly or falsely is a completely random matter.

Your task is to determine the identities of A, B and C by asking three yes-no questions; each question must be put to exactly one god. The gods understand English but will answer all questions in their own language in which the words for yes and no are da and ja in some order. You do not know which word means which. After reading this, I confidently grabbed the pen and started to work it out.

The first thing I did was to figure out a question that would identify who can't be random or who can only be either true or false. This will, by process of elimination, help me reveal the identity of random and once I have done that, it will be easier to work out the other two. So to make it easier for myself I broke it down into two simple steps. The first step I realised was that if I insert if and only if into a question that is either true or both false, I would get a true answer.

It is like inserting a multiplication sign between either two positive or two negative numbers. The number that I would get would always be positive, so inserting if and only if between either two true or two false questions would always get me a true answer. For the second and final step, I would need to find out if da was no or yes, to do this I would ask a question something like this:

"Does da mean yes if and only if Pluto is a dwarf planet?"

Now I was ready to solve this riddle. To god A I asked "Does da mean yes if and only if you are true and if and only if B is random?"

I then heard an answer echo through the room from what sounded like a speaker system. It said "ja," so this made god B either true or false. I then asked god B.

"Does da mean yes if and only if Pluto is a dwarf planet?"

Then again an answer echoed through the room the answer was "da" so this then made me realise god B was true. I then asked god B one more question knowing now it is true.

"Does da mean yes if and only if A is random?" and because god B is true he must say "da" which is yes, which means god A is random and god C is false.

As I finished writing this down, I sighed in relief but nothing happened. No secret door opened no mysterious mechanical noise echoing through the walls. Even though I had finished this puzzle there was nothing happening.\

Suddenly the walls started to shake. It looked like they were phasing into something else, the room gradually got bigger and bigger then changed shape, and when this madness had finally finished, I looked around and I could not fathom what my eyes were seeing.

Chapter 17

What I saw looked like something not from earth. The room changed completely its shape was now circular, all the walls were now white and on the walls were large metal pipes as well as four metal columns with a bright blue light emanating from them. These columns all went up onto the ceiling and met at this peculiar looking silver, circular device that was on the centre of the ceiling.

This device had five monitors on it as well as black wires hanging down from it. On the monitors were images of space, the ceiling looked as if it was made from large, silver metal plates. The floor was a light brown wooden colour and finally in the centre of the room was a circular metal table with one metal stool beside it. The legs of the stool looked like a person's legs when bending down.

I then sat on this stool completely confused. Where am I? What is happening? Then suddenly a metal panel the size of a door slid open and I saw the shadow of a person. I thought to myself, *Finally I will get some answers*, but as the shadowy figure came closer and closer and then finally came round the corner, I saw that it was not a person at all.

In fact it was not even human. What I saw was a being form another world. An alien floating in mid-air, its skin was light blue with pink in some places. It had no lower body; its upper body was stocky but very thin towards the bottom. Its arms only came down to where our elbows would be.

Its neck stuck out like a blow fish. Coming out of its back were four horn like objects and its face was very large, almost in the shape of a cross its eyes were almost non-existent being very deeply imbedded in its head. They were a very dark empty black colour, it had a nose but no holes to with which to breathe or smell. It also had the shape of a mouth but it looked like it was almost welded shut then on its chin either side were two little spikes.

Finally, I saw two holes on its almost cross shaped face, one on the right side of its face near the edge of its head and the other on the left side of it face near the edge of its head. I then thought to myself, *This is how it must breathe*, and as I thought this, I heard a voice in my head.

"Hello, human, my name is Talock and I come from the planet Zalga."

After hearing this, I looked around the room to see were this could be coming from. I slowly realised it could only be coming from the alien being but how, I thought could it speak without moving its mouth? So I asked it.

"Yes, uh hah…hello my name's Zac. How are you speaking to me, because I can hear your voice but your mouth isn't moving."

Talock then replied, "It is simple, on my planet this is no great feat. I am using telepathy. This allows me to speak directly into your mind. On my planet, we have evolved passed the point of speech, as you have already noticed, I have no real mouth, merely an orifice through which to feed."

I was baffled, so much to take in. Here was a real life alien standing, well floating in front of me. So many questions but first I asked, "I don't understand, I thought I was kidnapped, what's happening?"

Talock replied, "Yes, I took you to take part in this test. I placed five of your planets hardest puzzles in five different rooms. First the jigsaw, second the Rubik's cube, third the hardest Sudoku puzzle on your planet, fourth Einstein's riddle and finally fifth, the gorge boolos riddle, the hardest riddle on your planet.

"Many have tried this test and all have failed. You are the first to complete it that is why I have revealed myself to you because you are a very bright individual who will be able to take in this information and understand it."

I thought to myself, *so it was all a test to see if I was smart enough to get to see an alien life form amazing.* I then proceed to ask Talock some questions about alien life. "Talock, what are you doing here?"

Talock replied, "Observing."

I then asked him, "Observing what?"

But Talock stayed silent so I asked another question.

"What is it like on planet Zalga?"

Talock replied, "You are not capable of comprehending or accepting the discoveries of my planet."

I replied, "Try me."

Talock then replied, "The origin of the universe, the nature of so called life it is known." I was shocked did Talock know the meaning of life? I had to ask.

"So you know the meaning of life?"

Talock replied, "Not meaning, nature meaning is something that is ascribed nature is objective reality." I was blown away I then suddenly thought of another question.

"So you know how the universe was created?"

Talock replied, "Yes."

I was now in disbelief but I couldn't stop, so I asked another question, "So you've seen God?"

Talock then replied, "My race has evolved past a need for superstition, the need for a God and any other myths."

I then asked Talock, "So what happens when you die?"

Talock then replied, "Death is a human construct. It does not exist; you will experience and have experienced every instance of so called life. You, me, him we are instances of the same life separated by what you call death."

I then thought about what Talock had just said, so on planet Zalga there is no death they all experience each other's lives but then I heard Talock answer my own thought in my head.

Talock said, "In essence, yes." I was taken back but I remembered he had telepathy so he can project his thoughts into my head and read my thoughts as well.

Then I carried on asking him questions. "How do you speak English?"

Talock replied, "Learning your language is essential to understanding your species."

I then replied, "So you just learned English because you're smart?"

Talock replied, "Relatively, yes."

I then asked another question, "So how was the universe created and why was it so perfectly made for us?"

Talock then replied, "There are an infinite number of universes each with different physical properties. Virtually support life but not such as you know it. We exist in a universe that does support so called life that is all."

I then asked another question. "So, Talock, I noticed you don't have a lower body how do you have sex, you know erm…reproduce?"

Talock replied, "On Zalga we do not reproduce like you do here on earth because we have no genders. Instead, we are all born from a flower called Ellina."

I replied, "I'm just lost for words, so what does the flower look like."

Talock replied, "Ellina is as beautiful as a sunset but as small as a rosebud. Ellinas colour is dark purple with light purple tips."

"Wow the flower sounds beautiful. So um, is there any reason you revealed yourself to me?"

Talock replied, "Yes, the council of five has sent me here to tell you about their existence."

I asked, "The council of five, what is that?"

Talock replied, "The council of five is a group of five alien species that help protect your race against less peaceful species. The council meets here on earth on the last ten days of August, the reason being that earth has been receiving too many visits from new alien species in the past five hundred years. The alien species that make up the council of five are the Orela, Egarot, Ginvo, Redan and the Emerther.

"Very little is known about the alien species that are part of the council of five but it is agreed that the Emerther race is the most important. Not only to the council but amongst every known race. The Emerther are related to the Solipsi Rai but are much older and advanced in every way. They helped found the council.

They met with USA president D. Eisonhower on three different occasions. They also met with two high ranking USSR leaders again on three different occasions. They tried to meet with president R. Nixon but he refused them saying it would be too dangerous, as they could maybe read his mind and find out delicate national security secrets concerning the relations with USSR.

The species that are part of the council of five, previously known as the council of nine, have been protecting earth and your human race for as long there are alien records of it. Some say they have been protecting the planet for millions of years even before humans existed. The presence and arrival of the council of five on earth can cause cosmic events that could affect the earth's atmosphere for example floods or hurricanes.

The reason that the council is meeting is to discuss possible threats to humans and the Earth, as well as the fact that so many new races have been visiting earth in the past five hundred years. The council also monitors human evolution and has monitored it since you and all other humans were just a single cell organism. The main goal and purpose of the council of five is to monitor human life and protect it, so that humans can join us and other species in development and enlightenment among the stars."

After hearing all this information I was so amazed. Aliens protecting the human race, amazing but I didn't know what Talock wanted me to do with this information, so I asked, "I'm sorry but what exactly do you want me to do with all this information. I'm just a bank manager."

Then Talock replied, "Never forget." As Talock said this I suddenly felt faint and my body crashed to the floor. My vision became blurry and the last thing I saw was Talock floating away from me. When I awoke I was back home in my bed. Had it all just been a bad dream? I thought so.

I ran down stairs tripping on some loose bit of carpet, but when I eventually got downstairs and saw everything was as I left it. I sighed in joyful relief. It was just a bad dream. I made myself some toast with butter evenly spread and a cup of coffee.

I went to my front room and turned on the TV. It was the news. "Good morning this is Mike Blacksmith reporting to you from the channel nine newsrooms with some breaking news. There is major flooding in parts of the country today. I repeat major flooding in parts of the country today!"

I thought back to what happened in my dream and what the alien Talock said. "When the council of five meet on earth it can cause cosmic events that could affect the earth's atmosphere for example floods or hurricanes." But I thought it's just a coincidence. Then something else popped into my head from my dream, that Talock said. "The council meets here on earth on the last ten days of August."

So I went to check my calendar and I saw that it was the thirty-first of August, the last of the tenth days. I just thought it was another coincidence and thought nothing of it, but that was a mistake because as I did this, I got a skull crushing headache as if someone was hitting me in the head with a hammer.

Then a flash of blue light entered my mind and started to flash over and over and over again, until suddenly I saw a bright purple pulsating light coming from the middle of my front room. Then a loud buzzing in my ears and when I looked up right before my eyes was Talock.

"Never forget."

Then suddenly my headache stopped, the blue flash of light stopped, the buzzing in my ears was gone, the pulsating purple light was gone and Talock vanished into thin air. I realised what I had experienced was no dream, it was reality. It was as real as the skin on my body and the hair on my head.

Alien life is real, they are up there above us among the cosmic vastness of deep space. Some of them watch over us and protect us, others waiting to destroy our whole way of life.

Wrath

1

The year is 2079. It has been four years since the first nuclear bomb was dropped on my small village, Shirakawa-Go, which is located in Japan. My village has many residents. There are 1,630 people living here and 588 houses. All of the houses have the same design. They are made from a hard and dense wood and are triangle shaped with three floors.

I can't remember much from that day but this is what I do remember. I suddenly saw a bright light like the sun had exploded, and as I looked around, pieces of wood were flying through the air like a hurricane was passing through. Raging fires were everywhere and as far as my eyes could see, there were people running and screaming, some of them bleeding from their eyes, mouth, ears everywhere you could possibly imagine.

I saw one man running down a cobbled street while his body was blazing like a forest fire. I tried to get up but my body was weak. I looked down and saw that I had a piece of wood, about 8 inches thick, stuck in my leg. The sight of blood disgusted me and I started to feel faint.

Everything went dark and as I drifted slowly into unconsciousness, I could hear a voice say, "Hurry up and suck them dry before we get caught!"

2

When I woke up, I was in a hospital. The hospital was extremely unclean and had dried blood covering the floor. My bed was a hard stiff white mattress on top of metal springs that kept on poking my body. I tried to get out of bed but I felt a rapid rush of pain to my leg. I looked down and I saw that the wood had been removed and my leg had been bandaged up.

I looked and saw to my right a beaten and withered table. It only had two things on it, a glass of water which I would never touch (the water was a brown colour) and next to that was a letter. I reached for the letter; it was in a smooth ivory coloured envelope, smooth as silk and stiff. I thought to myself who ever sent me this has a lot of money.

Before I ripped into the letter and devoured its contents, a doctor strutted towards me with a puffed-up look on his face. His hair was a black, greasy ooze bouncing around on his head and as he strutted towards me, I could see his eyes were charcoal grey. They were almost shark like his eyelids were heavy his eyelashes were dark and dense.

His eyebrows were bushy and almost wing-like his face was a very thin shape. I also saw that his skin was tanned. It had a warm glow or a golden brown tint like turkey after cooking. I then saw as he took his final steps towards me that he was wearing a plain white doctor's coat with denim jeans, collared T-shirt and brown trainers.

When he finally gets to me, he says, "I see you're recovering well, no thanks to me." He gave me a grim smile.

I replied, "Yes thank you, Doctor…I didn't catch your name."

He looked at me intensely. "My name…you can call me Doctor Ambrogino."

What a weirdo, I thought but I continued to talk to him to make him go away faster. "So how long do you think it will be till I am able to leave, Dr Ambrogino?"

He looked like he didn't know the answer, then suddenly he replied, "When I say you're ready to leave, is that understood? Now I will leave you to rest."

I just wanted to leave this place and go home, well whatever is left of home; anyway I looked down at the envelope. I opened the letter that I had been gripping tightly in my hands while I was talking to Dr Ambrogino. When I opened it, I saw that there was a pale white piece of paper inside. I pulled it out and read it.

This letter is addressed to Mr Haruto. This letter is to inform you that you must serve in the army and fight in the war against the vampire menace that threatens our world. If you do not comply with these orders, then we will treat this as an act of treason and either throw you in prison, execute you or feed you to the vampires that our government has captured.

You must now go to your nearest army sign up post with this letter, from there they will take you to the army base called Vortex. From there you will be enlisted into the ruby regiment were you will begin your training to eliminate the vampire hordes.

I started to think to myself, *So it is true, not just rumours vampires are real.* The more pressing issue that was on my mind was that World War Seven had officially begun.

3

The letter shocked me. My whole world had just been turned upside down. I would never see home again, the lush vast green grass that spread for miles and miles that would shine and sparkle like a crystal when the sun hit it. When it snowed, oh when it snowed it was like we lived in a fluffy cloud village.

When I stepped on the snow I would hear a crunch beneath my feet, and on the very pitch black nights when people turned their lights on, it would shine out through the windows and the snow would shimmer and shine like a shooting star. But as I reminisced about my home, not knowing if I would ever see it again, I thought back to what I had read in the letter and I remembered this specific part. "Feed you to the rouge vampires that our government has captured."

Vampires are real? I thought they were just rumours. I mean I've heard of people going missing and turning up looking like a dried up raisin but now that the government has actually confirmed it, it's mind blowing. They also included in the letter that they have captured vampires. Then something broke my train of thought.

A clip-clopping against the cold blood soaked stone floors of the hospital and as I looked, I saw it was him, Dr Ambrogino. He was walking towards me with that disturbing smile of his. When he reached the end of my bed, he started to talk to me. In his dead monotone voice he said, "I think tomorrow you will be able to leave, do you have anywhere to go?"

I didn't know if I should tell him about the letter I'd received. I thought about it and decided to tell him. "Yes, I have somewhere to go. I received a letter drafting me into the army, so tomorrow when I leave this hospital, I will go straight to the nearest army sign up post. From there, they will take me and train me to help defend the world from the vampire menace that is threatening this world."

As I finished saying this, I saw an expression emerge on Dr Ambrogino's face. It was like something was trying to crawl its way out of his mouth, and he was trying desperately to keep it inside and not let his words burst out like confetti. He calmly said something, "That sounds wonderful. I'm so happy for you."

He then turned and walked away at a very fast pace. The way Dr Ambrogino said it wasn't believable. His tone of voice changed to a higher tone and while he was talking, he was gritting his teeth and he was twitching like crazy. I am getting out of here tomorrow, so I just forgot about the whole situation.

4

I decided to get some sleep as it was getting late but a couple of hours into the night, I heard what sounded like a scream coming from one of the hospitals corridors. I struggled out of bed and started to go and search to see what that sound was. As I walked around in the dark and decrepit hospital, I heard nothing but silence.

Then suddenly I heard an echo of what sounded like a drop of water dripping onto the floor. I followed the sound until the echo abruptly stopped and I found myself at the end of a long narrow corridor. In the dark silence, I could hear what sounded like a crunching noise. I saw what seemed like shadows moving around in the dark. I shouted out "Hello, is anyone there?"

I waited but there was no reply, so I cautiously made my way down the corridor. The crunching sound got louder and louder, and the shadows I saw dancing around in the dark started to become clearer until suddenly I saw Dr Ambrogino devouring someone. The person's head was completely missing and blood was dripping down from the gaping neck all over the floor.

Then suddenly Dr Ambrogino started to drink the blood from the large gaping hole where the persons head used to be. It was then I realised the good doctor was a vampire. I turned and started to back away as I realised this but I slipped on the blood that was spattered across the floor. Dr Ambrogino slowly swirled his head round and stared at me.

I noticed that his eyes had changed colour from a charcoal grey to a dark emerald green. I could also see his veins, they seemed to give off a glow like they were absorbing and soaking in the blood he had just taken in. He started to walk towards me. I started crawling backwards rapidly clawing at the cold wall, trying to get back to my feet when I heard a loud voice say, "NOW!"

Then suddenly a wall in the corridor exploded, the rubble went flying through the air and gave me a loud ringing in my ears. I couldn't hear anything but I could still see at least. The explosion left a circular hole in the wall, from the that hole I saw twelve people enter the corridor. The hallway was illuminated with a bright light. I could see the figures clearly.

They were all wearing black and red outfits that covered them from head to toe. Their heads were covered by some kind of helmet which covered their whole face and neck. It had a blacked-out visor and a large circular breathing device down on the right. In the middle of the helmet a torch was attached.

The helmet was black with small red lines coming of it in many directions. Their bodies were covered by lots of armour plates attached to them that were very sleek and small. It was like some modern day samurai armour outfit. This armour also had red lines coming off it. They were wearing black leather gloves.

Around their waists, they wore belts and attached to those belts was a lot of equipment that I couldn't really make out. They also each had guns. Their guns were black but also transparent. The gun also had a medium sized scope on the top of it and the magazine clip was made from some kind of plastic I assumed because I could see the bullets through it. The gun also had the word Apostolatus engraved into it.

Then suddenly they all surrounded Dr Ambrogino. He grinned morbidly and then they all shot their guns simultaneously, all twelve of them. I couldn't hear the noise of the guns but I saw a large cloud of smoke fill the corridor. It came from the barrel of the guns and now I couldn't see anything.

Slowly my hearing started to come back, I heard a voice say, "Is it dead?" then another voice reply, "Go check." Then there was a silence and I heard another voice, "Target down check the civilian." I heard loud heavy footsteps coming towards me, then I saw someone standing in front of me.

I couldn't see their face but I could see from the shape that the person had breasts so it was a woman. The figure offered me a hand up, I accepted it and started to ask questions, "Who are you?"

The person replied in a colloquial tone of voice, "We are Apostolate, the Roman Catholic Church's union of exorcists and undead fighters. We are many with our numbers going up to 50,000 but not very many of us have ever come in contact with the paranormal. The Roman Catholic Church has had much experience against heretics and heathens in various inquisitions, but few real supernatural entities were ever encountered until the twelfth century formed by Opus Dei.

"In Francos Spain, our group the Apostolate was born out of conflict between nationalist forces and republican partisans empowered with supernatural abilities, since then the union has waged a secret crusade against the undead with limited info but vast resources and vampires are the most dangers. Now that vampires have exposed themselves and the world is at full scale war with them, we have been ordered to help with the vampire threat known as The Sect of Blood."

5

My mind was overloaded with information. So these twelve people work for the church and hunt down and kill vampires, but now the world is at war with them they have been ordered to help the army kill vampires. OK so they are Special Forces. I then asked another question, "The Sect of Blood, who are they?"

The woman replied, "The Sect of Blood is who we all are fighting in this war. They are a sinister cult of vampires who believe that humanity must join the undead in order to evolve to a final form, become immortal. Make the world clean and depopulated and enrage God, so that he can bring about the second coming. They have many doctrines but one main enemy. Us, the Apostolate."

So these blood vampires are who I will be fighting against when I finish my army training; maybe I could ask one more question. "What are those weapons you have?" She looked like she didn't want to tell me but then she answered.

"The weaponry on our belts includes wooden stakes, silver bullets and many glass vials filled with holy water. The silver bullets are hollowed out and filled with a mix of holy water blessed by the pope himself and liquid silver to pack an extra punch, but enough with the questions, we have to move out. Maybe we will run into each other again."

I thought to myself, *Wow these people are cool*, then suddenly she asked me something. "So you got anywhere to go now this has happened, I don't think you should stick around."

I instantly replied, "Yes, I have been drafted to the army to fight against the vampires in the war."

There was a long pause then the woman replied, "Really, what regiment you in?" I had to think for a while then I remembered.

"The ruby regiment."

There was another long pause then she said something, "The vortex base, right? We are heading in that direction, we could drop you off if you want."

I thought that would be cool getting to ride in a car with these vampire hunters. I replied, "Yes, that would be very nice of you."

"There is one catch, we will have to knock you out so you don't see our faces, is that OK?" She said. I thought it's definitely worth it.

I replied, "Yes, I'm OK with it." The next thing I know I'm seeing the butt of a gun lunging towards my face, and then I was falling towards the ground and suddenly everything went dark.

6

When I woke up, the first thing I saw was a large white metal sign that read, *Welcome to Base Vortex. Warning! Intruders will be shot on sight.* I realised that I was tied to a tree just outside the perimeter of the base. All around the base ran a large shimmering metal barbed wired fence. It formed an enclosure making sure nothing and no one could get in or out.

I saw a guard at the entrance and shouted to gain his attention. "Hello…hey can I get some help please?" The guard glanced at me covering his eyes with his hand, so that the sun didn't impair his vision. He then quickly ran off into the base and within moments he was back, this time another man was with him.

This man was black and of a stocky build. He began to walk towards me at a fast pace, his walk looking more like a march. When he reached me at the tree I was tied to, I saw that he was wearing a light black and grey uniform. The top of the uniform looked like a coat.

There were seven badges or medals on the right side of the coat and on the upper left side, there was a large letter embroidered onto it. On the left arm of the coat, there were two white stripes that protruded outwards, on both shoulders were two black stripes that also protruded outwards. On his trousers were holsters one on the left leg and one on the right. The holsters were black and had a gold line that encircled them.

He was also wearing black boots that had grey laces. He looked very frail and beaten. The top of his head was bald but around the sides he still had hair, it was black mainly with shots of grey running through it. His eyes were a brown hazel colour and they had heavy bags beneath them as if he hadn't slept for weeks.

I then noticed his mouth, his mouth was metal. Well the lower part of his jaw was anyway and going up from that metal bottom jaw were two thin metal lines that looked like they were imbedded into his face. When they reached under his eyes, there was what looked like bolts or hinges to keep the metal jaw in place. Then the lines carried on behind his ears but attached, and protruding out of his metal jaw was a yellow circular deceive.

Then suddenly he spoke in a stern tone of voice. "My name is Field Marshall Loch. I am in charge of all operations here at Base Vortex. I had information passed onto me this morning that a new recruit would be getting dropped off but I didn't expect it to be like this so…do you have your drafting letter with you?"

He spoke but his mouth didn't move. No it can't be I thought. I heard the words he spoke, unless that yellow device that is attached to his metal jaw and is protruding out must be a speaker or maybe a speaking aid of some kind. That must be it, he must have lost the bottom part of his jaw while fighting vampires as part of the elite group, the Apostolates.

That would explain the large letter A that he had on his uniform as well as all the medals and badges. He must have helped kill hundreds of vampire scum, but got his bottom jaw ripped off and that must have affected his way of speaking somehow. Then he asked me again, this time in a much sterner tone of voice which snapped me out of my train of thought. He said, "Well do you or do you not have your drafting letter?"

I saw the look on his face and realised he was losing his patience, so I speedily replied, "Yes, it's in here." As I said this I made a pointing gesture with my head towards the pocket that was on my hospital gown. Then Field Marshall Loch went to reach into my pocket.

The only thought that went through my head at that moment was *I hope that that woman who is part of Apostolate and who dropped me off here, had the common sense to put the letter somewhere on me.*

Then Loch slowly took his hand out of my pocket and to my relief, there it was, my drafting letter. Loch then proceeded to read it and when he finished, he crumpled the letter into a tiny ball and threw it to the ground. He then spoke to me, "So you're in the Ruby Regiment? I'm in charge of that regiment. You're not going to be a trouble maker, are you?"

I replied, "No."

The look on his face then changed to a little smirk and he said, "As soon as you enter this base, you do as I say and you will refer to me as Sir or Field Marshall Loch at all times. Understand?"

"Yes, Sir," I replied. He grunted then called over the other guard that was at the front gate. The guard came dashing as fast as a whippet, when he reached us, Loch told him to cut me down from the tree and bring me inside.

7

The base was extremely large. It looked as if it was embedded into the side of a mountain. There were three buildings on the left of the base; two of them were very small and compact. The third one was behind them and was very tall.

In front of them were four dark green coloured tanks and on the right side of the base were two very large, what appeared to be housing units for people to sleep in. They were also a dark green colour. The ground around the base was mostly sand except for a stone pathway that lead up to the main building. This building was the largest of them all.

It had in front of it a turret that was currently unmanned as well as a dark green van, then on the top of the building there were two, large, what looked like robot turrets on the right. There was another platform that was raised on the right which held a helicopter. On the left there was a sniper tower, and further to the left built on top of a small mountain was an extremely huge gun with four long barrels, two on each side. There were also varies small buildings built into this mountain as well as a sniper tower to the very far left.

As I regained my focus, the guard dragged me to the right of the base where the sleeping quarters were. The guard then dragged the large metal door open and gestured me to go in with his hand. I slowly walked in and when I got inside the lights came on automatically.

Then to my amazement, I saw an endless, vast, never ending row of small houses or what looked like houses. I looked at the guard behind me in astonishment, but the guard just pointed at one of the small house looking units. I walked up to it and when I reached the door, it had a name plate on it.

I could see that the name that was imprinted on the name plate was indeed my name. It was in all capitals HARUTO. I tried to open the door but it was locked, then suddenly the name plate on the door vanished to reveal a rectangle shape imbedded in its place. From that rectangle shape, a blue light shined.

I leaned over to look at it then that blue light flashed and the name plate came back into place. An automated voice came from the door itself and said, "Scan complete. Welcome Mr Haruto to your new home." I thought that it must have been some kind of eye scanner to verify and log who ever enters the house.

I entered what would be my living quarters while training here at the army base named Vortex. As I entered the room, I saw there were the basic essentials. There was a large single bed set up which had a purple blanket. On top of the bed was my army uniform.

The bed was against the wall opposite the door, then at the bottom of the bed was a small white fridge, a mini-fridge and resting on top of that was a black microwave. On the far left wall was what could only be called the bathroom. There was a toilet, sink and a shower. The toilet appeared self-flushing.

The sink had a mirror above it then the shower was enclosed to keep the water from flooding the room. On the far right of the room in the corner was a metallic table with a metallic circular stool underneath it. On top of the table was a large computer screen that was imbedded into the wall. The walls and floor were all metal apart from the bathroom area.

The bathroom floor and walls were bright white tiles. I made my way to the bed and sat down. I noticed a yellow piece of paper on top of my pillow. I picked it up and read it. *Welcome to Vortex. I hope you are settling in well. I entered your room earlier to drop of your uniform. We start training tomorrow at 0800 hours, so make sure to get plenty of rest, Field Marshall Loch.*

I finished reading the letter and threw it on the floor. Suddenly, the floor beneath opened slightly and the letter quickly vanished into the hole. I thought to myself how cool that was for a second. Then I decided to get some rest to prepare myself for the day of training that was to come.

8

I fell out of bed in shock. I was woken up by a very loud blaring siren that I assume came from some speakers here in the housing unit. I rose from the bed and suddenly the sound of the siren stopped. A booming voice replaced it.

"All recruits are to report to the cafeteria for breakfast. Then immediately after, you will report the courtyard, where Field Marshall Loch will be waiting to brief you on your first day of training."

I hastily showered then got into my uniform which was a green colour with some parts of it covered with metal plates. It was a one piece, so I just had to slip inside it then zip it up. There was a large back chest plate that slightly protruded from the middle section of the uniform, and arm and hand compartments that felt like they were mechanical.

Now I had my uniform on, I stepped out of my room only to see hundreds, if not thousands, of people like me who had been recruited to fight in this war. All I could hear was a sea of whispers stretching all the way back and echoing around the oval shaped metal walls. They were all walking to somewhere. I thought it must have been the cafeteria, so I followed them so that next time I would know the way.

It took a while but eventually we got there. The room was enormous with plenty of people sitting down and eating already. There was what looked like an endless line of white tables with a metallic border around the edge. Each table could sit four people, the chairs were also metal but they were a grey colour like the floor, and the lights were a rectangle shape one over every table attached to the ceiling.

I joined the line where they were serving breakfast, the line moved at a snail's pace. Someone behind tapped me on the shoulder. I turned around to see who it was and to my amazement, I saw it was a robot. The robot was a dirty white colour like it had mud stains on it.

The robot's feet did have toe shapes but not like you might think; it had four toes one big toe and three small ones. The three small ones were all connected like a ducks but the big toe was separate, and all the toes had casings covering them. The foot was made from what looked like a clear plastic shell because I could see inside.

The robot's shins had a gap in the middle where you would expect the bone to be, but where the bone should be, I could see lots of white wires going up through the leg. The robot's knees had a white disc on them but I could still see a large hinge behind it that enabled the legs to move. In the upper part of the legs, I could see nothing because they were covered by a white and brown leather material that was being held on by brown leather buckles.

The robot's upper body was also covered in metal plates, some large and some small, all of them different shapes. It was the same for the robot's arms they were covered in small and large white metal plates but the robot's hands looked extremely realistic. Maybe they were made from some kind of rubber, and finally the robot's face had three blue, circular looking things on it.

If I had to guess, I would say they were its eyes. The three blue circles went down in a straight line. The first one at the top was large and protruded out from its head; the other two were embedded into its head. There was also a silver looking grate were the mouth would be, it had several small lines in it.

I assumed that this was its mouth, it must be some kind of voice box, then the robot spoke to me in an enthusiastic tone of voice. "Hey, my name's Axel. What's yours?"

I was still in shock at what I saw, first I find out that vampires are real and now robots. It's amazing but I had to keep my cool, so I calmed down and replied, "My name is Haruto, nice to meet you, Axel. So what regiment are you assigned to?"

Axel responded, "I'm assigned to the Ruby regiment. I can't wait to start training. So what regiment are you in?"

I replied, "I'm in the Ruby regiment too so…"

But before I could finish my sentence, I heard a loud voice shout, "Hey keep the line moving would you, some of us want to eat today!" I looked forward, the line had moved far ahead of me. I quickly ran to join it back up. When I got there, I was now at the counters where they were serving food. The only problem was they only had one option for food, it was this blue slime looking snot porridge.

Obviously, Axel observed the look on my face because he said something, "Hey, the only reason its blue is because they have to make sure it lasts long and doesn't spoil, so they put it in a freezing chamber but other than that, it's got all the nutritional value your body needs. It is made up of rice, beans, grains, sugar, salt and raw honey." After hearing Axel say this, I thought those ingredients don't sound that bad, so I took a bowl full and went over to a table and sat down.

Axel followed close behind me. He sat opposite me. I wanted to find out where Axel came from so I decided to ask him but I approached the subject with caution. "So, Axel, where are you from?"

He answered like it was nothing. "I'm not from anywhere, I was made here at this base years ago when this technology was new. They tried to make me into a super weapon or some kind of ultra-killing machine, but their attempt failed because I had developed emotions and free will so they locked me up. They freed me only to train me to become a soldier in their war."

I had to admit to myself, I felt pity for him but there are bigger things at play now than his feelings. I replied, "I'm sorry that happened to you, Axel, but even you have to admit there are more pressing matters right now. I mean the whole world is at war with vampires, that is what we are here for, to train and learn how to stop them. Don't you want to be a part of that great victory?"

Then suddenly before Axel had a chance to reply, someone slammed their tray onto the table and sat down next to me. I looked to my right to see who it was and I saw a woman. She had short ginger hair and the tips of her hair all the way around her head were coloured a light cyan colour. Her eyes were also a very bright cyan colour, almost like diamonds shimmering in the sun's rays.

She was wearing a dark blue and black uniform. The uniform was not like the men's, it did not look like a one piece either. She was wearing black shorts and then the top part of the uniform was a dark blue top with metal shoulder pads as well as metal plates to protect her chest. There was nothing covering her arms but she was wearing gloves, they were a dark purple colour.

Axel spoke, "Yes, I do want to be a part of it. Thank you, Haruto, for inspiring me."

I looked back over to Axel and replied, "No problem, buddy, that's what friends are for."

Then the woman to my right spoke, in a colloquial tone of voice she said "Hey you guys, don't mind if I sit here, do you?"

Me and Axel looked at each other and shrugged. "No, we don't mind. My name's Haruto and this is Axel. What's your name?"

She looked reserved at first but then she replied, "My name is Luna. So what regiment are you two in?"

Axel replied in a cheerful voice, "Me and Haruto over here are in Ruby regiment, what about you?"

There was a long pause then she replied, "Me too."

Axel eagerly replied, "No way, we should all be friends and hang out. What do you say, Haruto?" I thought about it for a second, I mean Axel is a nice robot but I don't know this other person. Maybe I can get to know her as time goes on.

I replied, "Yeah, I don't see why not."

Then Axel asked Luna, "What about you, Luna, what do you say to us three being friends. I mean we got to have someone we can depend on while we train."

She took another long pause then replied, "I don't see what harm it could do, OK friends, it is."

Then suddenly I heard some static from a speaker above us. A voice spoke "All recruits will now look down at the end of the cafeteria. You will see an officer holding a card in the air with your regiment's name on it. You will line up in front of that officer and follow them to your regiment's courtyard."

There were dozens of officers standing at the end of the cafeteria shouting regiment names. I heard some of them, "The Titan regiment!" then another one, "The Silver Soldier regiment!" Then I heard mine, "The Ruby regiment!" I looked at Luna and Axel and said to them, "Come on, that's us."

I ran to the officer with the Ruby regiment card with Luna and Axel closely following behind me. When we reached the officer we got in line. Eventually, the officer stopped shouting and started to count how many people there were in the line. When he was finished he shouted, "This way and keep up!"

9

We followed him until we eventually reached a large open area with nothing to see. The only thing that there was to see was sand, all over the ground. But then in the distance I noticed something else. A man was waving us to come over to him.

We all rushed over and when we got there, we all saw it was Field Marshall Loch. He had told me he was in charge of the Ruby regiment. He started to speak. "There are twelve people to every regiment but do you have what it takes to survive training? If you do then at the end, you will be given a choice to join one of seven Elite Special Forces. I will now list these Specials Forces so you can think about your decision while you're here training.

"Number one, the Heller Institute is an anti-paranormal group that was started in 1875 by 14 researchers, explorers and veterans of the Civil War and Crimean War. It is under the leadership of Conrad Heller, a Lieutenant in the British army who saw evidence of occult rituals and the undead during his campaign. Originally for investigation and study only, the institute became a fighting force against vampires after World War One with the discovery of their influence over mortals.

"It is now an officially international non-profit organisation headquartered on Heller Estates in Scotland, staffed by intrepid hunters. Number two, the

Department of Public Sanity the United States Federal Shadow Bureau created after the government's first encounter with the threat of the supernatural in 1938. It is well funded and contains impressive equipment but possesses little hard knowledge of the supernatural and still believes vampirism to be scientific in nature.

"Not known for gentle tactics, the brutal D.O.P.S. is feared by both vampires and vampire hunters alike. Now we come to number three. The Brothers of Nevsky are a knightly order within the Russian Orthodox Church extending back to the fifteenth century vampire slayers. The brothers rely on Faith and God and have been somewhat successful in purging the supernatural from the northeastern parts of Europe for centuries.

"However, following the Russian revolution, the brothers were at the mercy of the Bolsheviks for decades and most were exiled to Greece. They continue to be a force to be reckoned with and possess great knowledge in fighting the undead threat. Number four, Apostolate, these are the Roman Catholic Church's union of exorcists and undead fighters, numbering about 50,000 but few ever come into contact with the paranormal.

"While the R.C.C. has had much experience against heretics and heathens in the various inquisitions, few real supernatural entities were ever encountered in the twentieth century. It was formed by Opus Dei in Francos Spain. The Apostolates were born out of conflict between nationalist forces and republican partisans empowered with supernatural abilities. Since the union has waged a secret crusade against the undead with limited info but vast resources. Vampires are the church's greatest threat.

"Number five, the Organisation is a small but highly trained division of the British Government founded in the nineteenth century, with the goal of controlling vampire society. The Organisation focuses its efforts on ensuring that vampires do not manage to gain any positions of power or authority within the British Isles. While vampires are generally terminated when discovered, the Organisation specialises in dealing with smart vampires.

"This may be simply because their small size requires them to prioritise more dangerous targets but investigations by the Organisation hint that powerful vampires have other plans. They may be actively trying to take control of the human race simply to ensure it does not succeed in wiping itself out at the end of the day. The Organisation is one more player of shadow politics and it's disturbing to consider the humanity lost in the process of infiltrating the vampire world.

"Number six, Night Hunt is a generational society stretching back to the Middle Ages. It is more of a giant long running family with strong martial tradition in fighting the supernatural. However, throughout the ages, it has faced many human enemies in the form of your typical rival clans, controlling kings and ruthless competitors.

"Sometimes their best friends are creatures less interested in harming humanity. Finally Number seven. Horus Agency is a small time detective's office that actually specialises in taking out and investigating paranormals and their activities. Maximum staff is three to seven people, not counting friendly contacts.

"Very informal, there biggest problems are law enforcement intervention and the threat of bankruptcy. So now you know what choices you have. That is if you complete your training."

10

As soon as I heard Field Marshall Loch say Apostolate, I stopped listening because that was the one I wanted to join. I knew I had to make sure I worked hard and focused from this moment on, if I wanted to make it to the end my training. I refocused and started to listen again to Field Marshall Loch.

"Now I will tell you what your training will be while you are here at Base Vortex. You will have three different types of training, the first will be hand to hand combat, the second will be weapon training and the final type of training you will all undertake will be learning about vampires, their weak points and how to properly kill/wound them. That is how your training will take place every day in that order. Do you understand?"

All twelve of us yelled back, "Yes, Sir," well I thought all twelve of us did. I heard Field Marshall Loch scream at the top of his voice, "You, come here!" I saw a skinny blonde man walk towards Loch with his head down. Loch then spoke to him, "You did not reply, son, did you?"

The skinny man replied, "No."

Loch looked angry and replied, "No what, soldier?"

The skinny man replied in a raspy voice, "No, Sir."

Loch smiled and called some guards over to him. "Throw this man off the base and send him home." I was shocked. Loch started to speak again to all of us. "If you're not going to take this seriously, then I haven't got time for you. Now go back to your rooms and get some rest because tomorrow is when the training really starts."

I made my way back to my room and got into bed. I lay there thinking about the events of the day. I had made two friends, one a robot which is pretty cool and a woman named Luna, who I don't really know that much about. I hoped I would get a chance to have a conversation with her tomorrow to try and find out more about her, but I need to get my rest now because tomorrow the real training begins.

I woke up still tired and had a cold shower to perk me up. Now I was awake, I put my uniform on and made my way to the courtyard. When I got there, I saw Axel and Luna standing in line in front of Field Marshall Loch with the other people in my regiment. There were only 10 left now, 11 including me. I ran over to them and stood next to them in line.

Then I thought to myself that yesterday was just a debriefing and today the real training starts, what is the first…oh yes that's right, hand to hand combat. I wonder who my partner will be. Then Field Marshall Loch began to speak in a loud, clear distinguished tone. "Good morning, recruits. Today your training begins but before I address everybody on today's training, I would like to know why you, Mr Haruto, are late?"

I knew it, I thought I had overslept, how could this happened? "I'm sorry, Sir. I overslept it won't happen again."

He took a long gaze at me and replied, "Make sure it does not." I thought thank God for that, and then he carried on speaking. "Now today your training will be in hand to hand combat. I will assign each of you a partner now, Mr Haruto, you are to be partnered up with…Luna."

He pointed over to a spot in the courtyard and Luna and I both walked over there. In the background, I could hear him partnering up the other recruits in my regiment. I heard him say Axel's name then, when he was finished he spoke "Now one of you will be the attacker and the other one will be trying to defend/block your partner's punches as they come towards you. Ready? Go!"

Like a speeding bullet, Luna started to throw punches. They came hurtling towards my face and body. I blocked most of them but some got through and one connected with my jaw. While my defence was down, she swiped me off my feet, I fell onto the sandy ground beneath me.

She spoke softly, "Serves you right for not keeping your defence up." She smiled smugly.

I got up and brushed the sand off me and said to her, "Let's go again."

"Your funeral," she replied, again she threw a barrage of punches towards my body and face but this time, I was ready. I blocked them and every time I blocked them, I could see that she was getting more aggressive, hitting harder and faster until her hands were just a blur. Then I felt a sharp pain in my stomach. I looked down and saw that she had punched me.

I fell to my knees; Luna spoke "I told you it was your funeral." I thought to myself, *Who is this girl?*

Then Field Marshall Loch addressed us. "You will now swap roles"

Yes now it is my turn to get a punch in, then Loch shouted, "Ready? Go!" I started to throw as many punches as I could, but I didn't even come close to the speed that Luna was throwing them before. As I threw my punches trying at least to get one hit in on her she looked unfazed. She was blocking every punch I threw, and then I had an idea.

I kicked sand up into her face and while she was disorientated, I punched her across the jaw. I saw her fall to the floor; suddenly Field Marshall Loch shouted, "Stop! Training is over for today. Now go and get something to eat especially you, Haruto, since you missed breakfast. Go on go!"

They all walked wearily into the base but I stayed to help Luna up. I reached out my hand so she could grab it, and begrudgingly she did. I pulled her up and she spoke, "That was a nice move you did, dirty but nice."

I replied, "Thanks." I noticed Axel running towards us from the far end of the courtyard.

When he got to us he said, "Are you coming to the cafeteria then or not?" Luna and I looked at each other and nodded, "Yeah sure, why not."

Axel then replied, "Ok come on then, let's go." We all walked together to the cafeteria.

11

When we eventually got there, we got in line to be served and Axel went to save us a table as he doesn't need to eat, so it was just me and Luna in line. I started to speak to her as we slowly edged our way up the line "That was really impressive what you did out there, I mean how fast you were able to punch. How are you able do that?"

She smiled and then replied, "If I told you that I would have to kill you." We both laughed after she said it knowing she was joking.

I asked her, "I wonder what they serve after breakfast?"

She then rapidly replied, "All they serve here is that blue stuff, it's not a five star restaurant, we are here to train that's it."

"I guess you're right," I replied then in no time we were at the front of the line. We took our bowls of blue mucus and were heading to the table that Axel was saving for us, when I noticed Axel was surrounded by these three guys. They were shoving him then suddenly one of them punched him.

I saw what looked like a metal cog fling from Axels face. I went to run over to him when Luna held me back. She said, "It's best to leave it, most people around here don't like robots because they think they are replacing humans."

I instantly replied, "That's insane. Throughout history people have always feared technology because they were scared it would make their jobs obsolete cars, the printing press, industrial technology, all of these things were met with fear in the past. People were afraid these things would put them out of work but in every case they did not because instead technology creates new jobs and more prosperity as a whole and the same goes for robots. There is nothing to fear because technology creates far more than it destroys!"

I turned to see she wasn't paying attention; she was looking over at Axel. So I turned to look and saw the three guys had pulled him onto the floor and were now stomping on him. When I saw this, I dropped my bowl and rushed over to help him. I lunged at one of them bringing him to the ground, I then proceeded to punch him but before I could get a shot in, he head butted me and pushed me off onto the cafeteria floor.

Luna must have seen this happen because she also then rushed over and helped me up. The three guys were now circled around us and we were back to back. One of them went to throw a punch at Luna but she blocked it and kicked him in the stomach sending him flying across the cafeteria.

I punched one of the guys in the jaw but he shrugged it off like it was nothing. Then suddenly an officer entered the cafeteria and yelled, "Stop this now everybody! Back to your rooms." I said goodbye to Luna and then walked back to my room hoping Axel was ok.

When I reached my room the door scanned my eyes and the door unlocked. I entered and went straight into the shower to wash off all the sand that was still on me from the training session in the courtyard. When I finished, I dried myself off then jumped into bed hoping that tomorrow I would see Axel in his usual cheerful energetic mood.

12

I heard a knocking at my door, I thought it be Field Marshall Loch, so speedily put my uniform on and ran to the door, but when I opened it I saw that it was Luna. "Come on, you don't want to be late again, do you?" After what she said I left my room closing the door behind me and we both made our way to the courtyard.

On the way there we had a short conversation. "Thank you for yesterday, helping me with those three guys who were hurting Axel," I said.

She replied, "It's no problem. I only stepped in because one of them head butted you." Eventually we reached the courtyard where we lined up with the others but as I looked around, I couldn't see Axel anywhere.

Then Field Marshall Loch began to speak "I heard there was a brawl in the cafeteria yesterday between some members of this regiment. The four members have already been dealt with. As you can now see, not everybody is capable able of making it through. Now there are only seven of you left, which of you will be left at the end of this training program I wonder?"

I realised after what he said the reason why I couldn't see Axel. He had been kicked out or maybe something even worse, but I don't understand why would they kick him out he didn't start the fight, did he? I guess if many people here don't like robots maybe they kicked him out for his own safety.

I focused myself and listened to what Field Marshall Loch was saying. "Now today is your weapon training so to the right of you on the ground you will find a black case. When you open it up inside you will see a black and red rifle, and a magazine clip that is already loaded with silver bullets. When you go for the gun, I want you to carefully load the magazine into the rifle and then wait my next instructions. OK, now prep your weapon!"

I knelt down and opened the case, when I saw the rifle it reminded me of the rifle that the Apostolates carried. In fact it looked exactly the same but I had to focus. I picked up the rifle and to my surprise it was quite light, I got the magazine and slowly inserted it into the rifle.

I stood back up, then when everyone else was finished, Field Marshall Loch spoke, "Now if you look down the far left side of the courtyard there are targets, one for each of you." As I looked down the left side of the courtyard I could just about make out seven large, white squares with a large black circle in the middle of them. I continued listening to Field Marshall Loch.

"Those are your targets, now you will all stand 4 feet apart from each other and when I say fire you will all fire simultaneously at the target in front of you. Is that clear?"

We all replied, "Sir, yes, Sir." Then we all turned to face the targets. I brought the rifle up to my chest and looked down the sight to see if I was lined up with the target, then suddenly Field Marshall Loch shouted, "Fire!" I pulled the trigger as fast as I could, sending silver bullets dancing out the end of the barrel.

I saw them shimmer in the sun as they went flying through the air. There was a whirlwind of sand that came up from the ground, probably because of the speed of the bullets. Suddenly it was over and all that I could see was smoke coming from my rifle and mist like sand in the air.

Field Marshall Loch spoke, "Very good, at least you all know how to shoot a gun so you're not completely useless after all. That's all for today go on away with you." We all put away the guns back in their cases and Luna and I walked back together.

While we were walking back she asked me, "Hey, you going to the cafeteria for something to eat?"

I thought about it then replied, "No, I think I will pass just want to get some sleep, thanks for the offer though." I made my way back to the housing unit and to my room. I slunk down on the bed depressed. I tried to get some sleep but all I could think of was Axel and how much of a good friend he was to me.

I thought if Axel isn't here to complete the training, then I will make it past the training for both of us. I will work twice as hard and make sure nothing and no one stands in my way.

13

I awoke wearily having gotten hardly any sleep the night before. I walked over to the sink and splashed some cold water on my face. Now I was at least somewhat awake. I got my uniform on and stepped out of my room only to find that everyone was lined up outside. I quickly joined them.

I saw Field Marshall Loch standing in front of me. He said, "Now today is the third training exercise and you will be learning how to kill/wound a vampire. You will make your way across this housing unit to that building there." He pointed to the far right of the base were I saw three small stone structures dancing in the distance.

He carried on speaking, "When you get there my regiment, Ruby Regiment, will be greeted by a man by the name of Professor Fakirs. OK now off with you." We all started making our way to the three stone buildings in the distance. When I eventually got there, I saw on one of the doors of these buildings a name in large bold letters, PROFESSOR FAKIRS.

I entered the building only to see my regiment was already inside. The room was very small, all the walls were made from stone but the floor was made of a grey marble. There were seven tables in the room made from a thin heavy duty glass and they were being held up by two metal poles that had been bolted to the floor.

The chairs were grey made from plastic, at the front of the room was a large screen embedded into the wall. The lights were R shaped and were embedded into the ceiling. I caught a glimpse of Luna, so I quickly walked over to her and sat down in the seat next to her. She smiled.

Then the man who had been sitting at the front of the room stood up. He was wearing black shiny shoes long black trousers and he was also wearing a white buttoned up shirt with many creases in it. His face was tanned and smooth, his eyes were a dark brown colour and he was wearing thick rimmed glasses.

He had a little bald spot on the top of his head in the shape of an egg and his hair was a light brown colour. His side burns were grey and there were also tiny bits of grey around the top and back of his hair. He began to speak in an intelligent tone of voice.

He said, "Whatever I say, I want you write it down so you'll be able to study it and refer to it." After hearing this, I opened the book that was lying on the table in front of me and picked up the pen next to it. I began to prepare to write everything down.

He began to pace back and forth slowly across the small room. He carried on, "So do you know that there are only six ways to kill a vampire. I will tell you these methods and you must listen carefully as your lives may well depend on what you learn in our time together.

"Number one, how to kill a vampire with sunlight, by far the easiest way to kill a vampire is via direct sunlight. Even before the first vampire became a vampire, he was cursed forever to have to hide from the sun. Any skin of a vampire that comes in contact with direct sunlight will be severely burned, but beware, there are some vampires that can survive in sunlight. In fact someone in this very room may be a vampire and we don't know."

We all slowly glanced around at each other with uneasy smiles. "Anyway as I said, sunlight is the easiest way to kill a vampire because all you have to do is get them in direct sunlight for about ten seconds or so, actually getting one into direct sunlight is not so easy. This is where being smart helps, if you can somehow trick or trap a vampire in a place where they will eventually be exposed to direct sunlight, you're golden.

"The problem with this plan is that vampires are very fast, very strong and very smart. They aren't going to simply let you stick them in a place where they don't want to be and stay there. The nice part about sunlight is that it shows up daily if you can survive through the night and make it somewhere where you can see the sun you're probably safe.

"The problem is this usually means you have to be outside prior to the sun rising which pretty much just makes you a prime target for hungry vampires. Still if you can wait out the night until morning, find the brightest path to safety and move quickly you should be fine. Now number two, how to kill a vampire with a wooden stake. This is still a classic; the wooden stake remains one of the best tools to use for vampire killing.

"All a wooden stake is a piece of wood with one edge sharp enough to pierce human flesh or inhuman flesh in this case. If you think of monsters in terms of sports vampires are those great offensive players, they can always score but are pretty crappy defenders. Sure their speed and strength give them a big advantage but the truth about vampires is, they are so used to overpowering their opponent with their offensive capabilities, that few have spent much time learning to defend themselves.

"Knowing this, the key to killing a vampire using a wooden stake is to strike first. Yes that means playing offense against the offensive powerhouse but in this game of life and death you only need to score. OK, enough with the sports analogy but the lesson remains the same, a vampire will let its guard down fairly easily and you should attack quickly and without hesitation.

"A vampire can heal from most injuries but a wooden stake through the heart is not one of them. Though they heal quickly, their skin and bones are just as fragile as any humans, so the key to killing them is to make it so they can't heal which brings us to number three. How to kill a vampire with silver. Again the curse of silver begins before the first vampire became a vampire when the Goddess Artemis cursed the first vampire, so that his skin burned when it was touched by silver.

"Using silver is a bit like a blend between sunlight and a wooden stake it doesn't work as well as either of those two options but it has advantages of its own. First of all unlike sunlight silver is highly portable you can carry an item of solid silver with you easily, secondly it won't kill a vampire to stab it in the heart with silver but it will slow down the healing process which can be very helpful. In order to actually kill a vampire using silver you'd probably need a lot of it. Silver is more helpful as a slowing or trapping agent.

"Vampires despite their strength, cannot break a chain of silver even no matter how strong they are or how hard they try. If you could somehow manage to handcuff a vampire to a tree, say using silver handcuffs, all you would have to do is wait until then sun rose the next day, and you would have yourself a fried vampire. Of course how you would actually manage to accomplish this task is another story, so on to number four.

"Killing a vampire with fire, at first fire seems like an easy fix to the vampire problem we currently find ourselves in. But there is a problem; yes fire will burn vampires just like it burns humans. Sunlight and silver burn a vampire and cause its healing process to slow dramatically because vampires are inherently cursed by these two elements.

"So whilst fire can burn just as well as sunlight or silver, it does nothing to slow the healing process of the vampire because vampires are not cursed with a weakness to fire. If you're going to use fire to kill a vampire, you're going to need to have a big fire and have the vampire trapped in it for a very long time.

"This is because the vampire heals as it burns, the hotter the fire, the faster it burns but you're still basically trying to beat the speed of the vampires healing process. Should the vampire be mostly burnt but then escape the fire, it can still survive. This is another situation where tying a vampire down with silver to immobilise it, would be very handy if you could manage it."

The professor took a sip of water before continuing. "Number five, how to kill a vampire by removing its head. Removing a vampires head is not easy. Though their bones and flesh are as fragile as ours, they are fast and tremendously strong which make it a difficult task to achieve. If you're really intent on removing a vampires head there are two good ways to do it.

"The first option is to use a silver knife and cut off the head. This will still likely be a bit of a chore but the silver will stop the healing process and slowly wear down the muscles strength, so with enough patience and time, this will work. Secondly is to have another vampire tear the head off your vampire of choice.

"Vampires are built strong enough to tear each other's heads off easily, though it's highly looked down upon for a vampire to kill another vampire. So convincing one to do this for you would not be easy, plus you would still want to burn the head and body separately to prevent the vampire from healing.

"Now number six, the final method we use to despatch a vampire. How to kill a vampire using a disease? The term vampire disease is tricky because it can refer to two different conditions. Most of the time when someone talks about vampire disease they are referring to Porphyric Haemophilia.

"This is a condition caused by a bacterial strain carried in the blood and saliva of every vampire. A human who comes in contact with the blood or saliva of a vampire can easily become exposed to this bacteria. Once exposed, an infected human only has about 72 hours to begin specially engineered antibiotic treatments before the bacteria becomes incurable.

"In essence, this vampire disease spreads through the human body changing the genetic chemistry of the blood and skin. The first symptoms of infection may include photosensitivity or photodermatitis (sensitivity to light of the eyes or skin). Muscle weakness or seizures can occur as well as inconsistencies in the nervous system such as a slow or rapid heartbeat. Eventually the bacterium behind this disease settles into the body and lives there creating a perfect environment for it to exist in.

"At this point the human body has been completely transformed with the curses but not the benefits of vampirism. In order to gain immortality, strength and speed, the host must drink the blood of a vampire. The other vampire disease refers to the condition known as Sangue Debolezza, which translates to blood weakness in Italian.

"The origins of this rare vampire disease remain unknown but we do know that if only affects vampires. The symptoms of Sangue Debolezza include severe exhaustion and chronic headaches followed by nausea, which eventually lead to starvation in many cases. It has been difficult to acquire new information about the disease because only vampires can acquire it.

"Needless to say, they do not subject themselves to medical examination of free will, and according to most sources, it is a very rare condition. It is the only known disease that can kill a vampire. Oh and one more thing, did you know that there are three species of vampire, not just one?

"The first is the Sanguinarian vampires. This type of vampire requires blood in order to remain healthy. Most often Sanguinarians need to feed at least once a month usually more or their body begins to deteriorate. The amount of blood a Sang needs depends on the individual. Some Sang vampires need only a few drops once every couple of weeks while others need more than that either by feeding more frequently and consuming blood.

"Usually the symptoms that the vampire experiences will vanish for a short period of time before they once again need to feed. The symptoms of the Sang vampires include blood cravings, metallic taste in mouth, fatigue, lethargy, hunger pains, thirst that won't go away, irritability, brain fog and bloodlust.

"Now the second species of vampire is a psychic vampire. This form of vampire needs to take in more energy than any other vampire, though the exact cause of psychic vampires is yet unknown. It is suspected that psychic vampires burn though energy too quickly and then for whatever reason cannot compensate easily themselves.

"For this reason, they need to feed on non-psychical energy such as Chi or Prana. This can be done in a number of ways such as feeding on the energy given off in crowds at a concert for example, or feeding directly from a group or individual. If a psychic vampire does not feed, they will experience symptoms such as fatigue, lethargy and headaches.

"Of course many of these symptoms imitate other conditions many of which are known medical conditions, so I would advise you if you see anyone with these conditions on base, take them to a doctor so they can make sure they are not a vampire. Generally speaking when they feed the associated symptoms will vanish for a period of time before they reappear once more, resulting in the vampire needing to feed again.

"This time period in between can vary but most psychic vampires feed daily and usually a psychic vampire will feed unintentionally on their own kind.

"The third is a very rare species of vampire they are a hybrid form of vampire, half human and half vampire. Not much is known about these vampires apart from the fact that they are the only form of vampire that can survive in sunlight and also have extreme strength and speed."

After all that information that had just bombarded my brain I was stunned but at the same time amazed. I now had all this new knowledge on vampires that I could use to help me, no help the world win the war. Then suddenly the professor began to speak again.

"Well now that's all wrapped up with, I hope you feel confident by now that you would be successful in killing a vampire and when considering how to kill a vampire, feel free to blend any of the above suggestions together. They all work if done right, and if done wrong, well chances are you'll be dead. Good luck." He gave us all a cheeky grin and shoed us from his room.

After that, everyone made their way back to their rooms. On the way back, I saw Luna, I decided to try and strike up a conversation with her but she ignored me. I don't know what was wrong with her, maybe it was something the professor said but it couldn't have been, he was helping us, teaching us the best ways to kill/wound vampires.

I couldn't wrap my head around it, so I just left it and went to my room. When I got there, I fell into bed and thought to myself I need to catch up on the sleep I missed last night. I don't want to be late for training tomorrow, who knows what might happen if I am.

14

I was awaked up by the sound of an alarm and a banging on my door. I wondered what is this, what's happening? I heard shouting outside my room, so I rushed to get dressed. I stepped outside to see hundreds of officers banging on the rooms of the other recruits waking them up.

When all the other recruits were out of their rooms, the officers told us to follow them. So we all followed closely behind until eventually we arrived at the courtyard. It was already filled to the brim like a tin of sardines with recruits. We were told to line up behind hundreds if not thousands of other recruits.

All I could see were the back of people's heads for miles and miles. Then I heard on a speaker system Field Marshall Lochs voice.

He said "We have had reports that The Sect of Blood and its army have attacked a village in Japan. The village is called Shirakawa-Go. Every attempt to try and defeat them has failed, so you recruits are the last call to arms. Now I cannot force you to go, so this is your one and only chance to leave, but know if you leave, you may as well hand the world over to those bloodsuckers yourself!"

There was silence as we all waited to see if anybody was going to leave but nobody did. He continued speaking "Very well. So as you might not survive this, I deem it only fair and right that you go join your Special Forces group now, and they will brief you the rest of the way. So if you go to the very far end of the courtyard, a member from each of the Special Forces groups will be waiting. Make sure you pick wisely."

This is it! I thought, but before everyone made a scramble to the far end of the courtyard Field Marshall Loch said one last thing, "Let's hope what little training you have had is enough. Ladies, gentlemen, it has been an honour."

Everyone in the courtyard saluted and shouted, "Sir, yes, Sir!"

After that, everyone ran to the far end of the courtyard. It was like a riot everyone pushing and shoving each other trying to get to their favourite first. When I had made my way through all this commotion, I saw instantly the Apostolates. Their armour stood out from the rest, the sleek black and the fine red lines.

I ran over to the Apostolate who was there and said, "I want to join your Special Forces group please." The person then looked down at me and gestured me to follow. I followed closely behind and eventually, I was lead to a dark miniscule room. Inside the room, there were 11 Apostolates and Luna, all the Apostolates were wearing their armour, so I couldn't make out what they looked like, except of course for Luna, who was wearing her normal uniform like me.

I sat down on a cold wooden bench next to Luna, then suddenly she stood up and started to speak. She said, "I told you we might run in to each other again, didn't I?" I thought to myself this is impossible, she is the woman who saved me that night in the hospital. How could I have not recognised her voice?

I was mystified. I replied, "Why were you here?"

She then smiled and replied, "I wanted to see if you were good enough to join our ranks and you have proven yourself, so welcome. You are the thirteenth member of the Apostolates. Your uniform is in the corner. Once you have it on, I will brief you on the mission."

I walked over to the corner of the room there I found my amour. The black metal plates that covered the armour thin, but sturdy and protective, and the helmet made from toughened plastic with a blacked out visor so no one could see our faces. The belt that held our equipment made from a fine but durable velvet material. Once I had on my new uniform, I went back over to Luna and gathered around the other Apostolates to listen to the briefing.

"Ok so we have had reports of The Sect of Blood and their army ravaging a village in Japan by the name of Shirakawa-Go. Our mission is to go in there and take out every last vampire. This is it, we are the last defence. This is where the war ends. We are wheels up in 15 minutes so any last things you need get them!"

When she had finished speaking, I thought to myself, *Who is this person, it's a completely different Luna from the one who I was training with*. Then it hit me. The name of the village, I don't know how I hadn't realised until now, Shirakawa-Go, that's my home where I grew up. So after all this time, it looks like I will be returning, and my journey will end were it all started, home.

15

Fifteen minutes later and a helicopter had arrived at the base. I stepped outside with the other Apostolates to board it. As I looked around the base, I saw people running around like headless chickens, scrambling about. I refocused on the task at hand and Luna started to speak.

She said, "This is a Quantum Stealth Helicopter. Q.S. is a material that can make anything or anyone invisible, it does this by bending light waves around the person or object. The material removes not only your visual, infrared and thermal signatures but also the shadow as well. Oh and when it is attached to a vehicle like we have it here the vehicle makes absolutely no sound."

I thought that was incredible, we all then boarded the helicopter and strapped ourselves in. The helicopter took off and Luna began to speak again, "Now when we approach the village the helicopter will go invisible. We will repel down and carry out our mission."

A few anxious hours later, we had reached the village, but it was night time and night time is not our friend when dealing with vampires. Suddenly the helicopter went invisible and Luna shouted, "NOW!" We all repelled down the ropes until we reached the ground.

When I looked around, I saw corpses and body parts everywhere. Gallons of blood all over the ground and houses like someone had just got hundreds of tins of red paint and thrown them everywhere. I nearly passed out because I hated the sight of blood, but I had to stay strong if I was to complete this mission to end the war.

We all gathered around Luna, she told us what to do. "Now we have infiltrated the village we are to kill every vampire and end this war. We will all stay together so follow closely behind me!" We all followed Luna in a line watching, seeing if we could spot any vampires as we slowly made our way through the village.

We made our way to centre of the village, then all of a sudden Luna put her hand up, meaning for us to stop. So I made my way up to the front of the line and stood next to Luna and said, "What is it?" She didn't reply she just pointed in front of her.]

I turned my head and looked and what I saw next I couldn't believe. I saw hundreds, if not thousands, of vampires crowded tightly together in the centre of the village. All of the vampires were wearing grey and red hoodies with the hoods up. They were also wearing lime green joggers and black pumps, and surrounding the vampires was a mass of dead bodies.

Some were eating and tearing the flesh off people's bodies, so they could get to the blood inside. I was horrified when suddenly on the roof of one of the houses I saw a vampire. The vampire screeched and the rest of the vampires looked up to the vampire on the roof who pointed in our direction.

There was a moment of silence, then suddenly Luna shouted, "RUN!" We all then started sprinting, we didn't know where we were sprinting to, we just knew we had to get away from this legion of vampires that was closing in on us. I looked around as I was running and saw vampires jumping from roof to roof catching up to us.

I thought is this it, is this where I die. No I thought, I have to survive, if not for me, for Axel. So I ran and I ran and eventually we reached a barn and Luna shouted, "Everybody in!" We got inside and Luna locked the barn door. I thought to myself how is a barn going to stop hundreds of vampires, they're going to just smash through the wood like it was made of paper.

Then suddenly from the ceiling above us I heard a creaking noise. I whispered, "They're on the roof," and everybody including me aimed their rifles towards the roof but not another sound was made. We all relaxed until out of nowhere a vampire burst through the roof sending bits of wood hurling through the air, the vampire started to attack the squad.

It clawed two of the squad members faces off and then it ripped two squad members heads clean off their bodies. It ripped a huge chunk out of another squad members neck. The remaining eight of us were backing up shooting it as it came slowly forward slicing and grabbing at us but our silver bullets only slowed it down and then suddenly I felt it grab me.

It pulled me into the air and sunk its pale fangs into my neck piercing my skin. From behind me, I heard a scream that sounded like Luna, "NO!" She ran towards the vampire and staked it straight in the heart, after this it dropped me. I saw blood gush out of the vampire, some landed in my mouth but I didn't have time to react everything was going blurry. I fainted falling to the floor.

16

My whole body began to shake. It can't be, I thought. He is just a myth, a legend, a fairy-tale nothing but a made up story. I wanted to confirm my suspicions, so began to speak to him. "So what is your name?"

He chuckled in an undermining tone and then replied, "I have had many names given to me in my centuries of life. Some call me 'The Undying One', others call me 'The Black Prince'. Many know me by the name of 'Dracula' but you may call me Silas."

I was petrified, I could hardly breathe. So it is true, I thought it's not just a myth, he's real. Dracula is real but I didn't understand why he was underneath my village in Japan. So I asked him. I said, "So, Silas, how did you end up underneath this village?"

He glared at me then replied, "Later in my life, I moved back to Italy. Now I was a vampire, the first of my kind. I went to Florence where I created the first vampire clan. The humans there volunteered themselves because they wanted power and immortality, and were willing to trade their souls for it.

"The curse would be the same for every vampire; their souls would remain in the underworld until they went to retrieve it, then they would never be able to leave. My clan began to grow in size and strength until finally they began to fight amongst themselves creating a civil war within the clan. Because of this vampires, left to form their own clans.

"So I came here to Japan and slept underneath the earth waiting, knowing that when I awoke, I would never trust anyone again human or vampire. I would wipe the earth of them all!" It was then realised why Silas had awoken. This war between vampires and humans is the perfect time for him to take advantage, and kill as many vampires and humans as he can here right now, then he would move on to the rest of the world.

I couldn't let him do that, so I went to lunge at him but he tightened his grip around Luna's throat. Luna began to claw at Silas's hands trying to break them free of her neck but he was too powerful. Suddenly he snapped her neck as if it were just a twig and threw her aside like a piece of trash. I shouted "NO!" and ran over to Luna.

I fell to my knees crying. Then Silas spoke, "So pitiful, how fragile humans are and how easy they are to break." He began to laugh. I stopped crying and wiped away my tears. I became angry and suddenly I felt a rage inside me. I leapt up and lunged towards Silas, punching him across his face.

He looked at me calmly, smirking and spoke, "Well then, it looks as if your vampire powers have finally shown themselves. Right, let's get on with this, I have wasted enough time." We squared up to each other. Silas had an animal like gait. I could feel energy pent up inside me, coursing through my veins, it seemed to be growing stronger, urging me to attack, to taste blood.

Then we lunged towards each other. He backhanded me sending me flying through the some of the houses. I felt an ache but nothing more. I coughed up blood and wiped it away slowly. Silas grinning at me like a wolf would grin at its prey. I had to stop him, keep him from destroying life all over the planet, but more importantly, I had to do it for Luna and for Axel.

I began walking towards him then suddenly felt myself flying. I had launched myself at Silas like missile. Silas was caught off guard and I threw another punch. This time I made him bleed, but it didn't faze him, he just wiped it away and carried on. Suddenly he was gone. He re-appeared behind me, kicking me in the back sending me flying again, this time face first into the ground.

I got up then thought to myself there is no way I can beat him in a fight. He can run faster than a speeding bullet, his strength is far beyond any other vampires and he has an amazing sense of smell. I need a plan, then it came to me if I can just hold out till the sun comes up then the sun will burn him to death and perhaps I will survive.

I put my plan into action, I played offense, not attacking him but letting him attack me, that way I was sure to last longer. I span round to look at Silas. He said, "What are you waiting for? Are giving up already? Oh my you have no idea what you are capable of, too bad. I thought you might make this interesting or fun, but no. It appears you are just like the rest of the dumb cattle."

"No! I am not giving up; I will fight you until one of us is dead, whatever it takes, and however long it takes. Do you want to give up?" Silas scowled at me and then lunged towards me throwing punch after punch. I managed to dodge most of them; every time he missed his rage grew. This made him throw his punches faster.

After a while of him throwing punch after punch, kicking out and lunging to no avail, he looked like the devil himself. Then suddenly he spoke, "Enough of this!" He growled and grabbed me by the scruff of my uniform. He said, "Any last words, you disgusting hybrid?"

I replied, "As a matter of fact, yes, I do have some last words." I waited, hoping that I could find words. Then I saw it, the sun slowly started to rise behind Silas. The sky turning a strange shade of orange, it almost looked as if the sky were on fire.

"Well?" Screamed Silas. "What, what do you have to say?"

"My last words? I don't think you will like them." I hesitated, giving the sun more time to rise higher. "Is it me, or has it suddenly got hot?"

Silas looked confused. He looked at me puzzled; the sun rose and now fully covered every inch of the village. Silas turned to see it and began to scream in agony. He dropped me to the ground; I stepped back and watched as his skin began to flake away and burn.

Suddenly, Silas transformed into a black mist and fled towards the forest that surround the village. Before I knew it he was gone, the only thing he left behind was his long coat. I picked it up from the floor and put it on and swore to myself that from that day, I would hunt down Silas for as long as I walked this earth, or my name isn't Haruto Van Helsing.

The Great God Anu

1 December 1926

My name is Thomas Reed. I am a journalist for the Crack Of Dawn Chronicle. I have been working for this particular paper since I was eighteen years old but have been interested in journalism for as long as I can remember. My first job that I can conceivably remember was working for a small newspaper stand in my old home town of Snowport.

In fact that small newspaper stand is, or was, the only source of news my home town had access to. I say is or was because since I have moved away, I now don't know if that newspaper stand is still in business. That's right, when I was fifteen, I moved out of my home town to a big city.

At first, I was very dazed and not very confident in myself. I mean I come from a small town where about one hundred people live and that's stretching it. So for me moving to a big city where thousands of people live, I have to say I was not very confidant.

But the whole reason for me moving out here was to get a job at a large well known newspaper company, so I had to buckle up my boot straps and focus on my goal. I started going to interviews at every single newspaper company that I could find but every single one of them turned me away, until one day, this stranger approached me while I was sitting on a park bench enjoying some well needed fresh air.

The stranger was a few feet away from me, I saw that it was a man. He was wearing a grey well pressed suit and trousers as well as a grey waistcoat. He also was wearing a white shirt that was buttoned up all the way and a black tie that had white dots decorating it and a fedora sat atop his head.

I glanced and saw that he was wearing a silver ring on his left pinkie finger, and in his right hand he was grasping a cigarette firmly, as if it were his life support. The man had deep black hair and a long protruding nose, his face looked very smooth but his lips stood out from the rest of his face, almost like he was wearing lipstick. His eyebrows were thick and bushy like a caterpillar, he had wrinkles and bags surrounding his eyes.

His eyes were a brown but sometimes when I looked, it was as if his eyes had no colour what so ever. The man sat next to me on the park bench and started to engage in conversation with me. He said in an appealing tone of voice, "My name's Howard but you can call me Mr H. I've heard you're looking for a job in journalism, is that correct?"

I was taken back. How did this stranger who I have never met before know I was looking for a job in journalism? Had he been following me? I proceeded with the conversation, "Yes, that is correct, but how do you know?" I replied.

Howard then glanced at me smiled and replied, "I own a newspaper company called The Crack Of Dawn Chronicle, and I got a letter on my desk this morning saying every newspaper company in the city had been turning this one kid away. I'm not surprised if you haven't heard of it, it's not well known around here but if you're looking for a job, my doors always open"

Howard then went to walk away but I grabbed him by his wrist. I replied in a brittle tone of voice, "When can I start?"

Howard smiled then lit his cigarette and took a puff and replied, "First thing tomorrow," and that's how I got my start working for The Crack Of Dawn Chronicle newspaper.

At first I got stuck with the stories no one else wanted to write, for example 'Cat Stuck up Tree' or 'Hat Stuck up Tree' or 'Woman Finds Hat in Tree'; just lots of tree related things. It wasn't until a few years later, when I broke the story on the 'Recovered Writings of Mr Robert Smith' that I finally started to get good stories, and people started to respect me at my job.

I mean don't get me wrong, I don't believe anything that was in Robert Smith's diary/journal. I mean if you ask me, I think he was a wacko, but I just knew that when it was found, it was ether gonna be me that broke that story first or someone else, and I rather it be me and now look at me. I have my own office.

I'm one of the best journalists in the business and all thanks to a chance encounter and a lucky one off story that skyrocketed me to the top of journalism. I will always stay at this newspaper company because this is where I got my start and I'm faithful and thankful to Howard for taking a chance on me when no one else would.

"THOMAS!" Suddenly I hear an ear piercing scream that breaks me from my daydreaming and reminiscing of the good old times. It awakens me and slams me down onto my cold wet slab of reality. I hear it again. "THOMAS, I WANT YOU IN MY OFFICE NOW!" I recognised that voice, it was Howard.

I reassured myself that is was nothing bad as I entered his office for the first time today. As I entered I looked around and saw that his office was bombarded with papers and books from floor to ceiling. They were bursting from the shelves like a tsunami of knowledge.

He even had to pile some books up on top of his desk, the walls were also covered in papers concealing the colour of the paint on the walls and even stopping light from entering through the windows. Then I saw him, he had changed since the first time we met on that park bench all those years ago. His hair was almost non-existent and what little hair he did have was grey.

He had grown or tried to grow a moustache but it had not worked, there were just clumps of stubble all around his face. The wrinkles on his face had grew more defined, the bags under his eyes had grew bigger and looked like two overgrown grapes. Instead of wearing his trademark fedora, he has taken to wearing a top hat.

He was sat in a shiny leather chair behind his large dark brown polished desk. I saw one of his hands twirling a cigarette around his fingers as the other hand lay rested on top of a letter on his desk. He slowly motioned me to sit down with his black and yellowish stained fingers, but as I looked, I thought to myself, it would be pointless because the books Howard has piled on top of his desk were stacked.

So if do sit down I will not be able to see his face. So I replied, "No thank you, Sir. I would rather stand."

Howard paused then tapped on the table and replied, "Yes, OK whatever you like." Then there was a long an awkward silence. Howard continued to tap on his desk. I thought to myself has he forgotten why he called me in here?

So I asked him, "Sir, why did you call me in here?"

He replied in an orotund tone of voice, "Oh, yes, well you see I got this letter here, well just look inside." He then handed me the letter. I took the letter from his hand unfolded it. I saw a large symbol drawn on the paper. The symbol was strange, I had never seen anything like this before.

It was a large ring and inside the ring was some sort of creature with a large head. The top if its head looked like a triangle, then at both sides of its head were two axe like edges, protruding outwards. Coming down and out were eight tentacles four each side, wrapping and curling around each other.

When I saw it, I thought it was very odd but I thought nothing of it. It had obviously touched a nerve with Mr H, so I then spoke, "If you ask me, Sir, I think it's just some kind of prank."

He quickly replied, "No…No its not, look at the address from where it was shipped from!" I then looked at the address and to my disbelief I saw that it read Snowport, my home town and just a few minutes ago, I was reminiscing about my home town and the small newspaper stand.

Then Mr H spoke again and refocused me. "You see it's not a prank. If it was a prank, someone could have just slipped it under my door but it came from a distance you see. You see."

I replied to Howard in a cautious manner. "Well, Sir, what do you want me to do about this?"

Mr H then scoffed and replied, "I want you to go to Snowport and find out what this is. Even if it's nothing, at least it will put my mind at ease. So will you do this, Thomas?" I know this wild goose chase is going to be nothing but I'm just going to say yes, so I can visit my home town after all these years, so accepted.

"Of course, Sir. I will make sure this story is as good as done by the time I come back."

He replied, "That's good to hear, Thomas. Now go and get ready. I want you on the train tomorrow."

I replied, "Yes, Sir. Oh and one more thing, is it OK if I sleep in my office again?"

Howard scowled at me and snapped, "Yes, but really, Thomas, you must find some accommodation eventually." Then I left Howard's office and walked across the corridor to mine. I entered my office and crawled up into a ball on the floor like a fox. Before I went to sleep, I started to get excited that I was going back to my home town after all this time, and I wondered how much had changed since I moved away to the big city.

2 December 1926

I woke up the next day ready and raring to go. I got up from the floor and stretched, as I did this I looked around. My office was a very small square room, it had a small beaten down wooden writing table in the middle, and on top of it I kept my typewriter and other items, such as a few pencils and paper for making notes. There was a chair and also a solid wood, perhaps oak filing cabinet which I could lock.

In this, I kept files and notes that may help me when I'm writing a story for the paper. In right corner of my office is my large heavy duty iron safe. I don't keep anything in there but I have it just in case. On the wall above that is my calendar, my clock and a mirror.

This is a moment I feel like I need to spruce up as I have just woken up. I approached the mirror and saw that my fluffy light brown hair was a complete mess, so I brushed my hands through it to tidy it up and proceeded to make sure the rest of me was up to scratch. My emerald green eyes were fine, no bags had formed around them, and my pale smooth skin was as fine as ever except for the stubble. I was happy with what I saw and went to put my suit on.

I grabbed my notepad and a pencil to make notes if there is actually a story at Snowport and grabbed some money to buy a train ticket. I left my office and headed towards the elevator. Suddenly I ran back, grabbed the letter that had that strange symbol on it to take with me, in case anybody in Snowport could recognise it, which I highly doubted.

Anyway, I then made my way down the corridor to the elevator leading down to the first floor and onto the street. As I started getting closer to the elevator, the noise of clicking and clacking on typewriters grew louder and louder. I turned the corner and then I saw a barrage of never ending desks filling the room.

The room was very large, it had twelve circular light's hanging from the ceiling and two rectangular columns in the middle of the room. There were four windows on each side of the room which was filled with, if I had to guess, 20 desks. There were 3 people to a desk, and then in the middle of the room was a stern looking woman standing up against one of the columns with her arms folded.

She gave me an intense look and pointed to a sign above her that read 'Training in Progress'. I realised what was going on and so I continued on my way towards the elevator. The clicking and clacking of the typewriters faded away into silence as the elevator doors opened and then closed behind me. When I eventually reached the first floor, I went straight outside because the first floor is just for people who want to buy our newspaper directly from us, and the second floor is for the workers.

I didn't want to get caught up in all the buying and selling that's not my job, my job is to find a story then write it. So as I got outside, I turned around to look at the building for a moment, just to appreciate how much I will miss it while I'm gone. I looked at the two storeys building in the shape of a warehouse. From the outside, it looked much bigger then it felt on the inside.

I decided to walk to a busy part of the city and hail a cab, after a couple of minutes, I was lucky enough to get one. The cab had a black roof and the body was yellow then imprinted on the side in black it said *NO.5*. The front of the cab was also black with a two light's connected to the windshield the cab bonnet had holes in it, I think to let heat from the engine escape.

The wheels where grey and rubbery the rims where also a bright yellow, and there was a step to help me climb into the cab. I climbed inside and said to the driver, "Take me to the train station please and be quick about it." The cab sped off. I started to think about this whole predicament, I'm pretty sure I'm not going to find anything down at Snowport.

If anything it's just probably some kids fooling around, but the way Howard reacted to the symbol was strange. Suddenly the cab came to a grinding halt and I went springing forward out of my seat hitting my head on the roof of the cab I then whispered to myself "Ow," and as I looked out of the cab window, I saw that I had arrived at the train station. I paid the cab driver and went to buy a ticket for a train to Snowport.

The first thing you noticed when you walked into the station was a small rectangle shaped box protruding out of the wall. It had a large square space the size of a window, so you are able to speak to the man or woman about buying a ticket. I walked over to the ticket booth and saw a woman. She had short brown hair, round thick reading glasses as well as an unusually long neck.

Her eyes were a deep dark blue colour; she was wearing dark red lipstick. She was also wearing a black and white flowery dress. She was young, I noticed because she had no wrinkles and her skin was very smooth looking and every time she smiled in the left corner of her mouth, I would notice a dimple form. I asked "Do you have any trains heading for Snowport?"

She then looked down at a small skinny book that was on an even smaller and skinnier desk that she had in front of her. She flipped through the pages then abruptly stopped, and then after a few moments replied, "We have a train arriving in just a few moments that is heading to Snowport with no stops, and should arrive there in a reasonable amount of time. Would you like to buy a ticket?"

I thought to myself no stops, so as soon as I get on that train, I am stuck on it well its only for what, a couple of days. Well as long as nothing at of the ordinary happens it should be fine. I smiled and replied, "Yes, thanks." I handed her the money and waited a few moments while she sorted out the ticket for me. She finally handed me the ticket and I rushed onto the station's platform.

I saw a cluster of people surrounding the platform form, people from all different angels and from all different walks of life. I saw what seemed to be a postman pushing a cart full of large boxes across the station. I saw a small child running around pick pocketing people as he made his way through the large crowd waiting for the train, and then my eyes were drawn to a woman standing on the far side of the platform.

She wore a long white gem encrusted dress with no sleeves that came down to her knees. Her shoes were a bright white colour, she also had a long pearl necklace. On her right wrist she had a black leather watch and on her pinkie finger, she was wearing a silver ring. On her left arm, she was wearing a silver bracelet. Her hair was as black as the night sky, her eyes a pale blue colour and her lips were blood red.

My gaze was broken by the noise of the train pulling in to the station. The train was black with a thin yellow line going across the middle of it and all of the trains wheels were a dirty red colour. The train came to a stop at the platform and when they opened the doors to let the passengers off, I quickly hopped on board and went to find my room.

I looked at my ticket and saw that it said my room was 5B. I went to the fifth cabin and here the woman in the gem encrusted dress was. She smiled at me with her red lips and then entered her room 5A. Her room is right next to mine, coincidence…yea probably.

My birth was as expected. There were three large square windows that gave a view of the passing surroundings. A long brown leather seat stretched along one side of the room to the other, this would become my bed later. There was a fold down table beneath the window which I could use. Above my bed was a metal rack where I could store my bags.

A small built in corner wardrobe was one side of my compartment and the other corner a door to a small bathroom, containing a sink, mirror and a small shelf to hold a hair brush, razor and toothbrush. The windows had blinds that you could pull down if it gets to sunny or if you just wanted some privacy. I pulled them down and turned on the light. I locked the door and lay down for a while then went to sleep thinking about that woman with the blood red lips.

3 December 1926

I was awoken by the noise of the train's wheel's grinding against the track. I decided to make my way out of bed and to the dining car for something to eat. I walked what felt like a never ending corridor filled with rooms shielded behind wooden doors. I could hear the whistling of the steam coming from the train's engine.

When I eventually got to the dining car, I saw 12 tables, 6 on the right side of the room and 6 on the left side of the room. They were all square tables of differing sizes to accommodate parties of 2 to 6 people. The chairs were all a light brown shiny leather colour with metal going around the rim. Covering all of the tables were bright white table cloths and on all of the tables in the middle was a small glass vase filled with water and white and pink flowers.

A salt and pepper shaker sat next to the vase. There were water glasses and silver cutlery laid out ready. Large windows ran the length of the dining car with heavy maroon coloured curtains framing them. I took a seat on the left side of the room at a small table. A waiter appeared out of thin air and came over to me.

He was wearing black trousers with a white tunic covering his top half. He was also wearing white gloves. His black hair was shaved away very finely. I could see he was very stressed from doing this job. He greeted me in a very thick French accent.

"Would you like anything for breakfast, Sir?"

I pondered for a moment and replied, "Yes, I will have a slice of toast and coffee please."

The waiter replied, "Yes, right away, Sir." He ran off to the kitchen and as I waited for my breakfast I saw the woman with the ruby red lips.

She entered the dining cart, pausing to look around as if searching for someone. She began to walk towards me, then and sat in the empty seat across from me. In a velvety tone of voice she said, "Hi, my name's Lola, what's yours?"

I sat spellbound by her beauty for a moment then replied, "My name…Yes my name…my name is Thomas Reed."

She smiled knowingly and replied, "So what's your destination, Thomas?"

"I'm just visiting my old home town, have you heard of it? Snowport it's called." I asked. The smile seemed to melt from her face and she began to look slightly uncomfortable.

Quietly she replied, "I'm sorry, excuse me but think I'll go back to my room now."

Confused, I asked, "Was it something I said."

She said, "No I just feel tired." She got up out of her seat and went to walk away, but before going she reached out to me for a handshake. I shook her hand and noticed that ring on her pinkie finger again but this time I looked more closely. What I saw baffled me, engraved on the ring was the same symbol, that strange looking creature the same symbol that was drawn on the letter that my boss Howard had received.

I pulled my hand away in shock then heard Lola's voice, "Is something wrong?"

It took me awhile to reply but eventually I said, "Um…no I'm fine, thank you, bye." I ate my breakfast in a bemused state and walked back to my room. I locked the door and sat pawing over the letter Howard had given me with that symbol. It was the same as on Lola's ring without a doubt.

I jumped on my bed and lay back but all I could think about was that engraving on Lola's ring and how it matched the symbol on the letter perfectly. I tried to wrap my head around it but I didn't understand how it was possible. I knew I had to find out more to solve this puzzle that was enveloping around me.

4 December 1926

I had travelled the length and breadth of the train the previous day looking for Lola. I did not find her. If she ate it must have been in her compartment because I waited at meal times to see her. I didn't get much sleep last night as all I could think about was Lola's ring and the engraving on it.

I had stayed up almost all night thinking about how she could have a ring with the same symbol that was on that letter that my boss, Mr Howard, had received. I heard a strange sound, almost like chanting coming from somewhere, so I got out of bed and walked over to the dividing door. I pressed my ear against it then faintly I could hear her voice. I heard her chanting and mumbling strange words to herself.

I did manage to make out a few words of what she was saying but they were unlike any words I have ever heard before. The words sounded like this "La meela dd mee ray teeso mee Tesso." She chanted this several more times and every time it got a little louder, and I could hear the intensity in her voice growing then suddenly she abruptly stopped. I heard her leave her room and slam the door behind her.

I thought to myself this could be a perfect time for me to enter her room and maybe find out something about this symbol that has suddenly appeared in my life, as well as trying to understand what strange words she was chanting to herself. Maybe even try and see why she acted so strangely when I mentioned I was going to Snowport in our conversation yesterday.

I unlocked my door, opening it slowly till there was just a sliver for me to peek through. I slowly poked my head out slightly and peeked out into the corridor scanning to see if anybody was there. The corridor was indeed empty so I made my way out of my room and approached Lola's room. When I came to the door, I pushed down on the handle gently as not to make too much noise.

When I pushed the handle all the way down, I heard a clunk sound so I softly pushed the door open and entered her room, and gingerly closed the door behind me. I looked around the room. It was similar to mine, mirror imaged. On the small table were two pictures encased in a golden frame.

I couldn't make out what the pictures were so I carried on looking around the room. Her train ticket was laying on the bed. As inspected her train ticket, I saw that she was also travelling to Snowport. This was more confusing. If she knew of the town and perhaps even lived there why had she felt uncomfortable when I mentioned Snowport yesterday?

I replaced the ticket on the bed and carried on examining the room. I looked under her bed but I saw nothing except a few dust particles floating around. My attention turned to her trunk. Upon opening it, I could see it had three draws. I tried to open the bottom draw, it was stiff so I had to shimmy it out and when I finally got the draw all the way out, I saw that there was indeed nothing inside.

I then tried the draw above it but all it contained were a few stockings and a sewing kit. If there is nothing in this next draw then I don't know where else I can look because this is the last draw. I grabbed the draw by its handle and pulled it open. I must have used too much force because the draw flung out past me as fast as a speeding bullet and hit the floor making a loud thud.

I froze and listened to see if anyone had heard what had just happened. It felt like minutes passed before I realised no one could have heard anything, no one had come to check the noise. I saw that the draw was now broken and splintered all across the floor, but inside the draw was a large book. I picked it up.

The book cover was a black leather type material and in the centre of the front cover stood out a white symbol. As I took a closer look at this symbol I saw that it was that strange creature looking symbol again. The same symbol that was on the letter delivered to my boss Mr Howard. The one also engraved on Lola's silver pinkie ring.

I examined the book some more and noticed that on the spine of the book was some very unusual writing. I couldn't understand any of it but the writing read *νεκρός νόμος εικών*. Just as I was about to open the book, I heard someone stomping down the corridor. I quickly grabbed the book and tried to hide it in my suit.

The book was very heavy but I eventually did it, and then rushed out of Lola's room and made my escape back into my room next door. I bolted my door and placed the book onto the small and petite looking table that was in the middle of my room. I then went to bed now knowing that there is a story to be had in Snowport.

It just might have something to do with this somewhat curious and unusual symbol that is popping up around every corner, first with my boss Howard and now on this train with Lola. I know one thing is for certain, if I want to find out more about what is happening, I need to find out what secrets are held within the pages of that sinister and unfavourable book for me to uncover.

5 December 1926

Today, I was awoken up from my slumber by a deafening scream coming from what sounded like Lola's room. I got out of bed, opened my door and stepped out into the train's corridor leaving the door slightly ajar behind me. Lola was standing in the corridor displaying a rollercoaster of emotions, looking upset and angry at the same time. She was talking to a man standing next to her.

I hadn't noticed this man before; as a matter of fact I hadn't even seen him board the train. He must have seen me looking in their direction because he started to walk over to me and as he approached, I saw that he was walking with a limp. He had very pale almost ghost like skin, a big thick black scraggily bushy beard that covered almost his whole face, his lips were nuzzled tightly somewhere underneath.

Coming off his beard were clean thin side burns that connected to his black hair which was covered by a grey flat cap. His eyebrows were very thin and a grey sliver colour almost blending in with the colour of his skin, his face was devoured by wrinkles he looked beaten and tired, the bags under his eyes scrapping across the floor as he approached me. His eyes were a very dark almost black colour they showed no emotion.

He was wearing a light grey coat with a white shirt and a black jumper as well as some black trousers and green leather boots. When he finally reached me he spoke in a deep but at the same time toneless voice:

"Hi my name is Raymond…Raymond Richardson, do you have any idea what has happened here?" As he said this, he brought his right hand up and rubbed his beard, I noticed on his pinkie finger he wore a sliver ring, the same as Lola's. Engraved on the ring was that strange creature looking symbol again.

Raymond looked at me and raised one of his eyebrows and said, "Is something wrong?"

I replied in a cautious manner. "No, no…sorry so um…what did you ask me again?"

Raymond stopped scratching his beard and said, "What I asked was do you have any idea what has happened here?"

I instantaneously replied, "No, sorry, what has happened here?" But of course I knew what he was referring to, he was referring to the book, that ominous and mysterious looking book that I had um borrowed from Lola's room yesterday while she was not there.

Raymond replied in a confident manner. "Well I will tell you what has happened here, shall I…shall I? Someone aboard this train has broken into this poor woman's room and stolen something of great value."

I replied in a curious manner. "Well, was the item of significant value?"

Raymond scoffed at the question and replied to me in an condescending tone of voice. "When I said value I think you misunderstood me, Sir. I did not mean value as in a monetary value, I meant sentimental value. Nothing can replace what has been stolen, no amount of money. For what has been stolen is sacred, and now the thief will have to face the wrath of our great God Anu."

I was completely confused by what Raymond had just said to me. Was he just a crazy old man or was he serious? I remembered that I saw a silver ring on his pinkie finger the same one that Lola wears and engraved on it was that strange almost octopus looking creature, the same symbol that was on the letter that my boss, Mr Howard, had received. I thought there must be something going on.

I then asked Raymond a question, "Who is Anu?" Raymond froze in shock as if someone had thrown ice water over him. I could see Lola behind him, her eyes darting around the corridor.

Raymond replied in a stuttering manner. "I…I…don't know what you mean?"

"Anu? You mentioned some God named Anu just now. Who is Anu, I've never heard of that God before?" Raymond started to sweat profusely his eyes darting around the corridor looking for any way out of this situation. He lifted his hand and wiped his forehead, then as he dropped his hand back down to his side I saw tiny droplets of sweat go fluttering through the air and splash land down on to the floor beneath.

Suddenly Raymond replied in a stern tone of voice "You must be mistaken, I never said such a name as Anu." He limped away further up the train.

I spoke to Lola. I said, "Sorry, but Raymond never did say what was stolen?"

Lola replied in a loud tone of voice. "It's none of your business," then went back into her compartment and slammed the door behind her and lock it. I turned and went back to my compartment, closed the door behind me, locked it then went and sat down at the small table and looked down at the book. I knew from my interaction just now with Raymond and Lola that there is something obviously very special about this book.

I examined the cover more closely, the only writing on the book was on the spine and it read as such νεκρός νόμος εικών. I tried to think of what language it could be, it was not English but the problem was that I didn't know any other language expect for a small amount of Greek. I thought back to my days when I studied Greek. I thought hard and I thought long.

Then suddenly it came to me the title of this book was written in Greek and the rough English translation of the title 'νεκρός νόμος εικών' is 'Image of the law of the dead'.

I got goosebumps all over my body just thinking about that eerie title. I thought to myself what could this book be hiding inside its pages? Raymond and Lola were too scared to even reveal its existence, so I cautiously opened up the book to the first page, it was blank.

There were no contents, no authors name but scrawled in the top right corner of the page written in black ink and in an old gothic script was an initial. The initial read *Mr C*. I turned to the next page and saw at the top of the page written in the same handwriting, in an old gothic script a title. It read, *Ancient Beings* and as I looked down at the page I saw hand drawn pictures of these very strange and very unearthly things.

Around the page were notes and writings explaining what the hand drawn picture was. On this first page, there was a drawing of what looked like a large maroon coloured rock, then sprouting out of that was what looked like large amounts of coral. There was a note beneath the drawing that read, *Vulthoom: A huge unearthly plant*. On the next page was another drawing that looked like a large black claw, underneath a note read, *Vhuzompha: Mother and Father to all marine life, an amorphous monster of prodigious size*. Then on the next page there was a large hand drawn picture of what looked like a Venus flytrap plant.

The drawing was long and a mix of bright and dark green. There was a brown vine growing from the green and attached to the vine was a large circular almost mouth looking head with blue spikes attached all around it. In the middle of it was a hole. Beneath the image was a note that read, *The Green God: A sentient plant-like entity dwelling within a series of subterranean caves*.

I turned the page to look at the next drawing and saw that for some reason there was no drawing on this page, but instead, it was filled to the brim with notes about the 'Ancient Being'. Before I read all these notes that looked like they had just been vomited all over the page, I got up out of my seat and went to check that I had locked my door. Yes, it was locked, so I made my way back to my chair, switching on the lights on in my room and pulled down the blinds.

It was getting dark as I sat back down and started to read these notes. The notes read, *The Anu are a group of cosmic beings that rule the universe from up among the stars, but some people refer to The Anu as The Watchers or Anunna, which in English is translated to Those of Royal Blood or Star Rulers because The Anu rule us all, they are our great gods…they are our Star Rulers…they are those of royal blood…they…*

The rest of the page was filled with writing from head to toe but the problem was that the rest of the writing was just complete gibberish. It was not in any language I could understand, and the only thing I saw on the page that I recognised were the words that Lola was chanting to herself, "La meela dd mee mee ray teeso mee Teeso." Since there was nothing else I could understand, I closed the book for the night and decided I would carry on reading it tomorrow.

I got, turned off the lights and lay down on my bed. I began to think about that Anu note that was in the book, that both Raymond and Lola so desperately wanted and tried to keep hidden. If I am remembering correctly, Raymond called Anu a great God, and that is what it says in that unnerving book as well.

'The Anu are a group of cosmic beings that rule the universe from up among the stars but some people refer to The Anu as The Watchers or Anunna, which in English is translated to Those of Royal Blood or Star Rulers because you see The Anu rule us all **they are our great gods**…they are our Star Rulers…they are those of royal blood…they…'

As I lay, drifting slowly to sleep I thought to myself, *I need to find out more about Raymond and Lola.* I decided that I would try to get a look at Raymond's room to see if I could find anything that might be useful in helping me piece this puzzle together.

6 December 1926

I woke up and sprang out of my bed ready for the day ahead. I washed and dressed and made my way to the train's dining car (making sure to hide the book and lock my door). I looked out of the windows and saw a white smoke fly past the train that had probably come from the trains smoke stack. As the smoke cleared I saw luscious bright green trees that stretched across the landscape, the sky had not a cloud in sight and was a clear ocean blue colour.

The golden rays of the sun shone through the window like beams of light from heaven hitting my eyes. I turned away and refocused as I approached the dining car. As I entered, I swiftly noticed Raymond sitting in there. I began to approach him when he looked up and saw me. I nodded as a greeting but must have scared him because the next second, he got up and started limping off down the carriage.

Should I follow? My growling stomach was against it. I decided to follow, trailing slowly behind him making sure as to not attract attention or he would know I was there. As Raymond limped further and further up the train, I gingerly followed behind hearing the thud of his limp with every step he made. He stopped and entered his room.

I cautiously went to the door and saw his cabin was 2C. I heard him grunting and groaning inside the room and then he began chanting that same sentence I heard Lola chanting, "La meela dd mee mee ray teeso mee Teeso." Then like with Lola the chanting got louder and louder until abruptly it stopped. I heard him coming towards the door.

I looked around for somewhere to hide and saw a broom closet, so I quickly stepped inside and closed the door. I heard Raymond step outside of his cabin and then limp back down the train towards the dining car. When I could no longer hear his limp, I stepped out of the broom closet and closed the door.

I approached Raymond's room and cautiously pushed down on the handle, it gave way easily and I slowly nudged the door open. The doors hinges creaked slightly but no one heard it so I entered his cabin and closed the door behind me. Raymond's cabin was almost a carbon copy of mine; all the cabins were little copies with small variations.

In the right corner of the room was a brown desk there were no draws attached to this desk. I looked over the top of the desk. There were a lot of things littered about. I saw a long thin silver lamp with a pink lamp shade. I also saw a pile of used tissues as well as an ice bucket with an empty bottle of champagne inside.

In front of the desk was a large dark green chair. I sat down and started to take a closer look at the pile of rubbish scattered about the top of the desk. I saw his train ticket, so I picked it up to get a closer look at it, as I read it I saw that it said that he was going to Snowport as well. I couldn't see anything else of any use and was about to give up until I saw something shimmering under the used pile of tissues.

I moved the tissues out of the way and as I did this, saw the ring with the strange symbol engraved into it. Raymond must have forgotten to put it on today so I picked the ring up, it was extremely heavy for some reason. The ring was an oval shape and I felt the engraving of that strange symbol, it didn't seem to be done by a professional. It seemed as though someone had just scratched it into the ring with a knife.

As I looked closer at the ring, I saw what looked like deep knife scratches, this deepened my theory that someone had just etched this symbol into the ring with a knife. I replaced the ring back on the table and stood up out of the chair. I took one last look around the room to make sure I hadn't missed anything, and as I was about to walk out of the room, I heard a thud then another thud come echoing down the corridor.

It was Raymond, he was coming back to his room. I panicked and in my panic I scrambled, my eyes darting around the room looking for somewhere to hide. As I heard him get closer to the door, suddenly my eyes focused on the bed I rushed to the bed and slide myself underneath it.

Then I heard the door slam open and as I looked out all I could see was Raymond's leathery green boots thumping up and down limping over towards the desk. Then he stopped and I heard him speak in a low gruff voice, he said "Where is it…where is it?" As he said this, I saw things from the desk come flying down onto the floor.

I assumed that he must be looking for his ring then I heard him say, "There you are." He turned around and started to walk back to the door, but just before he opened it, he took a deep breath in and said one last thing in a deep unnerving tone of voice, "We the Cult Anu offer our body to Those of Royal Blood…to the Star Rulers…to you the Great God Anu." He left the room slamming the door shut behind him.

I got out from under the bed and whispered to myself, "What the fuck? Did he just say cult as in crazy devil worshipping cult?" I started to ask myself how I had not seen it before. Raymond mentioned before a god named Anu but when I asked him about it he got uncomfortable and walked away. Then there's Lola, she has that strange book in her room and on the cover of that book is that strange octopus looking symbol, the one that is also engraved onto Raymond and Lola's rings.

Inside that very same book it mentions something about Anu, as I recall it says, "The Anu are a group of cosmic beings that rule the universe from up among the stars but some people refer to The Anu as The Watchers or Anunna which in English is translated to Those of Royal Blood or Star Rulers because you see The Anu rule us all they are our great gods…they are our Star Rulers…they are those of royal blood…they…" But I highly doubt it's just Raymond and Lola in this cult.

Then I remembered both Raymond and Lola are travelling to Snowport and that is where the letter was sent from, the letter my boss received that had the very same symbol. So I now knew something out of the ordinary was definitely happening back in my old home town of Snowport, and I wanted to find out what. I was still standing in Raymond's room, so I quietly left and hastily made my way back up the train to my room, passing Raymond and Lola in the dining car on my way up.

When I eventually reached my room, I entered and locked the door behind me. I sat down at the table and grabbed a pencil and my notebook that I had brought with me. I started to make a few notes about the things that I had found out and the things that I wanted to find out so I could write it all up for the papers when I returned to the city.

My notes read as follows *Lola and Raymond part of cult* as well as *Is Anu a person?* I put down my notebook and pencil and opened the book, that indescribable book. I opened it where I had left off last time then turned to the next page, as I turned the rusty decrepit worn page, I saw at the top of the next page a new title. This title read, *Human-Animal Hybrids*.

I looked down at the page and saw three strange distinct hand drawn pictures with even stranger writing surrounding the pictures. The first picture was of a creature that had a human's body but with no hands. It had long skinny chicken legs as well as a long feathery tail and an ostriches head and neck then underneath were the words, *The Shantak*.

Then the second image had three drawings the first was of a human foot with webbed toes like a duck, then the second was of a ducks foot then the third was of a human hand with webbed fingers, but for some reason there was no note explaining what this image was. Then the last image also had three drawings.

The first was of an old man with horns protruding out of his head as well as long goat like ears, then the second image was of goat then the third image was of a young boy with curly hair, a long goat like face as well as long goat like ears. I scanned the pages for a note to explain what this was but I couldn't find one. There was just gibberish filling the page again, so I turned onto the next page.

On the top of this page there was another title. The title read, *The Ninth Planet*. On this page, there was just one image, the image was of a large black circle, then underneath it were some notes.

The notes read, *The ninth planet is a super Earth sized planet in the outer region of our solar system. It exists in the greater cosmic universe, it is five to ten times larger than that of Earth and is four hundred to eight hundred times as far from the sun as Earth. Some believe that this is where our great gods Anu live.*

I then went to turn the page but realised I had reached the end of the book.

I stood up and grabbed the book off the table stuffing it in my suit trying to hide it as best I could. I unlocked my door and left my room closing the door behind me. I approached Lola's room and knocked her door to see if she was inside. I waited for about ten seconds then, as I could hear no sound and no one had answered my knock, I slowly tried her door.

It was unlocked and so I popped my head in. I saw that her room was empty, so I crept inside and put the book under her bed. I then quickly and quietly made my way back out of her room closing it behind me. Suddenly, Lola was coming up the train towards her room. I hurriedly ran back towards my room kicked open my door and locked it behind me.

As I threw myself onto my bed, I heard the trains whistle, then I heard one of the train's crew members shout down the corridor. "We will be arriving at Snowport tomorrow!" He shouted it repeatedly. I heard him walk further up the train yelling the same thing to the other passengers further down the corridor. I started thinking to myself now that I know something definitely out of the ordinary is going in Snowport, tomorrow it's time to find out what.

7 December 1926

I popped upright in bed having just woken up from a nightmare in a cold feverish state and gasping for breath. The only thing I could recall from the nightmare was these bright red glowing eyes that stared straight into my very soul. Then there was a knock on my door and a voice soon after.

It was a member of the crew and he said in a loud and clear voice, "Sir, sorry to wake you but we have arrived at Snowport, I thought I should let you know. You have ten minutes to exit the train and thank you for travelling with us. I do hope we will see you again soon." I quickly calmed myself, putting the strange dream down to recent events.

I got out of bed, hastily collected and packed up my belongings and swiftly made my way out of my room and towards the train's exit. As I exited the train and stepped onto the Snowport train station (if you could call it that, the train station was almost non-existent), all I saw was a large shed like house on the right side of the station as soon as I exited the train, which I assumed to be the ticket booth.

The platform itself was just rotting and rickety and made me wonder what stopped people from falling onto the tracks. Then suddenly out the corner of my eye, I saw Raymond and Lola exit the train. A man walked over to them, I could make out his figure but not what he looked like as they were standing too far away and he had his back to me.

I decided to try to move closer but then they started to walk away, so I hastily followed them until they turned a corner exiting the train station. As I turned the corner a few seconds after them they had vanished into thin air. Where had they gone? I thought I better ask around, that is when I saw the rusty old sign saying *Welcome to Snowport*.

I walked further into town, the town was surrounded by a large forest with trees that stretched up touching the sky. There were two different types of houses in the town, the small one storey house that looked like it was just about ready to crumble to bits every time you closed the door. It was usually poor people who lived in these houses.

Then the other houses were very large and had two and sometimes even three storeys and these houses were for people such as the mayor of the town or just very rich people. As I walked further and further around the town, I noticed that the streets were abandoned. I didn't see a single person roaming the streets that was until I saw a milk man come walking by dragging his cart behind him.

He was wearing a black and grey apron, underneath that he was wearing a white shirt with his sleeves rolled up as well as the buttons done up all the way. He was wearing a long black tie with black trousers and black shoes. His hair was an almond brown colour and his neck was very thin, his jaw line was much defined and his eyes were an ocean blue colour.

His nose protruded upwards like a pig's nose and his lips were also protruding outwards like a fish. I approached him and stopped him from walking so that I could ask him a few questions. I said to him, "Hi my name's Thomas. I used to live here and I don't remember it being anything like this. What has happened where is everyone?"

He replied, "My name is Francis and our town has always been like this. I think you must be mistaken friend." He then gave me an eerie grin and carried on walking down the street dragging his milk cart behind him. As I looked at him as he walked away I saw something on the back of his neck. I saw to my dismay that strange symbol carved into his skin.

I knew after seeing this that something very strange must be going on with all the people of Snowport, not just Raymond and Lola. I decided to follow Francis closely and eventually, he led me to a lake that was beside the town, but just as I had lost sight of Raymond and Lola, I lost sight of Francis. I stood close to the lake and looked around, it was deserted and then I saw at the side of the lake was a row boat.

The row boat was dark wood and looked very rotten. There was one light brown paddle resting inside the row boat, so I pushed the row boat onto the lake and then jumped inside it. I started to paddle out around the lake to see if I could find any clue as to where they had gone. Finally after what felt like hours of searching, I found a cave built into the side of a wall on the lake.

I paddled towards the cave, and as I approached I saw that the cave opening was a very small oval shape. As I entered, I had to duck my head down as to not hit it on the walls. When the row boat had made its way through the caves opening. I saw that inside the cave on the ride side was a path made from wooden planks.

I steered the boat over and jumped out pulling the row boat up onto the path so it wouldn't get dragged back out of the cave by the current. Then I started to follow the path, leading me deeper and deeper inside the cave. I looked around and saw that the cave had large white stone like columns inside it as well as many white stone spikes hanging from the walls of the cave, almost like it was manmade.

The walls of the cave were a grey and yellow colour, then as I continued walking down the path, it lead me deeper into the dark and mysterious cave. Until suddenly I heard a voice echoing down towards me. I cautiously made my way towards the voice until I came to a corner. As I turned the corner, I saw that I was now in the very centre of the cave.

It was a vast space, with dark brown and grey walls with bright green bushes sprouting out of the walls in many different places. I looked up to see then an enormous hole in the roof of the cave letting the sun shine in. As I became more aware and the light improved, I suddenly noticed what looked like the whole town of Snowport gathered inside the centre of the cave.

They were all wearing long black robes with hoods as well as a mask. The mask covered the whole of their faces and had a long protruding nose as well as plump protruding lips and protruding eyebrows. There were two deep spaces for eyes. Then three people stepped out from the crowd and started speaking.

These three were the only ones who were not wearing robes or a mask, they were just wearing their own clothes. As I looked closer at the three individuals, I knew I recognised them. It was Raymond, Lola and the one Raymond and Lola met up with at the train station. I could see him clearer now. He was wearing long brown trousers and black polished shoes.

He was also wearing a black velvet coat and beneath he had on a black velvet waist coat as well as a grey shirt and a black tie. His coat had decorations on its sleeves that looked like squids; he had short greasy curly black hair that came down to just above his eyes, thick bushy black eyebrows and thin almost non-existent lips. He also had deep dark brown coloured eyes and around his eyes was a black colouring that pulled you deep in to his gaze.

His skin was smooth and he had no wrinkles except for on his forehead. His ears were small and protruded outwards; I thought to myself finally I had found them, and then the one Raymond and Lola had met up with started to speak in an elegant manner.

"Hello fellow friends, for those of you who do not know me, my name is Conrad and welcome to the cave of wonders…the cave of cosmic creation…the cave of the Star Ruler…the cave of our great God Anu!"

The crowd beneath his feet clapped and the clapping echoed throughout the cave, and as this was happening I started to move closer to the crowd so I could get a clearer view of Conrad. Suddenly, Conrad put his hand up and the clapping abruptly stopped, he spoke again.

"Let us offer our bodies to the great God Anu." After he said this, everybody started to chant "La meela dd mee mee ray teeso mee Teeso" over and over in almost rhythmic like pattern.

I then thought to myself that's it, that must be what that chanting gibberish means it must mean that they are offering their bodies to this so called Anu. Then the chanting got louder and louder, and the voices of the crowd grew deeper and almost demonic until suddenly the whole cave shook. Then the crowd stopped speaking and the cave grew silent. It wasn't until a few moments later Conrad spoke.

"He is here…The One of Royal Blood…The Star Ruler…The Great God Anu!" Then suddenly the cave began to shake again, but this time with even greater force than before, sending bits of stone flying from the walls of the cave hitting people in the crowd below. Then the shaking stopped just like before and Conrad went to speak but before he could the water in the cave started to tremble and suddenly something burst out of the water sending water into the air like a tidal wave.

As the water came fluttering back down, I looked and saw this unknown creature. It was at least 150 feet tall, its lower body looked like a giant slimy snakes tail but its upper body looked more like a humans. It had 6 arms and 4 claw like fingers on each of its 6 hands. It had dark green skin on its upper body, then on its lower body it had dark green scales.

Its forehead separated leaving a gap in the shape of a V. It had 12 blood red eyes and its mouth was just a mass of black and green tentacles. I heard screams come from behind me, so I quickly turned around and saw everyone in the cave had gone insane. They were fighting and trying to kill each other and as I looked and saw this, I couldn't pull myself to turn away from the madness that had erupted and consumed these people's minds.

Suddenly, some blood splashed up and streaked across my face pulling my mind back into focus. I turned back around wiping the blood from off my face and looked up into the eyes of this 150 feet tall monstrosity. As I looked deeper and deeper into its eyes I started to lose myself in its gaze. As I gazed into the eyes of the creature, I heard a deep demonic voice in the back of my head.

It then whispered one word to me and after that one word, the voice vanished from my mind. After hearing that one word, I then knew who this creature was, this unearthly creature is…The Cosmic Being…The Great God Anu…The One of Royal Blood…The Star Ruler…The Watcher.

After gazing deeply into its soul, I had now gained the unknown and vast knowledge of the greater cosmic universe and all of the secrets that lay within the undying…the unfathomable…the immeasurable…the carnivorous…the inky jet black…cosmic void.

Change of Heart

Introduction

It's 3032 and Nazi Germany won World War Two, and now has complete and total dominance over the world as we know it.

1

I woke up from a long nights rest and slowly made my way out of bed towards the bathroom. The bathroom was a large rectangular room; the walls were black and the floor a light wooden colour. On the right side wall was a large cylinder shaped box this was the shower.

Inside the shower was a long wooden seat that stretched the length of the wall, then on the right side of the shower wall was a small keypad. This keypad allowed me to control the showers actions, and then next to the shower was the toilet. On the far left side of the bathroom wall was the sink that rested on a black marble counter top, and above the sink was an oval shaped mirror.

I turned the tap on the sink splashing my face with cold water in order to properly wake myself up. I grabbed a towel and wiped away the water that was dripping down my face and walked out of the bathroom re-entering my penthouse. It was very large room in which I had a king size bed covered in blue and white sheets.

There were two blue chairs back to back and a dark wooden table. There was a lamp sat on the top and a circular rug covered some of the wooden floor. Taking up the far right side of the room was a large rectangular fish tank resting on a black coloured table.

In the middle of the room sat a holographic console that allowed me to control the windows and the blinds. I could also change the theme of the blinds, so if I wanted it space or sunset or swastika, I would just use the console to make my choice. I could also play music from Abba to Mozart. I can select a certain song and then a hologram of Mozart playing the song would appear in the centre of the room.

In the far left corner of the room was my bar stocked with many alcoholic beverages. I also had a black leather chair and foot stool which I would sit in sometimes late at night and watch the view out of 13 large windows. But for now the sun's rays were illuminating the whole room.

I put on my black trousers, my double-breasted field-grey coat with white shirt and black tie. My jacket was very plain with its silver buttons and it had no braid or decorations. The only thing I wore on the jacket was the swastika badge that was sewn onto it as well as the iron cross badge that was also sown into the jacket.

Now I was ready to go out and greet the people but before I did that, I walked over to the windows and looked down upon the great nation that I had now inherited. For I am Lucas Hitler, the great descendant of Adolf Hitler, the man who is God of this world. I heard a loud knock on my door and called out in, "Yes, who is it?"

My bedroom door opened and a man entered and started to walk towards me at a slow pace. I saw he was wearing a black peaked leather cap with a silver skull and cross bones badge in the middle. He was also wearing an all-black velvet jacket as well as a black shirt and black tie, with black trousers and knee high shiny black leather boots.

Around his waist he wore a black and silver belt and attached to his belt was a pistol as well as a knife that had an eagle engraved onto the handle. He carried black leather gloves and attached to his jacket were many medals, passed down through the generations of his family. Attached to his tie was an iron cross medal and on his left arm an arm band with a swastika on it our nation's flag.

On his face, he wore a metallic mask. The mask was a black and silver colour, it had two large protruding circles where his eyes would be, and where the mouth would be there was a large silver metal plate with four holes in it, so I could hear his voice I presume. He began to speak in a muffled manner. He said, "My name is Max…Max Müller, and I am your newly appointed body guard because as of this very moment, you are now the nations new Führer."

2

I already knew I was the Führer, but to hear someone say it out loud made me nervous. I mean what if I don't do a good job of it? But I guess if I'm just half the man my great relative, Adolf, was then I will be fine. I replied, "I know I'm the new Führer but thank you for telling me anyway…so shall we go?"

I exited my room having Max trailing a few steps behind. When I finally exited my room, I heard the door automatically close and lock behind me. I walked towards the elevator at the end of the hall, there were no doors like you would expect there was just a large square metal plate and protruding upwards from that and surrounding it were bright yellow handrails to hold onto so as to not fall over.

I stepped onto the elevator looking at the keypad. There were 43 floors in this building not including the basement or the penthouse. I chose the very bottom floor in order for me to exit this hotel. The elevator started up and I heard a loud grinding noise, and just a few seconds later the elevator started to take me and Max down towards the bottom floor.

The ride down was very quiet except for the sound of the elevator gears. The elevator slowed down and came to an abrupt stop. I stepped out and into the hotel lobby. I looked around and saw that it was small compared to my room. There was a blue sofa that could seat three people hovering gently above the floor.

There were lamps doted around in corners and on low tables. There were fluffy blue chairs, a black and silver desk which was covered in newspapers; a large black leather chair also hovered above the floor. There was a long white counter built into the wall and holding documents, binders, three laptops and a white plastic cup.

There were three large square windows and metal blinds that covered them. The floor had a grey and yellow carpet covering it and the ceiling was grey. In the centre of the ceiling was a large circular light. I now noticed that no one was in the lobby, not one single person not even a member of staff.

I looked around and saw a note on the desk in the lobby, the note read, *Sorry. Staff have left to attend the welcome of our new Fuhrer.*

Oh how stupid of me, now I remember everyone has took today off from their busy working lives to greet me in public. I then made my way towards the hotel's exit, hearing Max's heavy footsteps following behind me. I turned around to take a look at the hotel building.

The marvel of it. I saw it towering high almost touching the sky and scraping the clouds. This towering hotel was made from white stone and resting on top of the hotel made from solid gold was a giant swastika. On both the right and the left side of the hotel from the roof just coming down to above the pavement were 2 giant holographic swastika flags glitching out.

I turned around having my back to the hotel to face the street, and I instantly saw 30 speakers attached to metal poles attached to cinder blocks that were drilled into the ground. There were 15 on the left side of the street and 15 on the right side of the street, then in the very centre of this was a water fountain. The water fountain had six different white stone statues surrounding it.

As I was about to carry on walking down the street, a giant life like hologram of my grandfather, Adolf Hitler, burst up from the water fountain. It was a hologram of him making one of his famous and impeccable speeches. I heard the speakers crackle and suddenly his voice was amplified a thousand times over. Whole crowds started flocking towards the hologram to see him and listen to his speech; it was like he hadn't even passed on.

Then I got bored and started to walk down the smoothly cobbled street and as I walked, I saw people look and stare at me. I even heard some people whisper to each other and their children, "Look that's our new Führer." Some people even came right up to me and gave me a salute, but Max jumped in front of me as if I was about to be assassinated.

I told him to calm down, that that kind of thing doesn't happen anymore, but he said you can never be too careful. Then as I walked and walked down this street having many people greet me along the way, I arrived at a large triangle shaped stone building. It was almost in the shape of a pyramid, at the front there were several elongated steps leading up into the building, and then just before the entrance there were 8 tall stone pillars and on the very top of the building was a giant hologram of a swastika flag flying in the wind.

I entered this building and as I entered I saw that this was a museum. I looked around and saw that it was a very large museum, on either side of the lobby there were 4 small, square glass cabinets. The floor was an oak brown colour; the ceiling was a metallic black and came to a point at the top like a pyramid.

I slowed and glanced inside the cabinets and that's when I realised this wasn't just any museum, it was a museum containing many of Adolf's possessions from when he was alive. I continued to look and as I looked, I saw that encased inside one of the small glass cabinets was his personal pistol that never left his side. It was a Walther PPK.

Then as I looked in the next cabinet, I saw the very first swastika flag approved by Adolf himself. It had many holes in it and was ripped in many places. In the next cabinet, a replica of the famous LZ-125, a blimp designed by Adolf himself, the replica was small it was a shiny silver colour and on the back of the blimp were two swastika flags.

As I moved round to the next cabinet I saw another replica but this time it was a replica of the first fighter plane ever made, it was the Messerschmitt Me 262. The replica was a silver and grey colour and on the wings of the plane there was a large black swastika. Then there was another small replica but this time it was of boat, but not just any boat, it was a replica of the first boat ever made during the war time it was the U-1.

The replica was small but at the same time very long. It was a deep black colour and it had small swastika flags attached to it. I looked around and saw nothing else, but then something at the very end of the room caught my eye, so I speedily walked down there. When I got there, I saw a large amount of medals all different sizes and shapes encased and protected behind glass hanging on the wall, and underneath every single one of them there was a gold plated sign and engraved into the signs were the words *Awarded to Adolf Hitler*.

There must have been thousands of medals hanging on that wall. I saw a few centimetres in front of the wall a black beaten worn down chair and rotting wooden desk. There was also a sign attached to these, the sign read *Adolf Hitler's office chair and desk*. Then out the corner of my eye, I saw the most amazing thing in the museum.

It was encased in thick bullet proof glass and floating in mid-air inside the thick bullet proof glass, it was Adolf's skellington and the uniform he was wearing when he died. His clothes were frayed and ripped and they had many holes in them, but the leather material that was on his clothes had stayed the same. My eyes could not believe what they were seeing.

The very man who made this great nation, no this great world of ours. He built it up from nothing and here I am staring at his…corpse. It's not good enough. There has to be a way for me to meet the man in person. There has to be a way to meet my own relative, but how I thought it's impossible, he's been dead for years.

I walked on out of the museum feeling pretty run down, and I think Max could see I was in a depressed state because he said, "I think I know how to cheer you up, my Führer, why don't we visit one of the churches."

I replied, "What…what do you mean churches?"

Max then replied, "Oh you don't know? Come then I will show you."

3

Max stepped in front of me and started to walk at a fast past up the smooth and narrow streets, and as I followed behind him, I heard his shiny leather boots make what sounded like a squeaking noise every time he took a step. As I followed behind Max trying to keep up with his fast paced speed, I saw more and more people came rushing over towards me. Before I knew it there was a massive crowd gathered in front of me.

Max had stepped in front of me putting his hand across my body but then suddenly I heard a man shout a question from the crowd. "Is it true…are you the great descendant and grandson of our lord Adolf Hitler?" I heard murmuring in the crowd, and then the crowd abruptly went silent waiting for me to answer.

I replied in a loud and clear manner. I said, "Yes, it is true I am a great descendant and grandson of Adolf Hitler, and that is why I am your new Führer." Then the crowd began to disperse except for one person. It was a little girl about six years old. She came skipping up to and then asked me a question.

She said, "Would you sign this for me?" She pulled out a copy of *Mein Kampf*.

"Sure I will little girl. What's your name?"

"My name is Mia."

I signed the book *To Mia, don't grow up too fast. From Lucas Hitler*. I turned to Mia saying, "There you go, now run along."

After Mia left, Max continued in leading me to this church he spoke of, so we carried on walking down the untouched stone pavement until finally we reached a large oval shaped metal building. Max said, "Here we are." The building was plain, there was no decorations on the outside of the building except for a large silver coloured hologram of a swastika flag in the very centre of the building protruding outwards. I cautiously approached the doors.

I proceeded inside the church and looked around. There were 36 dark wooden chairs inside, 18 on each side of the church. The chairs were placed 2 per row going all the way back towards the entrance. I also saw that every single chair except for maybe 3 or 4 were occupied, so I made my way to one of the chairs and continued to look around.

The church floor was a black and white chequered pattern made from stone; the ceiling was an oval shape made from metal and was an inky black colour. There were only three windows inside the church on the left hand side of the room, and they were very small not letting much natural light enter the church. Bright white lights coloured the front of the church where there was a large portrait of Adolf hanging high on the wall.

Also at the front of the church was a square podium and covering the podium was a black red and gold swastika flag. On the right and left sides of that podium were two small black and silver columns, and on top of the columns was a gold vase but the golden vases were holding up a candle. Then I noticed something, on top of the podium there was a book lying open.

I was curious so I went to go and see what book it was but before I could move my feet, a man threw open some doors that lay behind the podium and approached the podium. He began to speak, "You may all now be seated," he said in a soothing tone of voice. Suddenly I heard a echoing thud as the many people in church took their seats.

I decided to take a seat as well and as I sat down, Max came over to me and took a seat next to me. I whispered to Max, "What is happening?"

He whispered back to me, "Just listen." I turned my attention to the man at the front of the church standing behind the podium. As I looked at him, I saw he was wearing a grey jacket as well as grey trousers and knee high leather boots. He was also wearing black leather gloves and a white shirt with a black tie but attached to his jacket on the left upper hand side was a medal of the golden eagle holding the swastika symbol.

Then on the right side of his jacket in the upper corner was the iron cross medal, and on his left arm he was wearing the swastika arm bad. Around his waist, he was wearing a black and silver belt and engraved into the centre of the belt was the insignia of the SS. Attached to his belt was a shiny black leather pistol holster, then attached to his tie was a golden pin badge and on the golden pin badge was a swastika symbol.

His head was shaved all around the sides and back. The only hair he had as on the top and he had it swooped back like an eagle. His hair was a golden blonde colour his neck was thick and skinny at the same time, his ears miniscule and almost non-existent. His jaw line was sharp like a knifes edge, his nose looked bent and broken as if he had been in a fight.

He had deep unnerving eyes that stared intently, then suddenly he began to speak again in a loud and clear but also soothing manner. He said, "Hello and welcome, my name is Oskar. I am the priest of this church and today I want to talk about our divine and sacred God, Adolf Hitler, for you see he saved this world from itself…"

I didn't understand what I was hearing, so I leaned over to my bodyguard Max again and whispered, "Will you please tell me what is happening?"

Then Max whispered back, "Just listen." So I sat back up in my chair and continued to listen to Oskar.

"He saved the world from itself at a time when no one else would. When the world was on the eve of war who stepped up to save them from themselves?"

Then the whole crowd inside the church shouted back in reply, "HITLER!" and as they did this the word 'Hitler' echoed and bounced around the church's cold and hollow walls. Then Oskar replied to the crowd in a loud and clear tone of voice.

He said, "That's right, Hitler…Adolf Hitler! Well if not for him where would we be, well I will tell you where we would be…" He then stopped and there was a long and silent pause; until suddenly Oskar shouted out in a loud and larger than life manner, "DEAD!"

Oskar then continued to speak but this time he spoke in a normal soothing manner, "That's right, dead. If our sacred and divine God hadn't been there to put a stop to the war, then we would all be slaves or worse not even exist. Now if you would like to grab your bibles from under your seats and we can begin to pray."

4

After he finished speaking, I leant over and stuck my hand beneath my seat and started to feel blindly around until my hand caught on something. I grabbed the object and pulled it from underneath my chair and placed it on my lap. I looked and saw that it was Mein Kampf, I was utterly confused.

After all the things, I heard Oskar say and now this I needed an explanation. I leaned over to Max again and whispered, "Let's go outside. I need some fresh air."

"Yes, my Führer." I then stood up and walked towards the door that lead onto the street, and as I made my way towards this door, I heard behind me the noise of Max's shiny leather heeled boots hitting the stone floor with every step he took 'Click…Clack…Click…Clack'. I finally reached the door, swung it open and stepped outside, and then Max stepped out of the church a few seconds after me. "Are you going to tell me what was going on in there?"

Max then replied, "Yes, my Führer, right away. Well you see I brought you here to cheer you up because you see, you are a great descendant and grandson of a God."

"What do you mean?"

Max then replied, "Well ever since he saved the world when it was on the brink of war and gave us this new world…this prospering nation, he has gone down in history as a God. Everybody worships him in every church in every nation across the world, and also every copy of every religions bible has been thrown out and destroyed, and replaced with Mein Kampf because he is more than a man, he is sacred…He is divine…He is a God."

I thought to myself it all makes sense now what I had just heard, what Oskar had just been speaking about. Max had put it into perspective for me and explained it to me in a clear way. A way I was able to understand but there was one thing I still didn't understand that Oskar and Max were both saying. I decided to ask Max to explain it for me.

I said to Max, "What do you mean when you say Hitler saved the world?"

Max replied, "What I mean is there was a war…a war that started on 1 September 1939, and didn't end until 2 September 1945. This war was between the British and the Americans. It was a brutal and unforgiving war with many loses, and then one day during this war, the Americans decided to build a nuclear weapon. On the 6 August 1945, the American's dropped their nuclear weapon on the British forces, killing 80,000 people.

"That's when Hitler, an innocent onlooker thought to himself, no this is not right, there must be something I can do. So he did indeed do something. Hitler gathered the forces that he had requested from our German parliament and went to help the British defeat the Americans and end the war. When he defeated the American forces, the British forces that he had so kindly helped, turned on him and tried to kill him!

"He had no choice but to defend himself and then after he had defeated the British forces, the entire world looked on and knew there was only one right choice to make the world whole. They agreed that they would entrust Adolf Hitler to rule and lead them all into a new golden age of peace and prosperity."

After hearing all of what Max had just said to me, I started to think to myself, I am the great descendant and grandson of a divine and sacred God, as well as a hero who saved the world from devastation. I thought to myself, how come I have never heard any of this before. As quickly as that thought popped into my head I pushed it out of my mind. I knew deep down that my mother must have just forgotten to tell me all these amazing stories about my ancestor, Adolf, when I was younger.

I looked at Max and asked him, "Why was I not told all of this? I mean I know about him being a hero and a saviour, but I never really knew that he was so revered by all. I never knew he was looked on as a God. Why? Why would I not have been told this?"

Max looked down at his feet, he seemed to change slightly and spoke softly. "You are a descendant of a great man, a God. Your family didn't want you to feel special or privileged. They wanted you to have a real childhood and not bow under the pressure of duty and of living up to the legacy left to you by birth.

"They thought in time, you would find out for yourself and understand what was truly expected of you. But you have been preoccupied with having fun and being less that happy about performing your duties and responsibilities that now you are shocked upon realising how serious your life, your duty is."

I looked up at the sky and as I did this, I noticed that is was night time already. So I said to Max, "I'm going to make my way back to my hotel room…good evening." I started to walk away down the darkened street but Max carried on following me.

I knew this because I could hear the click clack of his shiny black leather boots on the pavement as he took his step. As I carried on down the dark street, lights began to flicker on around me and as I looked, I saw that on the buildings in every possible direction my eyes could see different shaped, different sized different coloured swastika flag holograms on every building protruding outwards.

Some of them looked like they were blowing in the wind while some of the others hung flat and did nothing. I carried on walking down the street until in the distance, I saw the fountain outside of my hotel. As I got closer, I saw a crowd gathered around it. Suddenly a bright flash of light exploded and I saw that coming out of the fountain was another humongous life like golden yellow hologram of Adolf making one of his speeches.

The crowd that had gathered around the fountain watching the hologram was clapping and saluting it. I made my way towards the hotel's entrance and past the crowd that had gathered around Hitler's skyscraper like hologram. When I eventually entered the hotel, I headed straight for the lift that was at the back of the lobby.

Max and I then stepped onto the lift and I pushed the penthouse button on the elevators bright blue keypad, the elevator began to move sending me and Max upwards. As the elevator went upwards towards my room I could hear the gears of the elevator grinding away beneath me. As I listened to that noise it made me feel very anxious and unsafe but finally the elevator stopped.

It had reached my floor, so I and Max stepped off the elevator and then entered my room. When I entered my room, the lights turned themselves on automatically and a few seconds later, I saw something in the corner of the room. Suddenly, that something came running towards me but then abruptly stopped in the centre of the room.

I looked and saw that it was a robot dog; it had four silver metal legs and a medium sized silver metal body. Its four paws were just big clumps of metal but under the metal, I could see some brown leather material. I assumed that was to hide the wiring then its head was just a large mouth made up of 6 sharp spikes. It had no eyes or nose, Max started to speak, "This is my present for you, my Führer."

"Oh. Max, you shouldn't have bothered, but thank you."

Max then replied, "I thought the dog could guard you during the night while I'm not here."

I replied, "That's a good idea, Max, thank you…goodnight."

Max replied, "Goodnight, my Führer." After that Max left my room. I locked the door behind him and then climbed into bed to get some sleep, but all I could think about while trying to get to sleep was how I needed to meet my divine and sacred ancestor, Adolf, and how I was going to achieve this impossible and momentous task.

5

The next day I awoke and sprang out of bed like a jack in the box. I went and got dressed, then heard a knock at my door. I then shouted out in reply, "Yes, who is it?" Then my door opened and I saw Max enter the room. He started to walk over to me and as he did this, I then heard his black leather boots click and clack against my floor.

When he reached me, he began to speak in a soft and smooth manner. He said, "Good morning, my Führer, I trust you have had a good night's rest?"

I replied, "Yes, but there has been something that has been eating away at my mind recently."

Max looked at me with a puzzled expression before speaking. "Well do tell me, my Führer; you never know I might be able to help you."

I took deep breath and replied, "Well you see the problem is that I have heard so many amazing things about Adolf and what he did for us and our great nation that I just have to meet him...I need to meet him but I know that this is impossible! That is what has been eating away at me all night."

There was a long pause then Max replied, "Actually I think I can help you there, come and follow me." Max waited while I put on my coat and then exited my room, and I followed swiftly behind him. We got on to the elevator and I looked over at Max and saw him looking down at the elevators keypad.

He reached out his hand and pressed one of the buttons on the keypad, the button he had pressed read basement. The rusty old elevator began to move downwards, and as the elevator moved downwards towards the basement, I heard a creaking and groaning noise that started to make me feel uneasy. The elevator came to an abrupt stop. Max stepped off the elevator and I followed him.

As I looked around, I saw above me a large red sign that was embedded into the grey stone wall. The sign read, *Top Secret Technology*. I looked in front of me and saw a large metal rectangular door. I slowly approached this door and as I started to approach the door, I heard a noise coming from the other side.

It sounded like a beeping or a buzzing, but then all of a sudden, the door swung open and as this happened, I looked and saw a man standing on the opposite side of the door. I looked and saw that the man was wearing a black and grey stripy jacket, long black and grey stripy trousers, a black velvet top with a black velvet scarf around his neck. He also had a bright white belt around his waist.

On his left wrist, he was wearing a black metal wrist band, his right hand was a robotic hand it was a bright metallic colour and only had four fingers. I saw his hair was shaven all the way around his head the only hair he had was on the top of his head, well at least I think it was hair, it looked more like blacked coloured pieces of thin wire. Then his ears were very tiny in proportion to his head.

His nose was also very small as were his lips. He had a tiny amount of black stubble under his chin and on his top lip. I then noticed that on the left side of his head going down from his hair line and ending just above his lips were 10 thick black lines. I didn't know what they were for so I just moved, offering him a nod and a smile.

Then I noticed that in his left ear was an black earphone that stretched and extended all the way towards his lips, and as I looked closer, I saw that it was embedded into his skin. Covering his eyes was a black rectangular shaped visor; this also looked like it was embedded into his skin.

Suddenly the man began to talk. He said, "Hello, my name is Leon; I am the head of the scientific department that is based underneath this hotel. So is there something I can help you with?"

Max replied to Leon, "Yes, as a matter of fact you can. Your new Führer here is in need of your services."

Leon then replied, "Oh, my Führer, please accept my apologies. I did not mean to disrespect you, I did not recognise you. Please tell me how can I be of assistance?"

I looked to Leon and said, "Well you see I wish to meet my ancestor Adolf Hitler. Is there any way you could help me?"

After I had said this there was a long and silent pause that seemed endless until suddenly Leon excitedly replied, "Well I think I can help you there. Come follow me, my Führer." Leon started to walk inside the base, so I followed on behind and as I did this, I then heard Max say something faintly.

"Well I think I will leave you in the capable hands of Leon for now, my Führer, goodbye." Max got back on the elevator and left me with Leon. We went through some security doors and on the other side was an incredibly large square metal room.

As I looked I saw that on the left side of the room was a robot, the robot had a head in the shape of a security camera. It had long metal arms and legs they were a dirty silver colour like it had been down here for years. It had 4 fingers and toes and attached to its back was a large metal radio with a medic sign engraved into it.

All of its upper body was covered in a thick brown velvety material. I assumed to hide all of the wiring, and I then noticed that in its right it was holding a human skull. On the right side of the room, I saw a large silver grey metal mech suit. The mech suit had thick metal plated legs and I could see metal bolts in the legs protruding outwards and attached to the right lower leg of the mech suit were 2 grenades.

Thick black wires were coming out and upwards towards the mech suit's leg joints. The leg joints were circular allowing the legs of the mech suit to have wide and free movement, the knee joints of the mech suit were a black rubbery springy material so that when someone operated it, the legs would act just like a humans. The upper body of the mech suit was a rectangular shape and had the SS symbol engraved in the centre of it in a bright white colour.

Then the shoulders of the mech suit were an oval shape and had 6 pikes protruding up from them as well as a black coloured swastika symbol engraved on the left shoulder. The right arm of the mech suit was a long cylinder shape and it had 3 long metallic fingers, and attached to the top of the arm was a small black minigun. Attached to the minigun was a small ammo box and engraved into the ammo box was a white swastika symbol.

The left arm of the mech suit was also a long cylinder shape but this time, the left arm had a metallic grabber or clamp and then attached to the top of the arm was a long flamethrower. The face of the mech suit was circular, it had a rectangular shaped hole in the centre for someone to look through when operating the suit. Then where a mouth should be, there was a large circular filter that you would find on a gas mask and this was protruding out of the suit.

Attached to this were two thick black tubes going into the suit. I assumed this is what would help the person inside the mech suit breathe, then also on the face of the mech suit was a white skull and cross bones symbol engraved into the top left corner. I turned my attention to the centre of the room and that's when I saw something very odd.

It was a large bell shaped object. It was a shiny black colour and in the centre it had a silver swastika symbol protruding out of it, I was intrigued by it, so I began to walk closer towards this object. Then suddenly, Leon shouted out to me, "Interesting, isn't it? This is what I wanted to show you."

6

"What is it?" I asked.

Leon replied, "This is what I call the Nazi Bell. Imagine being able to visit the moon, mars or even distant star systems with just a snap of your fingers." He sounded excited.

"That sounds good and all but how does that help me?" I queried.

Leon then replied, "This can help you because it can also travel in time as well as space, but in the wrong hands, it is capable of destroying everything and everyone in its path or perhaps even altering time itself. That is why we keep it locked up down here were no one can get to it." I paused and took in what Leon had just told me.

Then after a while I replied, "So are you telling me that this is a time machine."

Leon replied, "Time and space machine."

"So will I be able to use this to see my sacred and divine ancestor, Adolf?"

Leon then replied, "Of course you are able to use this. Let me just get the machine ready for your journey." Leon then walked away to turn on the machine and as he did this, I then thought to myself it is finally happening. I am about to go back in time and meet my ancestor, the god and hero of our new world…Adolf Hitler.

I heard a clicking noise, so I looked over my shoulder and I saw Leon. He had flipped a large black metallic switch, then suddenly I heard this loud buzzing noise vibrate through the room and then the noise abruptly stopped. A purple light began to glow from the Nazi Bell, filling the room.

Then I heard Leon speak. He said, "The machine is now ready for your journey."

I replied, "Is it safe?"

Leon smiled confidently. "Oh yes, perfectly safe." After hearing this, I stepped forward towards the Nazi Bell and stepped inside. As soon as I stepped inside, I saw a bright white light and heard a loud ringing noise, but then suddenly the noise stopped and the bright white light was gone.

As I looked around, I now saw that I was standing in a large square room. On the left side of the room was a rectangular black marble counter covered in varies papers and documents. There was a long blue sofa and embedded into the wall was a small fireplace. The walls of the room were a light brown colour and had 4 paintings hanging up in different places.

The floor was covered with a light grey carpet and a large long dark brown desk. Behind the desk was a maroon coloured chair and in front of the desk were three white leather chairs. I decided to walk to the desk to see what was lying on top of it, and as I walked closer, I then saw that on top of the desk was a small golden lamp with a white lamp shade as well as multiple books of different sizes.

I also saw a small black rotary phone as well as lots of documents and papers neatly piled and organised in stacks. I grabbed some of the papers and as I looked and flipped through, I suddenly saw one that stood out. The title of this document read *My Master Plan For War*. As I read it I saw that it had three phases.

Phase 1—Invaded Poland and start WW2. Then I saw phase 2.

Phase 2—Initiate Master Plan to clean the world of all Communists, Socialists, Social Democrats, Romanians, Jehovah Witnesses, Homosexuals, Polish people, Disabled people, Jewish people and Soviet's by having them all put in my concentration camps were they will be either shot, die of starvation, be exterminated through extreme labour or die in gas chambers.

Then phase 3 read, *Phase 3—Win the war and become a God!* Suddenly I heard a noise coming from outside the large rectangular shaped doors. The door creaked open slowly and I saw someone walk in. It was him, Adolf!

He was wearing a light brown suit and dark brown knee high leather boots, a light brown tie and a white shirt. On his right arm, he was wearing a swastika arm band. He had thin greasy black hair that looked like it had been slicked back with mud. His eyebrows were thick and bushy; he also had a big thick black moustache on his upper lip that looked like a caterpillar.

His eyes were large in proportion to his head and he also had a large forehead. Then suddenly he spoke, he said in a loud tone of voice, "Who are you?" But before I could reply I started to hear that ringing noise in my ears again, and I then saw a bright white light appear before my eyes. Before I knew it, I was back in the basement of the hotel back in my time.

7

I was dazed, confused. I couldn't think straight. What had I just seen? How could it be? I couldn't believe what I had read when I was back there. All of us, this entire new world is based on a lie! How many more lies don't we know about?

I wonder if it was him, Adolf who had started the war not the British or the Americans…Adolf! And he did it with one goal in mind genocide…the genocide of thousands of innocent people. My precious, revered ancestor Adolf is not a God, he was not a hero. He was not sacred or divine. He was a racist, psychopathic serial killer and we have all been lied to!

Our whole way of life has been built and shaped from the mind of a mad man who should have been killed! But I then stopped and thought if he was killed I wouldn't be born. I wouldn't exist, nor will Max and Leon or that nice little girl Mia. I needed time to think so I hastily exited the basement and made my way towards the elevator.

As I did this, I heard a faint noise from behind me, it was Leon. I heard him say, "Bye then." Then when I reached the elevator, I stepped on and pushed the penthouse button. As the elevator went up towards the very top floor of the hotel, I listened and cringed as its gears creaked. Then the elevator stopped, I finally reached my room so I stepped off and started to walk towards the door.

As I made my way towards the door, I saw Max standing to the right side of the door. He then spoke and said, "Hello, my Führer…"

I snapped at him, "Do not call me that, call me by name please. Lucas."

Max paused for a moment and then replied, "Is there something wrong, Lucas?"

I replied, "I just want to be alone for the moment, I need to think."

Max replied, "Ok, I will leave you." I entered my room and was glad to hear the door automatically close and lock itself behind me. I pulled at my clothes, tearing them from my body. They felt as if they were suffocating me.

I jumped into the shower and had it as hot as my skin would allow, trying to wash the disgust from my flesh, the dirt seemed endless. I eventually crawled into bed hoping that when I woke up I would have a solution to this problem that is playing havoc inside my mind.

When I awoke, I rolled out of bed for a solution had indeed formed inside my mind when I was sleeping. I knew what I had to do; I had to kill Adolf Hitler! It wasn't an easy decision to make, for if I killed him, thousands of people who were born in this new world would never exist…I would never exist. But if I didn't kill him he would kill thousands maybe millions of innocent people all over the world.

No, he could not be allowed to live! It was a hard decision to make but it must be done. I got dressed and ate breakfast in haste. I exited my room and walked towards the elevator, suddenly there was Max. He spoke to me, "Good morning, Lucas, do you want me to accompany you today?"

I replied, "No, I'm OK thank you, you stay up here." I entered the elevator and pushed the button that said basement and the elevator started to go downwards. As the elevator moved I heard that creaking and groaning noise again. It started to make me feel uneasy, then the elevator abruptly stopped.

I had reached the basement and so I stepped off the elevator, and started to make my way towards the top secret science lab. As I made my way, I passed multiple soldiers guarding the entrance and when I finally entered the lab, I saw many scientists rushing around franticly. I looked around searching for Leon and saw him running towards me.

"Sorry my…" he began.

I interrupted him saying. "Please, just call me Lucas."

Leon replied, "Ok. So why have you come to visit us again, Lucas?"

"I want to use the Nazi Bell one last time, if I may?" I replied.

Leon then replied, "Yes of course, let me just get it ready for you."

"No, I want to be in here alone when I use it, if I may?" I hastily added.

Leon then replied, "Oh…ok let me just show you what to do." Leon pointed to a large black metallic switch on the wall and said "When you are ready, flip this switch and when the purple light comes on, you are ready to go."

"Thank you for all your help, Leon, it is greatly appreciated." I spoke with a sense of guilt knowing that after my trip things would very different for Leon, for everyone.

Suddenly Leon shouted, "Ok everybody out!" Then everybody left the lab and when the very last person had left the room, Leon locked the doors. I was now completely alone in the lab with nothing but my own thoughts to keep me company.

8

I started thinking to myself, the healthy human mind doesn't wake up in the morning thinking this is its last day on Earth, but I think that it's a luxury not a curse to know you're close to the end. It is a kind of freedom, good time to take…inventory.

Outgunned, outnumbered, out of my mind on a suicide mission but the sands and rocks here stained with thousands of years of warfare…they will remember me for this because out of all my vast array of nightmares this is one I chose for myself. I go forward like a breath exhaled from the Earth with vigour in my heart and one goal in sight. I WILL KILL ADOLF HITLER!

I walked over to the black metallic switch on the wall and flipped it. A few seconds later, a bright purple light started glowing from the Nazi Bell but then something caught my eye. On Leon's desk was a tape recorder. I decided to tape myself saying something, so I clicked it on and said:

"This is for the record. History is written by the victor. History is filled with liars, if he lives his truth becomes written and the world is lost. Adolf Hitler will be a hero because all you need to change the world is one good lie and a river of blood. He's going to complete the greatest trick a liar ever played on history…but only if he lives!"

I stopped the tape recorder and placed it back on Leon's desk. I turned slowly, crossed the room and stepped into the Nazi Bell. As I did this, I saw a bright white light and heard a light ringing in my ears. Then it suddenly stopped and I was back in that room I had been in before.

I assumed it was Adolf Hitler's office. I started searching around frantically for a weapon, then suddenly I heard a noise coming from the door and then the door slowly creaked open, and I saw him! Adolf Hitler! He stepped in through the door. He started to approach me but before he could get a word in I lunged towards him.

He pulled a gun out from his holster that was attached to his belt. I stopped and froze. Suddenly there was a knock on the door a moment's distraction as he turned to look. I lunged forward, this time to grab the gun from his hand but we tussled and in the tussle Adolf fired the gun.

After hearing the gunshot, I stepped backwards clutching my stomach. I slowly looked down and as I did I saw blood but I did not feel any pain. I searched for a bullet wound and to my surprise I did not find one. Then I looked up at Adolf Hitler and saw that it was him who had been shot.

I began to chuckle at the fact that he had shot himself, first a low chuckle which quickly evolved into a maniacal laugh, load and shrill. I heard soldiers trying to break down the doors because they had heard the gunshot. Suddenly I felt a large pain in my chcst. I collapsed to the floor in agony.

As the room around me faded to black nothingness, I thought of one thing and one thing only…history is written by the victor…history…is filled…with liars.

The Coffee Shop

1

BEEP! BEEP! BEEP…BEEP! BEEP! BEEP! "God, Olivia, if you're not going to get up, what's the point in setting your alarm…honestly I don't know why I agreed to rent this flat out with you. For god's sake, WAKE UP!"

After a sudden scream sent shockwaves tunnelling down my ears, I slowly raised my eyelids. As I did this, I could feel the sleep that my eyes had gathered in the night weld my eyelids together, making it almost impossible for me to open my eyes. I nearly gave up and went back to sleep but I powered through it, and eventually my eyelids separated and sprang apart from each other.

I rubbed my eyes and let out a loud and long yawn. After this, I stretched out and while doing this I gave out a relaxing sigh. I got slowly up and out of bed. I made my way to the toilet, as I made my way I stepped on a plug. I screamed in agony and then started to limp around in a circle speaking to myself saying "Fuck…Fuck…Fuck."

I looked down and saw that my roommate, Emily, had left her hairdryer lying around AGAIN! I kicked the hairdryer under the bed with a swift swing of my leg, and then carried on into the bathroom. Our bathroom was just like any other ordinary bathroom.

A scum filled bathtub with a shower head attached in case you don't have the time for that cheeky bath. Then a mould filled sink and toothpaste stained walls, floors and taps as well as a lovely pink fluffy oval shaped matt to step onto when we come out the shower. The toilet…well we don't mention the toilet. I made my way over to the sink and tried to twist one of the rusty taps.

As I tried to do this, the tap broke off in my hand, and then flakes of rust fell to the floor. I groaned silently and decided to try the other tap, so I twisted the other tap. Suddenly, I heard a noise coming from the sink, it was a rumbling noise a groaning noise, and then it came spurting from the tap.

Milky coloured water, I cupped my hands under the tap and left them there until I felt like they had filled with a good amount of water. I then took my hands from underneath the tap making sure not to spill any of this milky coloured water on the floor, and then splashed the water over my face. I did this 3 or 4 more times till I felt like I was properly awake and ready for the day.

I went back into my bedroom and proceeded to pick out something to wear from my wardrobe. As I went back into the bedroom and opened my wardrobe doors, I saw that there was nothing hanging up in there. I shouted to Emily, "Emily, did you remember to do the washing last night?"

There was a long pause then Emily shouted in reply, "What washing?"

I sighed and shouted in reply, "What do you mean what washing…our clothes that we wear, you IDIOT!"

There was another long pause then Emily shouted in reply, "Well obviously I FORGOT!"

I shouted back in reply, "Well what am I going to wear today!"

Emily shouted back in reply, "How do I know!"

I shouted back in reply, "Well thank you…FOR NOTHING!"

There was another long pause until Emily replied, "YOU'RE WELCOME!" After our conversation ended and after hearing that Emily had forgotten to wash our clothes the night before, there was only one option left for me. I would have to go around my room and sniff through all of the dirty clothes that I didn't put in the wash and whatever pair of clothes smells the least dirty, I will have to wear.

So I started sniffing, there was a pink adidas track suit, so I picked it up held it to my nose and inhaled. I immediately threw it under my bed as it stunk to high heaven. There was a knee high pearl coloured dress with small bright blue flowers covering it head to toe. I held it up to my nose, inhaled and threw it straight back onto my bedroom floor in frustration.

After about an hour of picking up and smelling countless clothing items, I began to give up until near the bottom of the pile, I saw something. "It can't be?" I thought so I looked closer, it is, it is, its plastic wrap. So I started digging and digging until I saw it, a new and sealed package from Outdoor and Country. This must have been delivered ages ago and I must have just thrown it to one side and forgot about it, but thank god for my crap memory.

Then without a second thought, I ripped into the package like a rabid dog and inside I saw a bright grey fluffy blazer, as well as a dark blue top, and black skinny jeans. I proceeded to get dressed, then about 15 minutes later when I had finished getting dressed, I decided to comb and straighten my light brown locks. About 20 to 30 minutes later, I was ready…ready to see where the day may take me. I ran down the uneven and very narrow stairway then when I had reached the bottom. I slipped on my pale pink high heels and proceeded on out the front door, exiting to see what the day might throw at me.

2

I walked on down the trash filled streets thinking of a way of how I could possibly waste my time today. As I walked down the uneven sloppy slab placed streets, I passed many shops, such as The Purple Fire Cafe that I was a frequent visitor to, and always ordered a full English with orange juice and white toast on the side. Then there was the restaurant Pulp Kitchen.

I would go there if I wanted to go out and treat myself, and as I passed this I saw The Whimsical Jester Pub. This is where I would go if I wanted a good night out. Then a couple of paces down I came upon The Worthy Moon Salon. Again I would usually go here if I wanted to treat myself and get my hair done for a night out.

A little further down I came upon The Fabulous Mammoth Florist, they sold the most beautiful flowers for miles around and as I passed the florist, I smelt the overwhelming gorgeous perfume of flowers of all different kinds. Next, I came upon The Brown Dwarf Movie Rentals from which I would go every Saturday night to rent a film for movie night. Then again a few paces away was The Stormy Mask Dry Cleaner.

This is where I went if I had to get a stain out of my clothes that I could not remove myself. Then as I walked and walked and walked some more, I came upon a building that I had never seen or even entered before, and I have been in every single shop up and down this street, but this shop is not familiar to me. Then it hit me, it is a new shop, it must be. That is the only explanation for it else I would have heard of it before.

The shop was called Brewed Awakening. It was a coffee shop. I decided to enter the shop. The walls were a bright white colour; the floor was a light brown laminate flooring. On the right side of the room, there was a long white counter and behind the counter was a woman who was already serving coffee to the people that had gone in.

She was wearing a long sleeved shirt and a black apron covered her lower half and she had long black hair. On the left side of the room were six small square tables and paired with each table was one small light brown wooden stool. Adjacent the wall was a dark brown wooden bench and they had a large square window at the front of the shop to let in an extreme amount of natural light.

Just the average, carbon copy, chain company coffee shop, of which you see 20 a day. I joined the line and about 10 minutes later, I was at the front of the queue. I was now face to face with the woman who was standing behind the counter.

She began to speak in a chirpy tone of voice and said, "Hello and welcome to the best coffee shop in the world. What would you like to drink today we have…" She then began to list off every drink they served. "We have Espresso, Caffè Americano, Caffè Lungo, Manilo, Café Cubano, Caffè crema, Cafe Zorro, Doppio, Espresso Roberto, Espresso Romano, Guillermo, Ristretto, Caffè Medici, Café Touba, Canned coffee, Coffee milk, Double Double, Kaapi, Pocillo…"

Then she took in a long lung full of air and continued. She said, "Here are the infused options we have you can have your coffee Drip-brewed, French pressed, Cold Water Extracted…" She then paused like she was thinking of what to say next then she carried on with her sentence.

She then said, "And these are the boiled options we have to offer you can have your coffee Percolated or you can select from two of our boiled coffee options which are the Turkish coffee or a Moka or you could have your coffee Vacuumed but that does not fall under our boiled options it is its own selection." She then again paused and took in a big lung full of air and then continued with her speech.

She said, "And now these are the different combinations that we offer you can have Coffee with Milk, Coffee with Condensed milk, Coffee with espresso, Coffee with tea, Coffee with alcohol…" She than took a sip of water and then wiped the droplets away from her mouth, then after that she put the bottle back down and carried on with her speech.

She said "And now these are the flavours that we offer you can choose from Melya, Caffè Marocchino, Café miel, Café mocha, Café de olla, Café Rápido y Sucio, Miscellaneous…" I began to think to myself will this ever end then the woman behind the counter carried on with her speech. She said, "And for our iced options we have Frappé, Freddo Espresso, Freddo Cappuccino, Mazagran,

Palazzo, Ice Shot, Shakerato…" She paused again and looked down as if she was reading from a script, then carried on.

"You can also have your coffee instant or have your coffee decaffeinated we also offer a coffee-based-dessert named Affogato, so do you know what you would like to order today?" I was stunned at how much they had to offer I felt overwhelmed.

I then replied and said, "Yes, thanks, can I just have a black coffee?"

The woman behind the counter looked almost confused but then replied, "Yes, of course you can that will be no problem, so if you just find a seat, I will bring it to your table when it is ready." As I left the counter I headed straight for the table that was in the top right hand corner of the coffee shop next to the window. As I walked over to the table I could hear my pink high heels tippy tapping on the laminate flooring of the coffee shop.

When I finally reached the table I pulled the wooden chair out, the one that was facing towards the window and then proceeded to sit down. About 2 minutes later, a waiter appeared by my table holding my cup of coffee. He placed the cup in front of me as well as a little black book with a piece of paper in it. The waiter then walked away.

I picked up the little black book and opened it to see what it was, hoping it was going to be something interesting. Turns out it was just the bill, so I closed the book and placed it back down on the table. I put my hands around my mug of coffee and smiled as the warmth of the coffee made its way threw out my whole body.

I lifted my mug up to my lips taking a little sip to see if it was cool enough to drink, but it turns out it was not as I burned my tongue. I did not react because I did not want to make a scene in front of everybody that was currently inside the coffee shop. I placed the mug back down on the table in front of me and waited for it to cool down, and as I waited I looked out the window of the coffee shop.

As I looked out the window, I saw hundreds of people walking around calmly and tranquilly. It was as if they had not a care in the world, then suddenly I saw a man walking towards the coffee shop. This man stood out from everyone else and there was something about this man that I found extremely odd.

The man entered the coffee shop but he did not go up and order a drink, he instead walked straight up to the table that I was sitting at and then sat in the empty chair opposite me. He was wearing a black coloured tailored blazer and trousers as well as a maroon coloured shirt that was tucked into his trousers.

He had on a stripy maroon tie that covered the buttons on his shirt. He was wearing black shiny leather shoes and a black fedora that covered the top half of his face. I could see that he had well defined black stubble and his chin was also very well defined. On his middle finger on his right hand was a silver platinum ring with a black rectangular shaped onyx stone in the centre of it. I saw a grimaced smile come from the man's face as he began to speak.

He said, "Hello…Olivia, I am The Creator, and we have much to discuss."

3

I was baffled, how did this well dressed mysterious person know my name? Had he been following me and if so for how long days…weeks…months…years even. I had to find out so I went about speaking to him to try and find out as much information as possible.

I said "How do you know who I am, have you been following me?"

The man chuckled and replied, "Oh don't be so foolish. I do not need to follow you or anyone for that matter. I just know where people are every minute of every second of every day." After I heard this I didn't know what to say. Was he trying to misdirect me because he had been following me, or was he telling me the truth?

I didn't know what to think I would just have to press on I then asked another question. "So who are you?"

Again he chuckled then replied, "I have already told you my name. I am The Creator."

I chuckled in response to his answer then replied to him and said "Come on, that's not your real name, what's your real name?" He never answered so I moved on and said, "So what do you want money, its money, isn't it?"

I then saw that grim smile fall over the man's face. After this he replied, "Money…money…money, that's all you people think about, that's all anyone here thinks about. Well since you brought it up, let's see if money is worth the price you bestow upon it."

I went to reply but as soon as I opened my mouth, he cut me off and said, "Let's play a game. I want you to make a wish. Any wish at all no matter how big or how small. I will make that wish come true right now before your very eyes. The only stipulation is that I want you to make a wish related to money." I thought to myself what is he playing at, did he follow me for months just to try and creep me out, and if so, he is failing miserably.

I then thought to myself I still don't know anything about this person but apparently he knows everything about me, and I need to know how he knows so much about me, so I need to keep playing along with him even if it's just to find out more information about him. So with this in mind I then replied, "Ok I will play your game and make a wish."

A smile grew on his face ear to ear, then he replied, "So what will you wish for?"

I thought long and hard until eventually it came to me. "I wish for a £20 note to appear in front of me on this table." I started to laugh silently to myself because I knew there was no way this was going to happen. The Creator raised his right hand and clicked his fingers and as he did this, I saw in front of me the £20 note.

Impossible! I thought impossible. I picked it up and checked to see if it was real. I held it up to the light, I tugged at it I did everything humanly possible to check and see that it was not a fake. I could not find one single imperfection on it.

I concluded that it was as real as the nose on my face but it was impossible. I then began to speak to The Creator. I said, "How…how did you do it."

The Creator replied saying, "If you think that was impressive wait until you see what else I have in store for you."

I uttered "W…What do you mean…Who are you…what do you want?"

There was a long pause, then The Creator replied, "I am just a passer-by who has taken a special interest in you, and you should be pleased by this. I don't do this very often. The last time I did something like this was about 2,000 years ago give or take."

When I heard what he had just said, I couldn't believe my ears. First he makes money appear out of thin air and now he tells me that he has lived for more than 2,000 years give or take. I cannot believe him. I just cannot. He doesn't look a day over twenty-five.

I don't know if he is actually telling me the truth or if he is pulling my leg and stringing me along as a part of some sick game. Perhaps he is an escaped lunatic on the run from the police. No matter how much I ask him who he really is, he will never give me a straight and truthful answer; so I guess I will never find out who this man really is this so called…Creator.

4

I picked up my mug that was sitting on the table in front of me and took a sip of my coffee that I had ordered earlier. As I did this, the Creator put his hand in his pocket and pulled out a large bright silver coin and started to twirl it between his fingers. As he did this, the golden rays of the sun shone down and bounced of the coin hitting me in the eye.

I closed my eyes and put my coffee mug back down onto the table. The Creator laid his right hand flat with the coin in it, then suddenly the coin levitated. He then lifted his middle finger up slightly, and as he did this the coin began to spin slowly in mid-air. I was amazed. I said, "How are you doing these things…ok are you a magician?" After I said this the coin dropped suddenly onto the table making a thud sound.

Then there was a long pause and finally The Creator replied.

"A magician…I am not a magician. This magic that I present to you is real. It is of the gods. What magicians do is just cheap trickery, so please do not insult my intelligence again."

I replied, "I'm sorry. I meant no offence."

The Creator then said, "Does this look like a magic trick a magician could do?" The Creator raised his right hand and clicked his fingers and suddenly in a blink of an eye, it had gone from day to night. It was another impossible event that happened right before my eyes. I had to find out what was happening and fast.

So I said, "How are you doing all of these things that are deemed impossible…is magic real? Explain it to me for I have seen 3 extremely impossible things and I fear more are ahead of me, so for my sake explain it to me….who are…what are you?"

The Creator then replied, "Now you are asking the right questions, for you see I am not a man of flesh and bone. I am a Djinn."

There was a very long pause, then I replied cautiously, "What's a Djinn?"

The Creator then replied and said, "A Djinn is a type of interfering spirit often demon-like but not equivalent to a demon. We Djinn are self-propagating and can be either good or evil. We possess supernatural powers and can be conjured in magical rites to perform various tasks and services but we can also have a life of our own.

"But it is a rare occasion you see Djinn living a free life. We are also sometimes malicious and some of us are beautiful and good natured. We Djinn are created from the ashes of the smokeless fire. We can shape shift into any form be it animal or human but in are true form we are invisible to most people except under certain conditions.

"However, dogs and donkeys are able to see us. We were here on earth 2,000 years before you humans. As you and every human has free will, so do we and we are also able to understand good and evil. There are 3 different types of Djinn. The first are skilled shape shifters and may appear in any form; the second type are consistently benevolent and are venerated and loved.

"The third type is one who is consistently temperamental, treacherous, hostile and malevolent, the very embodiment of evil spirits. You humans may propitiate them but the motivation is fear, and all of us are unreliable and deceitful but the life span of my species is much longer than yours but we do die. There are male and female versions of us, and we can have children.

"We eat meat, bones and the dung of animals. We play, we sleep and we have pets, some of us have the legs of a goat, others a black tail, others a hairy body, others may be exceptionally tall and have eyes set vertically in their head and we can live anywhere on the planet but we prefer deserts, ruins and places of impurity like graveyards, garbage dumps, bathrooms, camel pastures and hashish dens.

"We can also live in people's houses. We love to sit in the places between the shade and the sunlight, and move around when the dark first falls. We also love marketplaces but we do have some limited powers. We Djinn are limited in our ability to get in touch with the deceased, learn about the future and what happens after death or be healed but we can appear to you humans as the spirits of the dead and communicate with the you humans through visions and voices, and it was us Djinn who taught you humans Sorcery.

"We will eat human food to steal its energy. We can also fall in love with humans and marry them, but when we Djinn falls in love with a human, we may interfere with the relationship or try to disrupt the marriage. Sometimes ordinary human acts can hurt or even kill us Djinn without you people even knowing, and when that happens, we Djinn often possess the offending people in order to take revenge on them, and others who are vulnerable to possession are those who live alone.

"We Djinn can affect the moods of you humans, changing your mood from happy to sad although, we are able to affect humans minds, bodies and mood we cannot affect and have no power over the soul. When a human becomes possessed by one of us, they will appear to be insane and exhibit signs of anger, anxiety and depression. A women's voice will sound like a mans and a man's voice will sound like a woman's.

"Physical symptoms include nausea after eating, headaches, frequent desire to fight, heavy shoulders, a constant feeling of dissatisfaction and a desire to commit suicide, and if one of us has possessed someone, sometimes an exorcism is needed."

After hearing all of this I was extremely baffled, but this explains how he was able to turn day into night with just a click of his fingers. In a blink of the eye how he was able to make a £20 note appear from nothing, and how he was able to make that coin float in mid-air and spin. As crazy as all of this sounded, I believed him.

Then suddenly a question jumped into my mind, so I asked him the question. "Well what kind of Djinn are you?"

The Creator then replied, "I am a master shape shifter."

I then replied, "So you can appear as anyone?"

The Creator then replied, "Anyone and anything." Then as he said this, I saw his face slowly change shape and colour and as I looked I saw that he had changed into Emily, my flat mate. I sprung up from my chair and backed away slowly.

The Creator then spoke, "What's wrong, don't be afraid. Can't you see now that you are nothing." I carried on backing away then a stranger got up and asked me if I was OK, but I looked over and saw The Creator click his fingers, then the stranger stopped speaking. I poked the stranger and as I did this, I saw to my horror that The Creator had turned this stranger into a cardboard cut-out.

I looked around the room in a panic and as I did this, I saw that The Creator had turned every single customer in the coffee shop into a cardboard cut-out as well as the tables and chairs. I was now trapped in this coffee shop with an all-powerful Djinn, so I tried to run past him to the exit but he clicked his fingers again and I went flying through the air and crashing down onto the floor.

I looked up and saw him walking towards me twirling that bright silver coin between his fingers and as the moonlight rays shone on down behind him he shouted in a low demonic tone of voice. As he did this, darkness creeped around the coffee shop slowly covering every inch of the light that it could find. He then shouted, "You are not worthy to keep the secrets of the Djinn!"

Suddenly in a blink of an eye, he was gone. He vanished just like that. I stood up and looked around the coffee shop and saw that every customer was back to normal so were the tables and chairs. I then walked back to my table and looked out the window, and as I did this I saw that it was a very sunny clear and cloudless day. I thought to myself it's like he was never here, am I going insane?

I was freaked out, so I quickly finished off my coffee paid then left. Then as I was crossing the road, I heard a loud screeching noise, so I looked and saw a large white van hurtling its way towards me. Before I knew it, everything went dark and I lay there on the ground bleeding to death.

It took every bit of strength I had left to peel my eyes open and when I did this, I looked around slowly through my squinting eyes and saw hundreds of people gathered around me talking to each other, but I could hear nothing, not a sound. Then suddenly I felt someone place something in my hand, so I looked and as I looked over to the right, I saw him, The Creator.

I looked in my hand and saw that bright large silver coin that he was always twirling around between his fingers, and as I looked at him, he nodded and I then saw that large grim smile fall over his face as he walked away. I then clenched my hand tightly and turned my head upwards towards the beautiful blue sky, and then with my dying breath, I gave out one last laugh as the world around me faded away into a cold and empty darkness filled abyss.

Angel of the Bottomless Pit

Introduction

This is the story of how I, Lucifer, was cast out from heaven and sent unto the fierce, fiery flames of hell.

Heaven

I

What happens to a human's soul when they die? They may find themselves in heaven if they have lived a virtuous life, among angels and gods in paradise. If they have not lived a good life, they may be banished to the depths of hell, to suffer in eternity.

What is heaven you may ask? Heaven is the place where God, angels and deities reside. It is the immortal soul's final resting place. It is located above earth stretching from the sky up to realms outside of the humans known physical world.

Heaven is both a place and a state of being it is viewed as a reward for a virtuous life. The dead may also gain entry by sacrifice, heroic deeds or great suffering and this place known as heaven is where my story begins.

II

Before my fall from heaven, I was a high and exalted angel and was the most beautiful angel ever created in all of heaven. My body was covered in precious jewels and my voice was that of a choir. My forehead was high and broad, my form was perfect and my presence was noble.

A majestic light surrounded me and made me brighter, and more beautiful than every other angel. I was also the first angel to be created by God, a thousand years before the creation of the world and man. I was a commander in God's army and was in charge of 350 thousand angles, but as my kindness grew so did my hatred and envy.

Then God created the paradise, Eden, and man in his own image and when hearing of this, my hatred and envy grew and grew till there was no kindness left to spare.

III

If that was not already bad enough, I started to get jealous of Jesus who was one with God before I was created. I then knew that no matter how intelligent or respected I was, God would always choose Jesus over me, and as much as I tried I just could not accept this. I did not make my feelings known though, and when all the other angels bowed to Jesus Christ, I followed, even though my heart was not pure.

Then suddenly God held a meeting with Jesus to discuss his plans for creation. I was not allowed to attend the meeting. I was not allowed to know God's plans for the future; this troubled me as I thought I was his favourite in heaven, and I wanted to be just as important as God himself but couldn't see how I could reach such a level of power. I left the immediate presence of God with my heart filled with envy and anger.

I gathered all the angels in secret, when they all arrived I introduced the idea of them worshipping me instead of Jesus. That I would take the place of the Son of God. The other angels did not reject the idea right way as they were discontented because they didn't understand God's intentions. Some of the angels decided to side with me and rebel against God and Jesus.

The remaining angels were loyal and believed that Jesus was the one they should be worshipping. The loyal angels tried to reach me and convince me of this, they wept and were anxious of what the future might hold but I did not change my mind. I turned from any angel who decided to remain loyal to Jesus; the angels who sided with me were promised a new and improved government where they would all have complete freedom.

The loyal angels again tried to warn me about the consequences of my actions but I was more certain than ever that I was doing the right thing for me and the angles that chose to follow me. I knew that there was no crime higher than that of rebelling against the government of God. Then suddenly God summoned every angel in heaven including me, and had everyone make their case.

I told God that I felt that I should be considered just as important if not more important than Jesus but God dismissed me, telling me that I would be found unworthy of heaven if I continued these thoughts. I told God that nearly half of the angels in heaven agreed with me, and I then proceeded to challenge God's word, saying that he wouldn't be willing to dismiss nearly half of his angels. God declared that such a rebellion was unforgiveable and that I and the angels following me would no longer remain in heaven, and so the heavenly wars began.

IV

War broke out in heaven and with the 200 thousand angels following me, against the 150 thousand angels still loyal to God and Jesus. I knew that they didn't stand a chance and that I would win this war, and finally get the power that I so rightfully deserved. As the golden trumpets sounded, sending shockwaves through heaven, the two armies charged at each other and collided like two waves crashing into one another.

As I was hovering there, flapping my large feathered white wings, I saw Michael and Gabriel at the far end of the battle field. I saw them order a small group of angels to defend God's throne. Michael and Gabriel then started to fly at an immense speed straight towards me, so I readied myself and drew my flaming sword. When Michael and Gabriel reached me, they stood there wanting to speak.

Michael was wearing his golden armour with his white wings outstretched and his long yellow hair flowing in the wind. In his right hand, he was carrying a long silver sword and Gabriel was wearing his long white and golden flowing robes with his small wings outstretched, and his short brown curly hair bouncing in the wind, in both of his hands rested a long golden spear. Suddenly Michael spoke in a deep but cautious tone of voice.

He said, "Come now, Lucifer, stop this foolish charade, give yourself up and God may have mercy on you." As his words burrowed deep into my ears, I felt the hatred rise within me once again like so many times before. I looked down upon the battle that was commencing below me. Michael and Gabriel and saw that my army of angels were losing.

This cannot be, I thought to myself. So I proceeded to swing my flaming sword towards Michael and as I did this Gabriel anticipated my attack and flung his spear towards my sword. As the tip of his spear touched my sword, it instantly broke and crumbled into three separate pieces. I was now without a weapon.

Then Michael and Gabriel started to approach me, their weapons aimed at my face. As they approached me, I screamed out in panic and in anger, "No! No! This is my kingdom, this is my world I am…GOD!" Then in the haze of my great anger, I transformed myself into a huge red dragon with seven heads and ten horns.

When I did this the skies of heaven turned black and every angel coward with fear, except Michael and Gabriel. I saw them standing to attention ready to attack. Every angel below stared up at the three of us waiting with anticipation for what would happen next and who would be the first to strike. Then suddenly Michael raised his sword and flew towards me, and as he did this the battle continued.

When I saw Michael swooping towards me with his mighty silver sword, I blew a volcanic fire from my mouth towards his general direction but he raised his sword blocking my fire, and all that was left was a large black mist. Through the mist I saw Michael, still charging forward and within a blink of an eye, he had cut off one of my seven heads.

I roared in pain and reached up with one of my claws to grab him but he dodged me, and then in an instant, he had grabbed on to the horns protruding from one of my heads and pulled with extreme force, until eventually the head had just popped off. I again roared in pain but this time louder, then I thought to myself, I am to slow in this dragon form to do any damage to him.

So I transformed back into my normal form and as I finished transforming back, Michael threw the dragon heads that he had cut and ripped from me straight at my feet. Michael landed in front of me, sending a gush of wind up into the air making his hair and wings bounce. He spoke in a loud clear tone of voice, he said, "Look around you, Lucifer, it's over."

I proceeded to look around the battle field and saw that all my followers were lying on the ground defeated, and I was now surrounded by these so called loyal angels. I looked at Michael and lunged towards him but he proceeded to kick me to the floor. As I lay on the floor I just laughed. Suddenly the golden trumpet was sounded a second time, and as this happened the skies of heaven turned back to a bright white.

Then the golden trumpet was sounded for a third time and when this happened, I heard a loud thud that shook the heavens, and I saw all the angels kneel and bow their heads in synchronisation. After this, I heard a voice that came from high up in the heavens, so high that even I didn't know where it came from.

The voice was the voice of God. The tone of God's voice and the manner in which he spoke was that of genuine compassion and comfort. God said, "Because of your pride and your selfish desire for power and might, you are to be cast out from heaven onto Earth for the rest of your days. As of this day, the name Lucifer shall be stripped from you and you shall forever be known as Satan.

"As for the 200 thousand angels that followed in your cause, they are to be made mortal and live on Earth alongside the descendants of Adam and Eve for the rest of their mortal lives." After God spoke, Jesus came down from high and then suddenly there was a crack of thunder and a flash of lightening that split the heavens open, and sent me and my followers falling down from the heavens to that little pathetic blue ball called Earth.

But as I fell, I had one last look up and saw all the loyal angles dressed in white robes with all their wings stretched out gathered around in a circle, and in the centre of the circle was Jesus. Behind all of them was a bright blinding golden yellow light that sent rays shinning down in all directions, and one of the rays hit me in my eye blinding me, so I averted my gaze but not before I shouted up to Jesus and God saying, "This is not over…it will never be over!"

I saw that I was extremely close to Earth, and before I knew it, I was hurdling towards a large lush forest. I saw a large rock protruding from the ground. I tried to move myself out of its path but I couldn't. Then in a blink of an eye, I hit my head on the rock and everything went black.

Purgatory

I

When I awoke, I stumbled to my feet and looked around to find that my wings my beautiful bright white wings were now a smooth slick leathery red and black colour like that of the dragon that I had transformed into earlier. I heard a twig snap in the distance as if it had been stepped on, so I concealed my wings and then waited for the stranger to appear from the shadows.

As I suspected, a tall hunched over man wearing a simple robe aged by use stepped out from behind the trees. He had long dirty blond hair that came down to his shoulders and a big bushy dirty blonde moustache that covered up his lips, and in his right hand, he was holding a wooden three pointed pitchfork. The man started to approach me, so I shouted in the man's direction and I said, "Stay where you are, what do you want?"

The man froze on the spot and replied in a calm voice, "Don't worry, my friend, my name is Samuel. There have been many stories passed around in my village of a monster living in the woods. I just came up to see the monster for myself but you my friend are no monster, you are but a man. If you wish you can come with me and it will bring me nothing but happiness to provide you with new clothes as well as food warmth and shelter and you can stay with me for as long as your heart does desire"

I thought to myself this man…this man is correct I am no monster but I am no man for I am a God amongst men. I replied to Samuel and said, "I will take you up on your oh so generous offer if it please you."

Samuel said in response to me, "You will not regret this, please follow me and I will lead you to my home." Samuel then began to lead me to his home using his pitchfork as a walking stick, and as we walked together through the dense forest, I began to ask him a series of questions.

I said, "Where am I?"

Samuel then replied, "You are in a small village to the south west of France in Clermont." Then as he finished his sentence, we exited the forest and I saw many stone buildings all stacked next to each other. We continued on down a thin narrow cobble stone road until eventually we reached his home.

We proceeded to enter his home through a beaten and withered old wooden door, and as the door opened I heard the rusty metal hinges creak and groan. Then the door slammed shut behind us and as I looked around his home, one thing drew my attention straight away. It was a small wooden cross that hung on one of the walls of his home, and as soon as I saw this, nothing else interested me, nothing else deserved my attention.

I walked towards the wooden cross that was hanging on the wall and when I was eventually standing in front of it, I asked Samuel a question. I said, "Do you believe that God will save your soul?"

Samuel said, "I do for God…"

I then interrupted Samuel and said "God is what? Divine, sacred…God is nothing but a fool who chose you pathetic bags of meat and bones over the more intelligent option." After I said this, I grabbed the cross off the wall and crushed it in my hand till it was nothing but dust.

Samuel started to back away slowly towards the door but he then stopped and said in a worrying manner, "What would be the more intelligent option?"

I turned around to face Samuel and then replied, "Well me, of course," and as I said this, I smiled and drew out my wings sending things crashing and smashing. I looked at Samuel and as I looked at him I saw that he had dropped to his knees clasping his hands together in prayer. I chuckled a little and then flung him to one side of the room with my wings, as he landed up against the stone wall, I heard a snap like that of a branch breaking.

It was his back, it had broken. He screamed out agony and slowly started to crawl towards the door. I grabbed his ankle and dragged him to me. I sat him up and proceeded to ask him some questions.

"Now then, Samuel, would you be so kind as to tell me what year it is?"

Samuel then replied, "Its 1095…what are you?" I thought to myself, 1095, how long was I out for? It must have been a couple of centuries at least. I then continued and replied to Samuel.

I said, "I am Lucifer…I am Satan…I am a God amongst men."

This struck fear in Samuels' eyes, he then asked me, "Whatever unholy being you are, God will not falter in protecting his people and…" but before he could finish his sentence, I snapped his neck. I then concealed my wings and grabbed Samuels's clothes from his body and changed into them. Then as soon as I dropped my angel robes onto the floor.

They puffed up into a ball of fire and when the smoke cleared I could see that there was nothing left of them but a small mountain of ash. I made my way out of this little village and towards to the town of Clermont located in the centre of France.

II

When I finally made my way into town. I saw hundreds, if not thousands, of these pitiful humans everywhere. They were running around like rats looking for a piece of cheese. Suddenly a little boy bumped into me as he was running across the street. He was wearing a drab, brown, sack like garment, covered in filth and his feet caked in mud.

His hair was very scruffy and his face and clothes were covered in muck and dirt. "Sorry, Sir." He then went to walk away but I grabbed the boy by the scruff of his neck and pulled him back so that he was facing me. The boy looked up at me with great unease. I knelt down till I was head height with the boy and then proceeded to speak to him.

I said, "What do you think you're doing bumping into me you little…" but before I could finish my sentence, I saw that a crowd had gathered in front of me. I then asked the boy, "What is going on?"

The boy responded, "Don't you know, Sir, Pope Urban II is on his way here now to bless our church. It is such a special occasion."

I snapped at the boy and said, "A Pope?"

The boy then said, "Yes, Sir, do you not know what a pope is, Sir?"

I then cracked a half smile and replied and said, "No, I don't would you please explain?"

The boy then said, "The pope is a central figure of power and influence, he greets many people from all walks of life hoping to seek an audience with God. In a sense God speaks through him, so his words are God's words. He also deals with many religious matters using his authority to weigh in on issues facing the church."

After hearing this, I let the boy go. He ran off and mixed in with the crowd of people. I stood up and thought to myself this is it, this is how I will act out my revenge on God for casting me out of heaven and onto this disgusting ball of dirt. I will pervert the mind of this Pope who has influence and who has power and who's word is like that of God. I will make him start a war but not just any war, a war in God's name…a holy war.

I advanced towards the crowd of people all packed tightly together. Then when I entered the crowd that's when I saw him. Pope Urban II was sitting on a white horse waving to the large crowd that had gathered to see him. He was wearing a long white robe that reached all the way down to his ankles on and the robe was three black crosses.

One on each of his shoulders and one in the centre of his chest. He was bald except for a thin line of hair circling his head. He also had a clean kept beard with bits of grey scattered about in it and sideburns that lead up to that line thin of hair, his eyebrows were also thin and almost none existent. His eyes were narrow and small his nose also small but smooth.

He had three defined lines that ran across his forehead and his ears were hidden behind his sideburns. Then suddenly he disappeared into the church. I looked up at the church, a large brown stone structure with two large stone spires pointing up towards heavens. The doors leading into the church were large and wooden there was also many little decorations scattered around the structure as well as many glass windows.

I then went to enter the church but as I went to do this, I looked and saw that there was a guard at the door of the church. I thought to myself how I would get in, then in the background, I heard a faint voice go by, "Sorry, Sir." That's it, I thought. I then turned around and saw that it was the same boy from earlier.

The boy also saw me and started to run but it was no use. I used the own boy's shadow against him. I grabbed onto the boys shadow and pulled, the boy then tripped and went tumbling straight into the stone street. I strolled over to him and lifted him up off the ground and put him back on his feet. I grabbed him by his arm and then knelt down again like before, till I was at his height and started to speak.

I said, "Listen to me…what's your name?"

The boy replied, "My name is Robert, Sir."

I then replied, "Listen, Robert, I have a job for you…"

Robert interrupted me and said "Oh yeah, why would I do anything for you, I don't even know you. We only met once before and you were not very polite."

"Well I'm sorry; look if you do this job for me, I will reward you with more food than you could ever dream of."

Robert looked me up and down and asked "What makes you think I need food?"

I then smiled and replied, "I know you're homeless and trying to rob people just to get by but if you do this one job for me you will never go hungry ever again. You will never hear the sound of your stomach rumble, your belly will be full for as long as your live so what do you think?"

There was a long pause for a moment then Robert replied, "Well what is this job?" My smile grew bigger and my pearly white teeth began to show through the cracks of my smile.

I said, "Do you see that guard there?" I then pointed towards the guard with my finger, and as I did this, Robert looked and saw the guard.

Robert then replied, "Yes, what about him?"

"I want you to distract him, understand?"

Robert then replied, "Yes." I released the boy and he ran speedily towards the church, and approached the guard at the door. Robert then proceeded to throw stones at the guard and as he did this, the guard swiped his hand towards Robert but Robert ran way and the guard gave chase. Now the church was unguarded. I made my way towards its entrance, but just before I entered the church, I felt someone tugging on my leg.

I looked down and I saw the little boy, Robert, panting like a dog, "I did good, Sir. I outran that guard. Can I have my reward, Sir, can I, Sir, can I?"

I then replied in a soothing manner and said, "Yes just follow me this way." I led the boy down the side of the church where no one could see us. I grabbed the boys' neck and lifted him up in the air. He began to kick his little legs and claw at my hand for freedom, as he did this I just smiled and smiled until my smile reached ear to ear.

Then without any extreme force or pressure I crushed the boys' neck until his bones turned into powder. I dropped his tiny lifeless body to the ground, and as I did this I said, "There is your reward, you filthy maggot. Now you will never be hungry again." I crept back out from the side of the church and entered the church.

When I entered the church, I looked around and saw many stone columns and many wooden benches facing a square shaped white podium that was at the front of the church, then suddenly a guard approached me and said, "Excuse me, what is your business here?"

I replied, "I have an urgent message for Pope Urban II."

The guard then replied, "He is through here, follow me." The guard eventually lead me to a wooden door with a black iron handle. The guard turned to face me and said "I will leave you to it then."

He then turned and walked away and as he walked away, I heard the faint cling and clang of his metal boots against the church floor. When the noise had completely faded away I opened the door that lay in front of me and entered the room.

I slammed the door behind me and there he was, Pope Urban II. He had spun around in shock at the noise of the door. He then began to speak, "Who do you think you are, well tell me this instant?" After hearing this I chuckled to myself silently and then thought to myself this is going to be fun.

"I am an angel of God sent down to guide you and give you divine wisdom."

There was a long pause but Pope Urban II finally replied, "Prove it, for all I know you could be some peasant come to rob or kill me. Come on, prove it before I have my guards deprive you of your head." There was another long pause then Pope Urban II said, "Ha I thought so. Now why don't you just pi…"

But before he could finish his sentence I drew my wings out and outstretched them. I looked upon Pope Urban II and saw him cowering on the floor he then spoke, "It is true you are an angel from heaven, and the almighty God has sent you down to guide me on my path."

"Yes, it is true," I replied.

Pope Urban II then stood to his feet and brushed his robes then spoke; he said, "So what does God demand of me?" I put my hand upon his shoulder to comfort him and then replied.

I said, "God demands that you, Pope Urban II, are to tell the people to take up arms and to take back the holy land that you, his followers, so rightfully deserve. You are to kill every non believer in this fight and you are to have no mercy for anyone, for if they do not believe in the one true God, then they have passed any means of salvation. You are also to create a military that serves God himself and you are to call this military The Knights Templar, and whoever follows these words will guarantee there selves a place in heaven."

Pope Urban II then replied, "If that is Gods wish, then let it be done." After this discussion, I concealed my wings and exited the room. I took a seat at the very back of the church and waited, and while I waited I chuckled to myself. I thought how easy it is perverting the minds of God's creations. God will soon see that it was a mistake to choose these fleshy sinful meat sacks over me.

After a short while, the church doors swung open and a mass of people started to rush into the church snatching up any seat they could get, and then when every seat had been filled, the church doors were slammed shut and Pope Urban appeared from the shadows. He walked slowly towards the podium in the centre of the church. As he did this he waved and the people in the church clapped and cheered.

When he reached the podium he stepped up and a sudden silence fell over the church. Pope Urban began to speak, he said in a loud and clear tone of voice to make sure he was heard. "I came here today to give this church my blessing, but I now come to you with a message from God almighty himself. A message of great importance, a message we cannot ignore.

"I tell you my friends that we must all take it upon ourselves to take up arms and take back the holy land that God himself gifted to us. From this day forth, the church shall have a military who shall fight for God and in God's name smite his enemies and show no mercy. This military shall be known as The Knights Templar. Any man who fights in this military shall guarantee themselves a place in heaven at the very side of God himself."

He finished speaking and a long silence fell over the church until suddenly everyone in the church cheered and applauded, and as soon I saw this, I knew my work had been successful in turning and perverting the minds of God's followers against him and against each other. I left the church for I knew that The Crusades were next to come, a war but not just any war…The Holy War…

III

200 Years Later

As the Crusades came to an end, I looked upon my work with great enjoyment. I walked through the streets that ran red with the blood of the innocent and laughed. For I had accomplished my goal of perverting the minds of these creatures that God loves more than anything that he had created. For I have showed God that these humans are no better than I, for they have slaughtered 9 million of their brothers and sisters, whether they be innocent or not.

They struck them down as if they were nothing but a lamb ready for the slaughter, and they did so all in God's name. They showed God that they are not worthy of his love and they were never worthy of his love because not only did they kill millions of their own, but the Knights Templar, the order who swore an oath to God himself were charged with heresy, homosexuality, financial corruption, fraud and spitting on the cross and for these crimes, they were all burned at the stake.

Then as I continued to walk down the street, I looked upon the mountain of corpses piled up high with flies and maggots, all converging on these rotting bodies and smiled for everything I have done has lead up to this moment. I wanted to see, no, I needed to see God's favourite creation lying dead in the gutter rotting away to nothing, for this is my ultimate revenge against God.

Let God look down upon his creations and weep, for now they are dead and dying, and they do so in God's name. Then suddenly just as I was reaping my reward, I heard a crack of thunder, so I looked up and saw a flash of lightening appear above the forest where I had first landed here on this disgusting mud ball. There was something familiar about that flash of lightening.

It reminded me of the flash of lightening that was struck when I was cast out from heaven, so I decided to go over to the forest and investigate. I made my way over to the forest post-haste but when I eventually reached the forest, I saw sitting on the rock, the very rock on which I had landed and became unconscious after being cast out of heaven, I saw him. Michael, the very angel, who defeated me and as I looked into his eyes, a great rage swelled up inside me like a volcano that was about to erupt.

I calmed myself down for I had already exacted my revenge. I then began to speak to Michael and I said, "Do you like what you see?"

Michael replied, "You are a fool, Lucifer. God sent you here as test to see if you could make peace with God's creations and if you did this you would be allowed entry back into the kingdom of Heaven, but your pride and your lust for power have darkened your soul and your mind. You are beyond saving, there is no place for you in heaven and now there is no place for you among God's creations."

I replied, "Do you think I care? Why would I want to go back up to heaven and live among you and the rest of God's puppets. As for God's creations, I have done what I set out to do. I have whispered in the ear of man and perverted them against God and each other.

"They will forever be a sinful breed of serpents slithering along in the dirt killing and spitting in the name of God for many centuries to come and you have me to thank for it!"

Michael then gave out a long sigh and replied, "God has created a special place for you and in this place, you will be God and have power over all. In turn he has named this place Hell…Hell is a place where God's creations will go if they have committed sins against God or against each other.

"Such as lust, gluttony, greed, sloth, wrath, envy, pride, breaking promises, lying, lack of integrity, cruel speech about those whom they differ, despairing of salvation, presumption of salvation, envying the grace that God gives to other people, obstinacy in sin, final impenitence, denying the truth, murder, adultery, stealing, bearing false witness against their neighbour, not honouring their father or mother, taking God's name in vain, making idols, having other gods before God, not keeping the Sabbath day holy."

Then suddenly as Michael finished speaking, he slammed his sword into the Earth and the ground began to rumble and groan. As Michael drew his sword from the ground, a large bottomless pit appeared. Michael grabbed me and tossed me down into the bottomless pit, and as he did this the ground closed sealing me inside for eternity.

Hell

I

I was falling for what felt like forever, when suddenly I landed. I brushed myself off and just as I did this, a bright burning wind blew past me and made me look up. As I looked up, I saw a lake of fire bubbling over onto the rocks, the black, molten rocks that everything in this place were made from. I walked towards the edge of the cliff that I was standing on and looked down.

As I looked down, I saw a never-ending pit of darkness and a furnace of fire. Suddenly flames of fire spat out from the furnace like dragons breath. Then suddenly, I heard a scream echoing through the cavern. I looked up and saw a human falling down and just at the last second before she hit the floor, I grabbed her and pulled her to me.

She looked at me; her face expressed both fear and awe for she had never seen anything of the like. I could almost hear her thoughts, would I eat her, kill her, was she already dead, was this a dream? Then a thought popped into my head, if God can have minions in the form of angels, and if I am now the ruler of my own kingdom, why can't I have my own minions.

I thought of a way to create my own minions, that's it I thought that's it every single human soul who enters my domain, I will punish and torture for all eternity for the crimes that they have committed. If a human soul who has been tortured loses all their humanity, then that human soul I will take and turn into a demon, a malevolent, dark and malicious spirit that will revel in pain, chaos and death. They will forget what it means to be human, some may even forget that they were once human.

My demons will engage in torture and destruction because it is fun and they all will follow in my agenda to cleanse the Earth because my demons will be superior to every human in every way. They will go forth into the world wearing their human skin and whisper, whisper in the ears of saints and sinners alike. No one will be safe. They will tempt and seduce for all flesh is weak as it is human. Yes, they will pervert and harvest these pathetic souls for eternity.

II

Present Day

Well that was the story of how I, Lucifer…Satan…The Devil, whatever your culture calls me, was banished from heaven and ended up ruling Hell. Bad, weak people get sent to me every minute of every day, and they get what they deserve. But believe me it is not over and it will never be over because no one can tame my unquenchable fire, not even your almighty God.

The Bogeyman

Introduction

We've all heard of or seen the bogeyman. He's a monster who hid under your bed and in your closet when you were a kid. He gave you nightmares and made you afraid of the dark. But what happens when a real life bogeyman exists?

The Babysitter

"No, OK I've told you, Charlie, it's time for you to go to bed now. If your mom and dad get back and you're not asleep, they won't be very happy and we will both be in trouble. So come on, let's get you to bed."

Charlie replied in a upset tone of voice, "Ok if I have to so why did my mommy and daddy call you again, I don't understand."

I replied, "Well, you see, I'm a babysitter."

Charlie replied, "What's a babysitter?"

I replied, "A babysitter is someone who temporarily cares for a child or children on behalf of the children's parents. So in other words, I'm here taking care of you, making sure you're OK while your mommy and daddy are out, does that make sense."

Charlie replied, "Yea I guess so."

I replied, "Ok good, anyway come on, let's get you up to bed." After talking to Charlie, I walked him upstairs to his bedroom and as I walked him up to his bedroom, he let out a big mouth-watering yawn. Then when we finally reached his bedroom, he rushed over to his bed and jumped under the covers.

I then walked over and kneeled down at the side of the bed right next to his head and spoke, "Ok is there anything you want before I leave you to go to sleep?"

Charlie replied, "Yes, can you tuck me in?"

I then replied, "Ok then." I then stood up and tucked the covers tight underneath Charlie and then walked towards the bedroom door. Then when I reached the door, I spoke and said, "Alright, time for sleep. Do you want the light on or off?"

Charlie replied, "Light on, please."

I replied, "Ok night."

Charlie replied, "Night, Abbie." After putting Charlie to bed, I then walked back down the stairs and made my way into the front room. When I entered the front room, I slumped onto the sofa and picked up the TV remote that was lying on the small round coffee table in the centre of the room next to the house phone. After this, I then started to flick through various channels.

As I continuously flicked and flicked, I could find nothing of interest, so I just left the TV on a random channel then threw the TV remote next to me on the sofa. After this, I decided to call my boyfriend, Daniel, but before I could reach for the phone, I heard a scream come from upstairs. It was Charlie, so I quickly rushed to my feet and ran up the stairs to his room trying not to trip on my way up.

When I reached his room, I saw him hiding under the covers shaking like a leaf, so I approached him then when I got to him, I slowly pulled the bed covers from over his head, and spoke to him in a soothing manner. I said, "What's wrong, Charlie?"

Charlie replied with shaky breath and said, "The bogeyman…I saw the bogeyman."

I replied, "It's just your mind playing tricks on you because you're tired."

Charlie replied with a raised voice "No, it's true…it's true. I saw the bogeyman."

I replied, "Ok…Ok calm down. How about this would you feel better if I looked around your room and made sure that nobody is in here with you." Charlie replied, "Yes please."

I then started to search his room. First I got on my hands and knees and looked under his bed. I then said, "No bogeyman under here." I then got up and walked over to his closet. I opened the doors and then said, "No bogeyman in here either." I then closed his closet doors and walked back towards the bed.

I then knelt down beside the bed and said, "Look, Charlie, there is no such thing as ghouls, ghosts, goblins or the bogeyman ok. They're just stories that some people that lived along…long time ago made up to make their children behave so if you see a shadow move in the darkness or hear a whisper in the shadows calling your name, it's just your mind playing tricks on your because you need to get some rest. So go to sleep OK, Charlie."

Charlie replied, "Ok, I'm sorry."

I replied, "It's OK, Charlie, just go to sleep if you need anything, I will be right down stairs, ok."

Charlie replied, "Ok."

I replied, "Ok, night."

Charlie replied, "Night." After this, I then made my way back down stairs and into the front room. I then again slumped onto the sofa and carried on with what I was about to do. So I then picked up the phone and called my boyfriend, Daniel. As I held the phone to my ear, all I heard was the dial tone, so I checked to see if the phone was plugged in.

As I checked I saw that the phone line had been cut, then suddenly I heard a noise come from upstairs. It was the floorboards creaking when I heard this, I decided to slowly make my way up the stairs. When I had finally reached the top, I saw a large shadow coming from Charlie's room. So I slowly and quietly tiptoed across the landing and peered into Charlie's room, and that's when I saw…that's when I saw the bogeyman.

The Crime Scene

RING…RING…RING.

"Honey, wake up and answer that phone."

I replied, "Ok…ok. I'm up…I'm up." I then leaned over to the bedside cabinet and picked up the phone. Once I picked up the phone I put it to my ear and spoke. I said, "Hello, this is Martin Gunn, Homicide detective, what can I do for you."

Then the person on the other end of the phone replied, "Yea hi, Martin, its Ethan…Ethan Higgins. Look I really need you to come down here to take a look at something and maybe give some advice if that's ok."

I replied, "Yea sure thing, that's OK and by the way this better be worth my time you know. It's my day off. Right anyway tell me where I have to go, and I will write it down."

Ethan replied, "Oh don't worry, we will send a squad car to pick you up, and sorry to ruin your day off but trust me it will be worth your time." After this conversation, I hung up the phone then got out of bed and walked over to the toilet. When I was inside the toilet I turned the cold tap on and just splashed my face and rubbed my eyes with water to wake myself up properly.

After this I then walked back into the main bedroom and started to get dressed so I proceeded to open my large closet doors. After I opened the closet doors, I looked inside the closet. This closet that held mine and my wife's horde of clothes. I then rummaged through dresses and dresses and more dresses and what felt like thousands of shoes until I finally found some clothes that I deemed appropriate to wear.

So after finding these clothes I then yanked them out of the closet and laid them down on the bed, so they wouldn't crease. I then walked over to my bedside cabinet and started searching in the draws on my knees for a tie to go with the clothes that I had selected. As I emptied the contents of the draws onto my bedroom floor, I could not find a tie, so I shouted down to my wife, Sandra.

I shouted, "Honey, have you seen my tie?"

Sandra replied, "What tie?"

I replied, "You know my reddish brownish tie?"

Sandra replied, "Oh that tie. I chucked it out."

I replied, "Now why would you do that?"

Sandra replied, "Well it was all ripped and torn. It looked ugly, just wear a different tie."

I replied, "Fine I will have to wear my blue tie." After this conversation, I took off my pyjamas and proceeded to get dressed. First I put on my black boxers then my grey socks, after that I then put on my dark blue jeans. Then I put on my brown leather belt to keep my jeans up. After this, I then put on my long sleeved white collared shirt butting it up all the way and tucking it into my jeans.

After this, I then puck on my dark blue tie that had white dots decorating it. I then put on a grey jumper. After doing this, I walked down stairs into the kitchen and sat down at the kitchen table. When I did this my wife, Sandra, greeted me "Morning, honey, have a goodnight's rest?"

I sighed then replied, "Yes, I can't complain, and you."

Sandra replied, "I too had a goodnight's sleep."

I replied, "That's good, darling…that's good."

Sandra replied, "Yes anyway, what would you like for breakfast?"

I replied, "I think I will just have two pieces of toast with a glass of orange juice."

Sandra replied, "Ok, darling." My wife then went on to make my breakfast but as she did this, I heard a knock at the front door, so I got up and went to answer it. Then when I opened the door, I saw a uniformed officer standing in front of me.

She then went on to say, "Are you Martin Gunn, homicide detective?"

I replied, "Yes, that's me."

She then went on to say, "Sir, I've been sent to take you to a crime scene were homicide detective Ethan Higgins is currently waiting for your input."

I replied, "Ok I will be right there." After hearing what this uniformed officer has just told me that she is taking me to an active crime scene, I am shocked why didn't Ethan just tell me on the phone. I mean we have been friends for years well if he didn't tell me on the phone there must be a reason for it.

So I put that thought out of my head and then put on my dark brown leather shoes and my light brown overcoat, then headed out the door, but just before I headed out the door, I shouted in to my wife and said, "Cancel that breakfast, darling, and I might be home late, bye."

Sandra replied, "Bye." I then started to walk towards the squad car when I reached the squad car, I entered the front passenger seat and then after we both clicked our seatbelts in, she started to drive me to the location of the crime scene. While she was driving started to ask her some questions.

I said, "Can you tell me what I will be dealing with when we get there?" The officer then replied, "I think its best we wait so Detective Higgins can fill you in on all the details when you get there."

I then replied, "Ok, if you think that's best." We then sat in silence for the rest of the car journey until eventually we reached the crime scene. I then exited the car when I exited the car I slammed the door shut behind me. As I looked around, I saw about twenty-five police officers and that was just outside the house.

I also saw a cascade of media vans and news reporters swarming around the place like vultures. I then walked up to the house until I came upon the police tape that keeps the media out or anyone else that is not authorised to be in the crime scene. When I approached the tape, there was a male officer on the opposite side who spoke to me. He said in a stern tone of voice, "Can I see some identification please, Sir?"

I then reached into my overcoat inside pocket and pulled out my badge, then showed it to him. The male officer took a close look then nodded his head, and lifted the tape. After this, I then put my badge back in my pocket and proceeded to walk towards the house but before I could enter the house, Ethan came striding towards me and said, "You're finally here. I just want your expertise on this one I mean you have been a homicide detective longer than anyone I've ever known. Come it's this way."

I replied, "So what are we dealing with?"

Ethan replied, "Just wait and see."

I then replied, "Have the forensic guys been in yet?"

Ethan replied, "No I made them wait to see what you have to say."

I replied, "So everything is in its original place nothing has been moved?"

Ethan replied, "No nothing has been moved."

I replied, "Ok good, let's do this then." We finally reached the top of the stairs and there on the landing right in front of us was a young girl laying on her side, and underneath her was a pool of blood. I then spoke, "Who is the victim?"

Ethan replied, "Abbie Johnson."

I replied, "What was she doing here?"

Ethan replied, "She was hired by the parents, Mr and Miss Dawson, to babysit Charlie Dawson while they went out for their one year wedding anniversary. The parents came home, walked up stairs found this. They're down stairs if you want to take their statement."

I replied, "Maybe later." I knelt over Abbie's body and saw that her throat had been slashed one quick and clean movement. She wouldn't have suffered for long. I then very carefully stepped over her body and walked into Charlie's bedroom, and I then walked closer to Charlie's body. Straight away I saw that pieces of Charlie's face were missing, both his cheeks were gone and a part of his nose.

This could either mean he is taking trophies or…or he is eating parts of the victim. I then saw that he had been stabbed several times in the stomach and his pyjama bottoms were on the floor by his bed, which could suggest rape. I then walked out of the bedroom feeling disgusted at what I had just seen. I then made my way back down stairs, and Ethan closely followed behind me. Ethan then spoke, "So did you see anything…anything that stood out?"

I replied, "Well this is just a hunch but you have two victims. One had a quick and clean death while the other one suffered in pain and agony but not just that, the killer spent more of his attention on Charlie. He stabbed him several times, he cut pieces off his face either to take as a trophy or to consume.

"There is also a suggestion of rape but we won't know that until forensics get in there, but I think that our killer only wanted to kill Charlie. That was his prime focus, maybe Abbie got in the way or tried to protect Charlie, so he had to dispose of her and then once he was done with her, he moved on to his real motivation, the child."

Ethan then replied, "So what you think we should be looking for paedophiles?"

I replied, "No, they wouldn't invade a home like this. In my mind, it's probably someone who has had homicidal and sexual urges, even fantasies rolled into one but has never acted on them until now. This person probably has never even done an illegal act before in his life until now. So this would be his first crime that he would have committed which makes our job a lot harder and if so, I would be very worried if I were you."

Ethan replied, "Yea why's that?"

I replied, "Well if this is his first crime, then I think he's only just getting started."

Then suddenly we had reached the bottom of the stairs. I went to walk out of the house but as I went to do this, Ethan put his hand on my shoulder and pointed towards the front room. I then looked inside and saw Mr and Miss Dawson sitting on the sofa. Miss Dawson was crying and walling with her head buried in her husband's lap. Ethan then said to me, "Aren't you going to interview the parents?"

I replied, "I thought this was your case. I thought you just wanted my advice now if you don't need me anymore, I need to get home to my wife after all it is my day off."

Ethan replied, "Ok thanks for all your help. Have a safe trip home and tell your wife I said hello."

I replied, "Ok I will. Bye, Ethan, sorry I couldn't have offered more help." I then walked out of the house and as I did this, I saw the uniformed female officer who drove me to the crime scene wave to me in the distance. So I started to walk to her and as I did this, I heard the frantic overlap of crazed shouting voices.

So I looked to where it was coming from and when I looked I wasn't surprised to see that it was the news reporters clamouring for a story. As I approached the police tape that surrounded the crime scene they rushed me like a mice to a piece of cheese and started to asking me hundreds of questions at once. As I was not in charge or even a part of this investigation, I ignored them and carried on walking to the female officer.

When I eventually reached the female officer, I just got in her squad car without saying a word, and then she drove me back to my home. When we reached my home, I said thank you to the female officer then exited the car and walked slowly up to my front door. Then when I entered my home, I shouted "Baby, I'm home!"

But there was no reply, so I walked into the kitchen. My wife, Sandra, was not there, so I went into the front room. She wasn't there either so I walked up the old and rickety stairs to check the bedroom, and as I did this every single step I stood on creaked and groaned but I eventually made it to the top of the stairs. Then I walked across the landing and peeked my head into the bedroom and as I did this, I saw Sandra laying curled up on the bed fast asleep.

So I tiptoed in the bedroom and pulled the bedcovers over her so she wouldn't get cold. Then I walked back down stairs trying to make the least amount of noise possible and went into the kitchen to make myself something to eat. I opened the fridge but all I saw was a half empty carton of milk and a carton of eggs, so I shut the fridge then as I looked around the kitchen. I saw a post-it-note stuck to the microwave.

So I approached the microwave and ripped the note off then proceeded to read it. The note said, *Sorry I wasn't awake when you got home so as an apology I cooked your favourite cheesy mash, fish fingers and beans hope you enjoy honey xoxo*. After reading the note, I kissed it then threw it in the bin. I then set the microwave to cook my food for one minute.

After I punched in the numbers, I leaned up the kitchen counter and just stared at the food spinning in the microwave until suddenly PING! It was done. Then I opened the microwave door and carefully took the plate out so I didn't burn myself. I then carried it into the front room and placed the plate onto the square oak coffee table that we had.

I then sat down on our dark brown, almost black, leather sofa and turned on the TV switching to various channels until I decided that I would watch the news. After this, I then picked up the plate from our coffee table and began to eat while watching the news. It was a while until I had finished eating all my food but after I did, I stood up and walked into the kitchen.

I then switched the light on and walked over to the sink, washed and scrubbed my plate, knife and fork clean then placed them on the draining bored to dry. After that, I then walked out of the kitchen into the front room switching the light off on my way out. I then slouched back onto the sofa and carried on watching the news.

That's when I heard the news reporter mention something about a murder, so I turned the volume up but I made sure not to turn it up to loud, so it wouldn't wake my wife, Sandra. So when it was at a volume I deemed appropriate, I leaned in and listened closely to what the news reporter had to say.

"If you're just tuning in hello and welcome to channel nine news. I'm your reporter for tonight Brad, and our breaking news tonight is that there has been a double murder right in the heart of our very community. The police haven't released any details, all they have told us is that they are pursuing all angles at this time. So safely secure your homes because there is a murderer out there hiding in the very depths of our community, and now the weather…"

As I listened to this my eyelids began to feel like weights I fought and fought to keep my eyes open and to stay awake, but I eventually caved and fell asleep upright on the sofa with the TV blurring on in the background.

The Investigation Begins

I was woken up by my wife, Sandra's feet pounding on the stairs as she walked down them. So as I was now already awake, I reached forward for the TV remote and switched the TV off that I had accidently left on when I fell asleep last night on the sofa. I then placed the TV remote back down on the coffee table and then stood up. As I stood up, I heard the bones in my back and legs crack like matchsticks. I just put it down to me sleeping in an awkward position.

After that I then made my way into the kitchen. When I got into the kitchen I made my way over to the kitchen sink, then proceeded to turn the cold tap on and splash my face with cold water. This is when I heard my wife walk into the kitchen and she said, "What are you doing?"

I then replied, "I'm just splashing my face with cold water in order to properly wake me up. I always do this in the mornings when I wake up."

Sandra then replied, "Oh ok…so what did Ethan want you for yesterday?" I hesitated at first but then replied.

I said, "He just wanted my advice on a case he was working."

Sandra replied, "What case is that?"

I replied, "Honey, you know I don't like to talk about work at home, plus it's not my case so I don't know any details."

Sandra replied, "Ok then so what would you like for breakfast?"

I replied, "I think I would like a couple of pieces of toast and a cup of coffee please." I then went and sat down at the kitchen table and waited for my breakfast. As I was waiting for my breakfast, I suddenly heard the phone ring, so I rushed into the front room and picked up the phone and placed it to my ear. As I did this I heard a voice.

The voice said, "Hello, is this Martian Gunn?"

I replied, "Yes who is this?"

The voice then replied, "This is Thomas Bishop, homicide detective. The Chief wants to speak with you right away when can you come in."

I replied, "Oh, Thomas, I will be down right away, and do you know what this is about?"

Thomas replied, "No, sorry, I don't."

I replied, "That's alright. I will see soon." I then hung up the phone.

As I did this my wife, Sandra, called me, she said, "Honey, your breakfast is ready." After hearing this, I then returned to the kitchen and sat down at the table and as soon as I sat down at the kitchen table, my wife, Sandra placed a small round plate in front of me with two pieces of golden crusted toast on it. She then placed a pearl white mug down that had coffee inside it. I then proceeded to scoff down the toast and slurp down the coffee.

When I was finished, I rushed to the front door, got my shoes on, then put my overcoat on. Just as I was about to walk out the door, my wife, Sandra walked up to me brushed to crumbs off my chest and kissed me on the cheek. I then said thank you and rushed out the door. After I did this, I made way over to my car, when I reached my car, I got inside and started to drive to the station.

After about 20 or 30 minutes, I had finally reached the station, so I parked my car got and locked it. Then started to walk towards the station and as I did this, I looked around and saw that the parking lot was filled almost to the brim with squad cars. There was only about 7 or 8 cars that weren't squad cars.

I then turned my attention to the building it was 3 stories high, not including the basement. It was a perfect square shape. The first floor was for uniformed officers, the second floor was for people who could understand criminals such as investigative psychologists or criminologists, people who could get inside the criminals mind and give us more insight into the crime, and the third floor was for detectives such as myself but not just homicide detectives, all kinds of detectives cybercrime detectives, narcotics detectives and cold case detectives.

We shared the third floor with Chief Anderson, the boss of the precinct and finally the basement is where forensics operate, and each floor can hold up to at least fifty people. After this, I then walked into the building and stepped inside the lift, there were 4 buttons on the lift's panel. One for floor one, two for floor two, three for floor three, then at the top there was a capital R, and if I pressed that, it would have taken me to the roof.

Then at the bottom the was a capital B for basement, and if I pressed that I would have taken me to the basement, where the forensics lab is. So I outstretched my finger and pushed the number three, and as I did this, the button lit up and the elevator doors began to close slowly and as the doors were closing slowly. I heard a voice in the distance shout, "Hold the elevator…hold the elevator please."

So as I heard this, I stuck my foot out to stop the elevator doors from shutting. Then as I did this, I heard rushed footsteps coming closer and closer until eventually, I saw it was Thomas. He then spoke and said, "Oh hi, Martin, thanks."

I replied, "It's OK now get it." Thomas stepped into the elevator and we continued to speak. I said to him "What floor?"

Thomas replied, "Floor three please." I then pressed the third floor button again and like last time the button lit up but now the elevator started to move, and within seconds, we had reached the third floor. In those few seconds that we were in the elevator, Thomas only said one thing to me and that was "Good luck."

I then exited the elevator and headed straight for Chief Anderson's office that was at the end of the room, and as I passed desk after desk on my way to his office, all I could think was what could he want. Then suddenly in a flash, I was standing right in front of his door, so I knocked lightly as to not disturb him. As I did this, the door opened and the person that opened the door was Ethan.

I didn't understand what was happening. I nodded at him he nodded at me, then I walked into Chief Anderson's office and closed the door behind me. I then looked around the office and saw a long rectangle wooden desk. On top of that was pens and documents nicely stacked and organised. In front of the table were two black leather chairs. Behind the table, I saw Chief Anderson sitting down also in a black leather chair.

The floor was covered with a bright blue carpet and the walls were painted a bright white colour and decorating the walls were all the medals and awards Chief Anderson had been given for his many years of service to the N.Y.P.D. I then sat down next to Ethan and Chief Anderson began to speak.

He said "You must be wondering why I wanted to see you, Martin. Well Ethan came to me yesterday and talked to me about the case that he was working on, and he strongly believes that he does not have enough experience to work this case. So I asked him I said who do you think has more experience than you, and your name was mentioned, and I have looked over your file and you do have a lot of experience.

"I mean you have been with us for many…many years now so effective immediately the case is now yours. Ethan will be working under as well as Thomas, and you will have any uniformed officer at your disposal."

I replied, "But, Sir…"

Chief Anderson cut me off and said, "I don't want to hear no buts or ifs ok. You're in charge of this case now, ok."

I replied, "Ok, Sir, thank you." I then stood up and as I did this Chief Anderson stood up and outstretched his hand for me to shake it, so I shook his hand. After that me and Ethan then left his office. As we did this, Ethan spoke, "I'm sorry, I…"

But I cut him off and said, "Its fine just bring me up to speed on what we have so far."

Ethan then replied, "We have nothing at the moment."

I then replied, "What, no suspect, nothing."

Ethan replied, "No."

I replied, "What about forensics, have forensics got anything yet?"

Ethan replied, "Yes but…"

I cut him off again and said, "Good, let's go down there now." We then headed for the elevator but as we walked to the elevator, I saw Thomas and nodded at him to come with us. He then joined me and Ethan, so then the three of us entered the elevator and made our way to the basement where the forensics lab is based.

Then a few seconds later, the elevator had arrived at the basement, so I stepped out Ethan and Thomas closely followed on behind me. I then stepped through two large rectangle doors that led me into a small square room, and in front of me was a large pain of glass that allowed me to see inside the room in front of me.

I then looked down and saw a metal panel with a silver button on it sticking up. I then proceeded to press this button and as I did this I heard a crackling come from what sounded like speakers or an intercom, then a short stubby woman walked in to the room in front of me. She was wearing a full body bright white protective suit that went up to her neck. She then preceded to wave at me through the pane of glass.

After that, she then approached the large white rectangle slab that was in the middle of the room, she then turned looked at me through the glass and waited. I then nodded. She then spoke and said, "Bring in the first victim, if you will." After she finished saying this, two tall men walked in the room carrying a body bag, they placed it on the slab and then left.

She then proceeded to unzip the body bag. When she had finished unzipping it, she began to speak. She said, "For the record, this is forensic specialist, Elizabeth Patrice, the victim's name is Abbie Johnson. The cause of death was a slash to the throat but looking further it looks as if a vascular structure has been perforated maybe the carotid artery.

"It also looks like the killer only slashed her once and there are no other wounds to be found on her body, and at closer inspection her windpipe has not been penetrated, so it was not a sharp blade. So it looks like she was caught by surprise because there are no defensive wounds, and I would say after the killer slashed her throat, she fell straight to the ground and would have been lying there bleeding to death unable to do anything."

I replied, "What about DNA, did you find anything?"

Elizabeth replied, "Oh yes." After she said that she then reached under the slab for a file. Once she had the file in her hand, she began to read it. "We didn't find any fingerprints or DNA at the scene expect for the victims and the parents."

I then sighed and whispered to myself, "The parents."

Elizabeth then said, "What?"

I replied, "Nothing, so do we have anything?"

Elizabeth replied, "Actually we did pull prints off the home phone, they are Abbie's but it looks like she was trying to call someone. The number is 0775552984."

After hearing this I leant over to Thomas and said, "Go and find out who that number belongs to and see where they were the night the murders were committed." After I said that Thomas rushed off. I then replied to Elizabeth "Anything else?"

Elizabeth replied, "No, shall we move on to the next victim?"

I replied, "Yes." Then as I said this the same two men from last time came in zipped the body bag back up and carried it out the room. Then a few seconds later they brought in another body bag and carefully placed it on the table, and as Elizabeth unzipped it, I leant over to Ethan and said, "Get Charlie's parents in. I want to get their statements as soon as possible." After I said this, Ethan rushed off. I then turned my attention back to the room in front of me.

Then Elizabeth said, "Shall we begin?"

I then hesitantly replied, "Yes."

Elizabeth replied, "Ok so…for the record this is forensic specialist, Elizabeth Patrice, the victim's name is Charlie Dawson. The cause of death was the several deep stabs made to the abdomen area but at closer inspection, if you look at the face, you can see three pieces of the victims flesh missing. The victim's cheeks and a chunk of the victims nose but looking closer it looks as if the killer has took a bite out of the victim's nose, that's why that chunk is missing.

"If I look closer, I can see small bite indentations in the nose but the cheeks look like they have been cut away and because of this, I suspect that the killer has eaten these parts that's why you see the bite indentations in the victims nose but I guess the killer found it too tough to bit off or chew so the killer switched to his knife for the rest."

I then replied, "Is…I…is there any evidence of rape?"

Elizabeth replied, "Yes, I have found evidence that the victim was raped but no semen was found."

I replied, "How old was Charlie?"

Elizabeth replied, "Six…Six years old."

After hearing this, I then whispered to myself "sick fuck," and then said to Elizabeth "Can you tell in what order he did these things?"

Elizabeth replied, "I can take a guess but that's all it would be, a guess."

I replied, "That's fine, go ahead."

Elizabeth replied, "Well by the looks of it, my guess would be that the killer was intending to rape Charlie, but he didn't know he wasn't home alone. So the killer was interrupted and because of this he slashed Abbie once across the neck. The killer then moved on to his intended victim, Charlie, this is when he raped him then stabbed him several times. Then when Charlie was dead or dying, the killer began the eat certain parts of Charlie's face."

I then replied, "So you think the killer might have been casing the house?"

Elizabeth replied, "It's hard to say."

I replied, "Ok, thanks for everything. Oh one more thing, did you pick up any DNA from the victim's bodies."

Elizabeth replied, "No."

I replied, "What is this guy a ghost. How can he not leave one single piece of evidence behind."

Elizabeth replied, "I'm not sure."

I replied, "Yea well, see you later." I then made my way back into the elevator and when I got into the elevator, I pressed the third floor button. Then a couple of seconds later, the elevator pinged and the elevator doors opened. I was at the third floor, so I then stepped out of the elevator and as soon as I did this, Thomas walked up to me and said, "I found out who that number belonged to."

I replied, "Who does it belong to then?"

Thomas replied, "It belongs to a Daniel Adams."

I replied, "Ok who's that?"

Thomas replied, "He said he was Abbie's boyfriend."

I replied, "Did he have an alibi?"

Thomas replied, "He said he was home all night alone, should I bring him in?"

I replied, "No, but I want him in first thing tomorrow."

Thomas replied, "Ok."

After this, I then carried on walking until Ethan intercepted me. He said, "Yeah, Martin, hi I got Charlie's parents to come in. They are waiting at your desk." After hearing him say this, I then looked over at my desk and saw Mr and Miss Dawson waiting nervously.

I then replied to Ethan, "Ok good job. First thing tomorrow I want Abbie's parents to come in and make a statement."

Ethan replied, "I knew you would say that so I already tried them unfortunately, they passed away a couple of years ago."

I replied, "Ok so what about friends?"

Ethan replied, "She apparently dropped out of school when she was fourteen and has been living with Daniel ever since, getting by on the money she makes as a babysitter."

I replied, "So Daniel is the only person we have that knows her, OK that's just great."

Ethan replied, "Do you need anything else?"

I replied, "No, now excuse me, I have to take the statement of two grieving parents." After this conversation, I walked slowly and campy to my desk then when I eventually reached my minuscule desk. I sat down on my round wooden swivel chair and opposite me were Mr and Mrs Dawson sitting in big comfortable black leather chairs. Then after I got comfortable, I pulled out a notepad and pen and began to ask them both a serious of questions.

I said, "So were where you when the incident was taking place?"

Mr Dawson replied, "We went out to the cinema to celebrate our one year wedding anniversary."

I replied, "Can anyone confirm you were there?"

Miss Dawson replied, "What are you saying…are we suspects?"

I replied, "No of course not, this is just procedure."

Mr Dawson replied, "Why don't you go and get a glass of water or something, honey, is that OK?"

I replied, "Yea that's fine."

Miss Dawson then walked off down the hall then Mr Dawson started to speak. "It's OK I understand that it's just procedure, it's just that she is a bit emotional, you understand."

I replied, "Yea I understand totally but can we carry on with the questions"

Mr Dawson replied, "Yes that's fine."

I replied and said, "Ok so can you think of anyone who could want to hurt you or your family?"

Mr Dawson replied, "No."

I replied, "No one have any grudges against you?"

Mr Dawson replied, "No, not me or my family. Everybody likes us in the neighbourhood but I know that someone had a grudge against Abbie every time she come round she talked about it."

I replied, "Do you know this person's name that she talked about?"

Mr Dawson replied, "Danny, no Daniel, yes. I'm sure it was Daniel."

I replied, "Did she mention a last name at all?"

Mr Dawson replied, "Let me think Daniel…Daniel A something."

I replied, "Daniel Adams?"

Mr Dawson replied, "Yes…Yes that was, it was Daniel Adams. Why is he a suspect?"

I replied, "Sorry, I can't reveal any details about the ongoing investigation at the moment, you understand."

Mr Dawson replied, "Yea I understand."

I replied, "So what exactly did Abbie say about Daniel?"

Mr Dawson replied, "She said something about them splitting up and him being obsessive or something like that, but I didn't take note."

I replied, "Well that's it if we have any more questions, we will call you."

After the questions Mr and Miss Dawson started to walk towards the elevator but then suddenly Mr Dawson turned around and said, "Oh I almost forgot. I placed cameras on the outside of the house, if that's any help."

I replied, "Yes that is helpful if you could bring the footage from the cameras down first thing in the morning."

Mr Dawson replied, "Yes, that's fine." He and his wife then entered the elevator and left. I then looked at the clock and sighed then decided it was time for me to head home as well. So I put my pen back on my desk and then picked up my notepad, I then got up and started to walk towards the elevator with my notepad in hand.

Then as I passed Ethan's desk, I threw my notepad right in front of him and said, "Type that up for me."

Ethan replied, "Yea sure." I then entered and as I pushed the button the elevators doors closed and the elevator started to move slowly, then after a few seconds I was on the ground floor. I then exited the building and made my way to my car but as I did this, it was too dark to see. So I pushed the button on my car keys and then my car flashed, and I saw it light up in the darkness, so I then started to walk to my car.

Then when I reached my car, I entered it turned the headlights on and then started to drive on home. Then about 30 to 40 minutes later, I was finally home. Then after I parked my car in the drive, I got out and locked it. I then walked up to the front door and as I did this, I looked in through the front window and saw that the TV was still on.

Then when I eventually reached the front door, I opened it and entered my home. I then shut the door behind me and walked straight into the front room. When I did this, I saw my wife, Sandra, still awake watching TV in the dark, so

I walked in and as I walked into the front room I turned on the light then passed out asleep on the sofa next to my wife, Sandra.

The Crimes Continue

I don't know how long I was passed out asleep for but my wife, Sandra, had to wake me up. When she did this, I rubbed my eyes and sat up straight on the sofa. I then looked around and from what I could see it was now morning. My wife, Sandra, then whispered something to me, "There's someone on the phone for you."

I then stood up and walked over to the phone, and as I did this I said, "Who could it be at this time in the morning?"

Then when I reached the phone, I placed it to my ear and said, "Yes, who is it?"

The voice on the other end of the phone replied, "It's me, Ethan. There has been another murder but this time…we have a witness." When I heard this, I was shocked.

I then replied and said, "What's the address, I will be right down."

Ethan replied, "You know the house on the corner of old Olson road?"

I replied, "Yes, is that where the crime scene is?"

Ethan replied, "Yes."

I replied, "Ok, I will be right down. In the meantime get forensics in there."

Ethan replied, "Yes, Sir, see you soon." After the conversation ended, I hung up the phone then smartened my clothes up as I didn't have time to change or had time for a shower. Then after I did this, I quickly kissed my wife, Sandra, goodbye then ran out the house to my car. I then entered my car and rushed to the crime scene, then when I finally reached the crime scene, I stepped out of my car and looked around.

When I did this, I saw 30 uniformed officers scattered around the crime scene. I also saw about 10 or 15 news vans parked in various location in front of the crime scene. After this I then started to walk up to the house and as I did this the news reports that were gathered around outside the crime scene, rushed up to me and they all started to ask me questions at the same time, but all of their questions just blurred into noise.

I could only pick out a few from the toneless overlapping of sound that they were spewing out from their mouths in my general direction. So I stopped and turned to face the reporters then went on to answer their questions. I then started to speak, "I only have time for a few questions."

Then someone replied, "Yes I'm Charlotte from channel five news and nine, have you any suspects yet?"

I replied, "No, we have no suspects at this time, next question."

Somebody else then replied, "Yes, this is Mike channel seven news at eleven do you think that this murder could be connected to murder that was committed in the Dawson residence, and is so do you think it is the same killer?"

Just as I was about to reply, Ethan said "Forensics are finished now, Sir, we can go in."

I replied, "Ok." I then walked away from the reporters and carried on to the crime scene with Ethan leading the way and as I did this I saw the forensic team pour out of the crime scene ducking under the police tape and putting the evidence into the back of large black vans. After all the forensic team had left the crime scene, I then approached the tape and showed my badge I then carried on walking until eventually I was at the front door of the house.

I was about to step foot inside the crime scene but as soon as I lifted my foot Ethan spoke, "I have to warn you, Sir, I…I um…I have never seen anything like this in all my years as a homicide detective."

I replied, "It's OK, Ethan, I think I can handle it. I mean I am fifty-four years old, nothing can surprise me anymore." Then after this conversation ended, I entered the crime scene and started to walk around. As I walked around, Ethan talked me through the events that took place.

He said, "It looks like the killer entered the victims back garden and broke in through the back door. I say broke in but the back door was open as they have a small dog that they have to let out every so often, so the dog doesn't wee or poo in the house, and it looks like when the sister went to lose the dog outside, she saw the killer standing in the kitchen, so she ran upstairs." After hearing Ethan say this, I then made my way upstairs and then replied to Ethan.

I said, "Do you think it's the same killer because if it is, we might have a serial killer on our hands."

Ethan replied as he followed on behind me up the stairs. He said, "Well, Sir, if it is the same killer we need find him and catch him fast."

I replied, "What do you think we are doing, playing a game? We are doing all we can with evidence that we have."

Ethan replied, "Yes, Sir, I know, sorry." Then as we reached the top of the stairs right in front of me was the door to the victims bedroom but the door had been closed and caution tape had been plastered over the door. I asked Ethan what this was about. Ethan then said, "I think it's best if you look for yourself."

After hearing him time and time again avoid the question or try to warn me from looking inside the crime scene, I began to think what did Ethan see in that room that had gotten him so scared. So I decided to go in as it was my job after all, but right before I entered, Ethan spoke. He said, "Don't you want more information about the crime, Sir?"

I replied, "Oh yes, carry on." Ethan then ran me through what had happened, well what we thought could have happened here at the crime scene.

Ethan then spoke and said, "Well after the sister ran upstairs, she went to her little brother's room and told him to hide under the bed. After her brother, Adrian, hide under his bed, she then exited his bedroom and as she did this she says she saw the killer's shadow as the killer walked up the stairs, so she ran into the bathroom and hid in the bathtub."

I replied, "So the sister is the witness, how old is she?"

Ethan replied, "She is twenty-five years old and her name is Zoe."

I replied, "Where were the parents?"

Ethan replied, "There mom committed suicide after constant physical abuse by their father, then because of this social services deemed Adrian not safe to live with his father, so Zoe, his sister, said she would be his parent/guardian and he could live with her."

I replied, "So the father has a history of abuse. Bring him in for questioning see if he has an alibi for last night, and see if Thomas has brought in Daniel yet, Abbie Johnson's boyfriend, and if Charlie's dad, Mr Dawson pops by with some camera footage. Tell him to put it on my desk and say thank you. Oh and one more thing, how old was Adrian."

Ethan replied, "Eight…eight years old."

Ethan then rushed off back to the station and as Ethan did this, I finally entered Adrian's bedroom. So I slowly opened the bedroom door ducking underneath the bright yellow caution tape, and as I did this I lifted my foot and took my first step inside. Then as I looked around, I saw the horrors that Ethan warned me about. Adrian, the eight old victim, was lying naked on his bed with one of his legs missing.

It had been cut off and the killer had taken it with him. Also his eyes had been burst, it also looked like the killer tried to cut off one of his arms but failed as it was just dangling like a piece of string. There was gallons of blood over the floor and as I looked around in disgust, I saw that on one of the walls of the bedroom was writing but it was written in blood. I couldn't make out what it said.

After seeing all this I felt like I had seen all I needed to see, so I headed back outside got in my car and then headed straight for the station. Then about twenty minutes later, I had arrived at the station, so I parked my car got out, locked it, then made my way towards the building. As I walked towards the building the only thing that kept repeating itself in my mind over and over again was *Who could have done this…who in their right mind could have done this.*

Then as I reached the building, I stepped inside then ran to the elevator then got in the elevator and pressed button three for floor three. Then a few seconds later, the elevator arrived at floor three and I stepped out.

Then as soon as I did this, Ethan walked up to me and said, "I spoke to Thomas. He said he tried to contact Daniel and Daniel didn't answer, so Thomas went over to his house. There was no one there but he phoned around, and it turns out Daniel tried to commit suicide the second Thomas phoned him and told him about what happened to Abbie."

I replied, "Ok so It can't be Daniel because he was in the hospital when the murder happened. OK what about Adrian's father, any leads?"

Ethan replied, "Yea but you're not going to like it. So it looks like after Adrian got took off him by social services, he started drinking heavily and after a couple of years, he died of alcohol poisoning."

I replied, "Well what do we have?"

Ethan replied, "Mr Dawson dropped those photographs off. They're on your desk and Zoe, the victim's sister, is waiting for you to take her statement over by your desk."

I replied, "Ok thanks. While I'm doing this, go down and wait for me in forensics."

Ethan replied, "Ok."

After this conversation, Ethan then entered the elevator and made his way down to the basement which is where the forensics lab is located. After seeing him do that I then walked over to my desk sat down in my creaky wooden swivel chair, and then started to speak to the victim's sister. I said, "So Zoe, is it?"

Zoe replied, "Yes."

I replied, "What's your last name?"

Zoe replied, "Beckett…my name is Zoe Beckett, and my brother's name is…was Adrian Beckett."

I replied, "Yes, I am sorry. Now you said you saw the killer, can you describe to me what you saw?"

Zoe replied, "Well he was wearing black jeans, black trainers, black leather gloves, a black jacket that he had zipped up and he was wearing a black backpack."

I replied, "Yes, thank you for that but what about the killer's face?"

Zoe replied, "Well you see, I didn't see his face because he was wearing a mask."

I replied, "Ok can you describe the mask for me."

Zoe replied, "Yes, it was a grey sack like mask, and I could tell that it was made from rubber but there was no features that stood out on the mask except for the eyes and the mouth. The eyes protruded outwards and where a white colour surrounding the eyes were large black circles and the eyes had small red veins that filled the edges of them. The mouth of the mask was open wide and had 14 white teeth protruding out from it, 7 on the top and 7 on the bottom, then the gums of the mouth were black."

I replied, "Did the killer speak at all?"

Zoe replied, "No, all I heard was screaming coming from my brother's room I tried to help him…I did…I tried!"

I replied, "You said he."

Zoe replied, "What?"

I replied, "When you were talking about the killer earlier, you referred to the killer as a he, why?"

Zoe replied, "Well when I looked and saw him standing there, it was obvious to me that it was a man. The way he was built and the way he walked."

I replied, "Ok thank you, that's everything. You may go home now." After this, Zoe got up and left and when she had left, I decided to look at the camera footage that Mr Dawson had dropped off. So I put the CD into my computer and then suddenly the CD had loaded up, so I pressed play.

When I did this, I saw nothing until a few seconds, later Mr Dawson's CCTV had captured the killer breaking in through the basement window that had been left open. But the odd thing was the killer didn't look around for another entrance, the killer went straight to that basement window that had been left open. It was like the killer knew it would be open, then I paused the video and zoomed in, and when I did this I saw the exact same description that Zoe Beckett had described.

As I saw this, my worst fear had come true, it is the same killer and we could be dealing with a serial killer. Then suddenly Thomas tapped me on my shoulder. This broke my concentration, so I turned to face Thomas and I said, "Yes, what is it?"

Thomas replied, "Forensics just emailed they are ready for you now if you want to head down."

I replied, "Ok come on, let's go." Me and Thomas then made our way to forensics, and after a few seconds we arrived in the basement where the forensic lab is located. We then walked up to the pane of glass that separated the room. We stood in front of the room the dead bodies got analysed in and as me and Thomas did this, Ethan walked in with two cups of coffee. He then gave one cup to me and kept the other one for himself, and after this happened there was an awkward silence.

Then Thomas said, "Fine I will get my own coffee, shall I." Thomas then walked out and as Thomas did this, Elizabeth walked into the room that was in front of us, looking very distressed and nodded at me. I then pressed the button in front of me, as I did this, I heard crackling come from what sounded like speakers or an intercom.

I then spoke and said, "Shall we proceed?"

Elizabeth replied, "Yes, OK bring in the victim." As she said this two tall slender men carried a body bag inside the room and placed it carefully onto the slab. Then Elizabeth proceeded to unzip the body bag and when she had fully unzipped the body bag, she began to speak she said, "For the record, this is forensic specialist, Elizabeth Patrice, the victim's name is Adrian Beckett.

"I can already tell that the victim died from his right leg being severed from his body. This would have made the victim die within 30 minutes or even less from lack of blood, and if I take a closer look I can see what look like saw marks on what's left of the victim's leg. Then if I look at the victim's right arm, I can see that it is partially cut.

"It looks like the killer has severed the victim's brachial artery, so if the victim didn't die from the previous injury, he would have certainly died from this."

I replied, "Did you pull any prints from the house or the body?"

Elizabeth replied, "No, nothing."

I sighed in frustration and replied, "What, nothing again? How can this guy leave no evidence behind at the scene, not even a single strand of hair or a piece of fibre from his clothes. I don't understand he's not a fucking…you know what forget it, do you have anything else for more?"

Elizabeth replied, "Yes, the writing on the wall at the crime scene we photographed it and cleaned it up, so we could read what it said."

I replied, "And?"

Elizabeth replied, "I have emailed it to Thomas, oh and one more thing, before you go, this boy was raped like the one before him. I mean we have to stop him, Martin, we just…have to."

I replied, "I'm working on it ok." After this, I then turned around and walked towards the elevator with Ethan closely following behind me. We both then entered the elevator, I then pressed the third floor button. The elevator doors closed then a few seconds later, we arrived at the third floor. So I stepped out with Ethan following.

I then walked to Thomas and said, "Now you had your coffee I believe Elizabeth emailed you something to give me."

Thomas replied, "Oh yes, sorry, I forgot I will just go and print it out now." I then saw Thomas rush over to the printer and as he did this, I went over to my desk and Ethan went over to his. I then sat down waiting for Thomas minutes had passed until finally Thomas came rushing over to me with a piece of paper in his hand.

He said nothing, he just held the piece of paper out towards to me gasping for breath. I then took the paper from his hand and when I did this, Thomas rushed back to his desk. I then proceeded to read what was on the piece of paper but just before I read it, I reminded myself that what I was about to read was written on the wall in the victim's bedroom using the victim's blood, and after I reminded myself of this fact, I started to read the piece of paper.

After reading this it became clear to me that we were out of our depths and desperately needed help from an outside source, so I decided to bring in a criminal psychologist in an advisory capacity.

A Break in the Case

When I made the decision to bring in outside help, I knew there was only one place I could go to get it is the second floor as the second floor was full of people who worked in the field of criminology and psychology. So I stood up and made my way towards the elevator when I reached the elevator, I stepped inside and then pressed the second floor button. The button then lit up and the elevator doors closed and a few seconds later, I had reached the second floor.

So I stepped out of the elevator onto the second floor and as I did this, I looked around and saw that there was hardly anyone here. I then thought to my myself I knew it was a waste of time in the back of my mind. I knew I just knew but then suddenly out of the three people that were in the room, one of them stood up and started to walk towards me.

He was tall and slender wearing black tight fitted trousers and a white long sleeved shirt with a brown blazer. Then when he finally reached me he spoke. He said "Hello my name is Michael Tannin. What are you looking for maybe I can help."

I replied, "I am working on a murder case, well 3 or 4 murders that are linked and we know that it is the same killer, so now we well know it's a serial killer. I was hoping for some outside help, oh and the killer has sent us a message. Well I think it's a message, I'm not so sure if it is meant for us or not though."

Michael replied, "Wow sounds like your overwhelmed, well I could help you if you want."

I replied, "What do you do?"

Michael replied, "I am a criminal psychologist."

I replied, "Ok that's great just what I was looking for, so you know I would only want you helping in an advisory capacity."

Michael replied, "Yes, of course."

I replied, "Great, well then welcome to the team, let's go." After this conversation, me and Michael headed to the elevator then when we had reached the elevator, we both stepped inside. I then pressed the button for floor three after I did this, the elevator doors closed and a few seconds later, we had reached the third floor.

I then stepped out and Michael followed on closely behind me then when I reached my desk, I sat down and walked him through what was happing with the investigation. I said, "So the first murder, the killer breaks in through the basement window, cuts the phone line, heads up stairs to kill Charlie, then Abbie, the babysitter, catches him in the acted. She tries to run but he kills her. We think the killer thought no one was home except for the little boy, and that was his intended victim. What do you think?"

Michael replied, "Well let me hear the other murders before I make a judgment."

I replied, "Ok so the second murder, Adrian. Same circumstances, the killer broke in through the back garden. The sister saw the killer then ran upstairs told her brother to hide under his bed, she hide in the bath. The killer killed Adrian and left, that's all the murders so far we hope."

Michael replied, "Do you have any suspects?"

I replied, "No."

Michael replied, "Ok, what about DNA?"

I replied, "No, the killer leaves nothing behind at the crime scene's not one fingerprint, not one piece of fibre, not even one piece of dandruff. It's like the killer doesn't exist."

Michael paused for a moment, he looked like he was in deep thought he then replied, "Say that again."

I replied, "Say what again?"

Michael replied, "What you just said, say it again."

I replied, "Ok umm…It's like the killer doesn't exist."

Michael replied, "That's it all the killers intended victims have been children. Anyone else the killer has killed just got in the way, yes?"

I replied, "Yes, why what are you getting at?"

Michael replied, "You mentioned someone who didn't die, who was that?"

I replied, "Adrian's sister. She saw the killer."

Michael replied, "Did she give a description?"

I replied, "Yes, but it wasn't much help the killer was wearing a mask."

Michael replied, "Of course he was, what did she describe the killer looking like?"

I replied, "She said that he was wearing black jeans, black trainers, black leather gloves a black jacket that he had zipped up and he was wearing a black backpack. She also said that the killer was wearing a grey sack like rubber mask."

Michael then whispered to himself, "It all adds up so far." He then replied to me and said, "Do you have a picture of this description"

I replied, "No, but we have CCTV footage from the fist crime and the killer is there wearing the exact some clothing and mask."

Michael replied, "May I see it?"

I replied, "Of course." After this, I then got the disc out of my draw and inserted it into my computer. I then waited for it to load, after a few seconds I then heard a ping and the video and loaded up, so I pressed play and turned to computer screen towards Michael. When the video was over, Michael replied, "And what about this message you told me the killer had left for you."

I replied, "Oh yes, sorry. I forgot about that." After hearing Michael say this, I fumbled around on my desk looking for that piece of paper flinging documents onto the floor until eventually, I found it. I then handed it to Michael then when Michael had it in his hands, he began to read it out loud to himself.

The letter read, Michael then shouted "That's it."

I replied, "What…what?"

Michael replied, "Don't you understand, it's been staring you in the face ever since you get this message."

I replied, "What?"

Michael replied, "Ok so a killer who leaves no evidence behind at any of the crime scenes, a killer whose main focus is to kill children, a killer who dresses in black and wears a sack like mask then we have the message. If we link all of these things together, I believe we are looking for…the bogeyman."

I scoffed then replied, "Yea OK, I don't know why I even considered this you can go now."

Michael replied, "No, listen to me. I can see how that sounded strange or even stupid but let me word it differently. We are looking for someone who wants to become a myth and legend, like jack the ripper for example, but this killer unlike jack the ripper is using the myth of the bogeyman to assert fear into his victims, and in doing this the killer is bringing the bogeyman from the fictional world into the real world.

"With every murder the killer commits, the more real the bogeyman becomes in the killer's eyes and in the eyes of his victims, but more importantly in the eyes of the public. If the public begins to think that the bogeyman is real then the killer wins and the killer will go down in history…the killer will become a myth…the killer will become a legend and the world will forever be changed as the bogeyman's name is echoed throughout the globe."

I replied, "Ok but what makes you think the killer is using the bogeyman myth?"

Michael replied, "Look it's obvious, the killer only targets children. The killer wears all black and a grey sack like mask and if that wasn't obvious enough, there's the message that the killer left for you which clearly tells you that the killer is comparing himself to the bogeyman. So let's take look at the similarities that the killer and the bogeyman myth have in common.

"Ok so the bogeyman sometimes referred to as the sack man in the myth is portrayed as a man with a sack on his back who carries children away, so if we compare this to the killer and what he was seen wearing. The killer was seen wearing a sack like mask and if that's not enough the killer was also wearing a backpack which you could call the modern version of a sack. Also the killer only targets children if that's not enough proof that the killer is using the bogeyman man then I give up!"

I replied, "It's enough…it's enough, just a bit odd that's all. So what type of person do you think we should be looking for?"

Michael replied, "I would say from looking at the CCTV footage from earlier that you're looking for a male, maybe mid-twenties, and the way he knew that the basement window would be open, it has to be someone who either the family knew or lives in the area."

I replied, "So are you saying I should take new statements from everybody?"

Michael replied, "I think that would be best. Now you know what you're looking for, you know what questions to ask."

I replied, "Ok, well thank you for your help."

Michael replied, "You're welcome." After the conversation ended, Michael then walked away towards the elevator, and made his way back to the second floor. After Michael left, I looked at the clock hanging on the wall above me and as I stared at the clock watching the hands tick…tock…tick…tock. I slowly began to feel sleepy until eventually I passed out asleep at work with my head resting on my desk.

The Bogeyman

I was woken up by a loud slamming noise, so I lifted my head from my desk to see what the noise was and as I did this I saw that someone had slammed there hand on my desk in order to wake me up. I stood up and then proceeded to look at the person who had done it. As I did this I said, "Who the hell do you think…" but I stopped halfway through my sentence as my eyes had now met the gaze of Chief Anderson.

Then said, "Chief Anderson, what a pleasure it is to see you. Can I help you with anything?"

Chief Anderson replied, "Can you step into my office for a moment please, Martin."

I replied, "Of course, Sir." I then followed Chief Anderson into his office then when we reached his office, he held the door opened for me and gestured me to sit down. So I entered his office and sat down after I did this chief Anderson then shut the door walked over to his chair and sat down he then began to speak.

He said, "How far along are you with the case?"

I replied, "Well I believe we just had a major breakthrough."

Chief Anderson replied, "Oh so do you have any suspects?"

I replied, "Well no, Sir, not at this time but…"

Chief Anderson cut me off and said, "But…but what it's been at least a week since the first murder took place and you have no suspect, no evidence of any kind and if that's not bad enough, I come in to work and I see you sleeping on the job. I mean come on, Martin, I thought you were better than that."

I replied, "Sir, I wasn't sleeping on the job. I stayed late last night working on the case and that's when I decided we desperately needed, so last night I went to the second floor and got help from Michael…"

Chief Anderson cut me off again and said "Michael, who is Michael?"

I replied, "Michael is a criminal psychologist and last night he helped me understand the killer. So we looked at the all the crimes until eventually we came to the conclusion that the person we are dealing with is not just our ordinary cut and dry killer. This killer wants to be remembered. This killer wants to be engraved on our brains and etched into our thoughts.

"This killer wants to be the source of our fears and nightmares, the creak on the floorboards, the whisper in the shadows that calls out your name, the shapeless shadow you see moving in the darkness. This killer is bringing the bogeyman to life."

Chief Anderson replied, "What absolute nonsense."

I replied, "Yes, I thought so at first too, Sir, but when Michael explained it to me in more, well simpler terms, I thought there is no other explanation, especially after I read the message that the killer had left at one of the crime scene."

Chief Anderson replied, "So you really think this is manic pretending to be the bogeyman, so what…so the killer can become famous."

I replied, "I don't think the killer cares about fame. I think the killer just wants people fear the name of bogeyman once more, and I fear the killer will go to any amount of length necessary to make that happen."

Chief Anderson replied, "Well you better catch this person then and fast. What do you have so far?"

I replied, "Well, me and Michael came to the conclusion last night from looking at CCTV footage of the killer and from a description that an eye witness had given that the killer is a male in his early or mid-twenties. We also thought that the killer had to have known the victims or at least he must live in the surrounding area, so today I am taking everyone's statements again seeing as this time I know what I am looking for."

Chief Anderson replied, "Oh right then, don't let me stop you. I hope you get results and fast because the mayor has been chewing my ear off about this case, so I don't have to tell you how important it is that you solve it and fast." I then stood up and went to walk out of his office and just as I was about to do this Chief Anderson spoke and said, "Oh and one more thing I have to tell you, I'm not taking the flak for you if you screw this up, so smarten yourself up get your act together and take this bastard down."

After hearing this, I then left his office and closed the door behind me. I then immediately approached Thomas and said, "I need you to bring in Mr and Miss Dawson back in, I have some more questions to ask them."

Thomas replied, "Yes, Sir." I then approached Ethan and said, "I need you to bring in Zoe Beckett. I have some more questions to ask her."

Ethan replied, "Yes, Sir."

After this I then went to my desk sat down in my chair and waited, and as I waited I went over the notes that I had made from the previous question's that I had asked Mr and Miss Dawson as well as Zoe Beckett. Finally Thomas said, "Mr Dawson is on his way up." When I heard Thomas say this, I prepared myself then behind me in the distance, I heard the ping sound of the elevator doors opening and faint footsteps that grew louder and louder until eventually they reached my desk.

I then looked up and saw that it was Mr Dawson. I then stood up and shook his hand then gestured him to sit down, he then sat down and got comfortable. I then sat down and began to speak to him. I said, "Sorry to have to bring you in again like this but I have some more questions for you, if that's ok."

Mr Dawson replied, "Yes, that's fine and I hope you don't mind that it's just me this time because you see, my wife didn't want to come. She is still grieving pretty hard."

I replied, "Yes, that's OK I understand. Now, Mr Dawson, in the days leading up to the murder was there anything out of the ordinary happening?"

Mr Dawson replied, "No, not that I can think of everything was as it normally was well except that we were having the house painted, so it was a bit of a mess for a couple of days."

I replied, "Who did you hire to paint your house?"

Mr Dawson replied, "I can't really remember, it was a while ago now."

I replied, "Well if can think back for me please, Mr Dawson, think back."

Mr Dawson sat silently for a couple of minutes until eventually he said, "Sam Marsh. Yes, that's right that was his name, Sam Marsh. We put an ad in the newspaper and he showed up almost the very next day."

I replied, "Well thank you, I think that will be all."

Then as soon as I had finished with Mr Dawson, Ethan came up to me and said, "I just got a call, it's Zoe Beckett. She's on her way up right now." After he said this, I then started to clean my desk. After I had cleaned my desk, I then flipped to a new page in my notepad, then suddenly the elevator doors pinged open. It was Zoe Beckett. When she stepped out of the elevator, she walked straight up to my desk and sat down.

I then spoke and said, "I am glad you could come and help us some more with this investigation."

Zoe replied, "As long as you catch the person who did this, then I will give you all the help you need."

I replied, "So on the nights leading up to the murder, can you think of anything that stood out or was out of the ordinary?"

Zoe replied, "No not really well. I did have someone over to paint the basement but that's not out of the ordinary."

I replied, "What was that person's name, can you remember?"

Zoe replied, "Yes of course, his name was Sam Marsh."

I replied, "Thank you, that's all the questions I have, you can leave now." Then as Zoe and Mr Dawson left in the elevator, I thought to myself this Sam Marsh was at both of the victims' residents leading up to the murders, so he would have had plenty of time to case the houses. He could have even cased the houses while doing his job painting, so I think we should see if we have anything on this guy.

So I then shouted Thomas and said, "See if we have anything on a Sam Marsh in the database and if we do email it over to me."

Thomas then replied and said, "Yes, Sir." Then a few minutes later after Thomas had searched through the database, I had an email popup on my computer. I then clicked on the email and started to read it and this is what it read, *Sam Marsh born May 1995 in New York to Ralph and Ellen Marsh.*

The child has been plagued by mental illness since birth as were all his family members. His brother and his uncle have been diagnosed with mania and were therefore, locked in an asylum while his mother has routine visual hallucinations. His father was seventy-five when he was born but died when he was just five years old.

His mother now widowed does not have the resources to care for him or his three siblings all by herself, so she has decided to leave them all in the care of a state orphanage and it was here that he conceived a passion for pain. The caretakers at the orphanage beat him and even encouraged him to hurt other children but while the other children lived in fear of the painful punishments, Sam revelled in them.

Sam came to enjoy and associate pain with pleasure which would seep into sexual gratification, then when his mother became mentally stable and financially self-sufficient enough to take him home in 2007, she removed him from the orphanage but the damage had already been done. After reading this email, I just knew, call it a get feeling or a hunch, I just knew that this was our guy. This was our killer, this was out bogeyman.

Then suddenly Thomas and Ethan rushed over to me at the same time gasping for air. When they had caught their breath, they both started to speak at the same time, so I said, "One at a time."

Ethan stopped talking and I heard Thomas say, "We have reports of a kidnapping. The description that was given matches the killers, what should we do, Sir?"

I replied, "I want this Sam Marsh's address now and I want a description of what the victim was wearing, what the victim looked like, OK let's go."

I then opened my bottom desk draw and pulled out my Glock 19 handgun that was attached to a holster. I then clipped the holster around my waist and made my way towards the elevator, and as I did this, Thomas handed me a piece of paper he then said, "This is the suspect's address and what the victim was last seen wearing and what she looked like."

I replied, "Thank you."

Thomas replied, "Let's get that son of a bitch, Sir." I then nodded and then me Thomas and Ethan entered the elevator and after a few minutes, we had reached the ground floor. We all then exited the building and entered a squad car. Ethan was driving, I was in the passenger seat and Thomas was in the back. Ethan then started the engine and sped off.

I then turned on the police radio while Thomas was checking his gun. I then picked up the radio and spoke into it. I said, "To all available officers, this is homicide detective, Martin Gunn, listen closely to the description I am about to give you. A young female, age ten, her height is 4 feet. She was last seen wearing a white felt hat with a blue streamer in the back of it. Her hair is dark, straight and bobbed, she has blue eyes and a sallow complexion.

"Her physical condition can be described as anaemic, she was last seen wearing a pink rose on her right shoulder. She has on a grey overcoat with a fur collar and cuffs. She is carrying a brown pocket book and underneath her coat she is wearing a white silk dress. If you have seen a ten year old girl matching this description radio it in straight away."

After I put down the radio, Ethan spoke. He said, "So where is Sam Marsh's address?"

I replied, "Ask Thomas."

Thomas then spoke, "Old Olson road, number 35."

When I heard this I scoffed and said, "I knew it he was right under our noses this enter time. He was just a few meters away from the victim's houses. OK let's go to his address now." Then as soon as I said this, Ethan put his foot down and turned the siren on as we headed to Sam Marsh's house.

After about 30 minutes, we got there. Then all three of us rushed out the car and made our way to his front door. Then when we got to his front door, we all got our guns in hand and took the safety off, then after we did this Ethan spoke, "What about backup, Sir?"

I replied, "We don't have time for backup, we have a little girl's life in the balance."

Ethan replied, "You're right, sorry, Sir." After this I then looked at Thomas and nodded. As I did this, he started to bang on the front door and shout police open up but there was no response, just muffled noises and bangs until we heard a scream. That's when Thomas broke the door down. After that all three of us entered the house, I entered first, then Ethan, then Thomas but as soon as soon as we entered, I saw him.

Sam Marsh standing in the hallway wearing all black and that grey sack mask but then he reached for something from around the corner and pulled it in front of him. It was the little girl. After seeing this, Thomas had moved closer and was now on my left side with his gun pointed towards him, and Ethan had also moved closer with his gun pointed towards him but I dropped my gun on the floor. After I did this, Sam took off his mask and threw it at my feet.

I looked at the mask that was now crumpled at my feet and I then looked up into the eyes of Sam Marsh, the killer not the bogeyman. The cold hearted murderer, rapist and cannibal, and as I looked into his cold dead blue eyes, I saw nothing. He was just an empty emotionless shell that enjoyed the pain and suffering of others. I then looked at his other features, he had fair skin.

His hair was a very dark brown almost black colour, it was trimmed and parted on the left with a loose strand hanging near his parting. He was clean shaven. He was a small and slender man and I would say that he had a face that would blend in with any crowd. After I took I his features I began to speak not to him but to the little girl.

I said, "Hey, it's ok…it's OK, look at me…look at me. What's your name?"

The little girl then replied with shaky breath. She said, "My n…name is Grace."

Then as soon as Grace said this, Sam pulled out a knife and put out against her throat. When he did this, Thomas and Ethan cocked there pistols. I then said, "Ok you want my attention, you have my attention. So what is it that you want?" There was a very long silent pause until suddenly Sam replied.

He said "I am the creak of your door left open at night. I am the whistle of wind or a trick of the light. I am the blink of a star shooting through space. I am the stranger next door. I am a mystery face. I am the tap on your window when others don't hear. I am the rattle of milk bottles when morning is near."

As soon as he finished saying this, he went to slice Grace's throat but Thomas and Ethan saw this and they open fire, shooting Sam more than several times in the chest. Sam then fell to the floor and Grace ran over to me. I then took her to the car and Ethan and Thomas came with me. I told Ethan and Thomas to wait with Grace, while I went back into the house.

So, I made my way back towards the house and as I did this, I heard Thomas calling for backup, then eventually, I made it to the house. I stepped inside but as I did this, I could not believe what I saw in front of me. I refused to believe my eyes for as I looked, I saw nothing. Sam Marsh…had disappeared.